BETWEEN
PERFECT
AND
REAL

RAY STOEVE

BETWEEN
PERFECT

AND
REAL

AMULET BOOKS • NEW YORK

For trans teens everywhere, and for teenage Ray.
Who you are is right and good,
and you deserve to be your fullest self.

PUBLISHER'S NOTE: This is a work of fiction. Names, characters, places, and incidents are either the product of the author's imagination or used fictitiously, and any resemblance to actual persons, living or dead, business establishments, events, or locales is entirely coincidental.

Cataloging-in-Publication Data has been applied for and may be obtained from the Library of Congress.

ISBN 978-1-4197-4601-7

Text copyright © 2021 Ray Stoeve
Illustrations copyright © 2021 Susan Haejin Lee
Book design by Hana Anouk Nakamura

Published in 2021 by Amulet Books, an imprint of ABRAMS. All rights reserved. No portion of this book may be reproduced, stored in a retrieval system, or transmitted in any form or by any means, mechanical, electronic, photocopying, recording, or otherwise, without written permission from the publisher.

Printed and bound in U.S.A.
10 9 8 7 6 5 4 3 2 1

Amulet Books are available at special discounts when purchased in quantity for premiums and promotions as well as fundraising or educational use. Special editions can also be created to specification. For details, contact specialsales@abramsbooks.com or the address below.

Amulet Books® is a registered trademark of Harry N. Abrams, Inc.

ABRAMS The Art of Books
195 Broadway, New York, NY 10007
abramsbooks.com

ACT ONE

". . . some consequence yet hanging in the stars
shall bitterly begin his fearful date
with this night's revels, and expire the term
of a despised life closed in my breast . . ."

—ROMEO

Romeo and Juliet, act I, scene 4

CHAPTER ONE

I think I might be trans.

I mean, I know I am.

CHAPTER TWO

I sit in the folding chair, waiting for my turn in the classroom.
The monologue in my hands looks more like an accordion
than a piece of paper, but I can't stop folding and unfolding it.
I have it memorized backward and forward, but I brought it
anyway, just in case I wanted to look at it before I go in.

"What are you trying out for, Dean?" Olivia sits down
beside me. Her waist-length brown hair swings forward, spilling over her shoulders.

I look down at the paper in my hands. "Lady Capulet, I
guess. There aren't a lot of roles for women in *Romeo and Juliet*."

"I know, right?" She rolls her eyes.

"What about you?"

She smiles. "I'm going for Juliet."

"Nice." I stare at the closed door. I want it to open, I want
to get this over with. "That's perfect for you."

"Thanks. I just feel like it's senior year, you know? I want to play a lead before I graduate."

I nod. I want to play a lead too. But there never seems to be a lead role for me. Tomboy lesbians don't get a lot of parts in theatre.

Even though, at this point, I'm pretty sure I'm not a girl. Or a lesbian.

The door opens. Blake nods at me, smiles at Olivia. He's bulked up since the end of last year, his usually white skin sunburned. He looks like he should be out on the field with the Jefferson High football team instead of here auditioning for the school play. Olivia jumps up and they kiss.

Mr. Harrison appears behind them. He's got his trademark bow tie on, a purple-and-green plaid pattern today. "Dean?" He smiles at me. His British accent is crisp, like the paper in my hands before I held it. "Come in."

Inside the classroom, it's just me and Mr. Harrison. I crumple the monologue and shove it into my back pocket. I've been here before, just me standing in front of the whiteboard while he sits a few rows back, one leg crossed over the other, twirling a pen in his fingers, but this time feels different. I'm not a scrawny, shaking freshman, a cocky sophomore, a jaded junior. Before, I never assumed I'd get a lead. I was always excited just to audition, but I knew a lead was a long shot. The seniors always got the leads. A few times I got a major secondary role, like last year, in the gender-swapped version Neil Simon wrote of his famous play *The Odd Couple*. In that version, most of the main characters were girls instead of guys. I played Sylvie, a friend of the main characters, who were both played by seniors.

But now I have a chance. It's my turn to shine. To be the star.

"How was your summer, Dean?" Mr. Harrison asks.

"Good."

He smiles. "I've got a few excerpts here of scenes from the play. We'll do a cold read first, then your monologue." He shuffles through the options as I wait. "Ah, yes, how about this."

He stretches out a hand and I walk over, grabbing the paper and bringing it back to the open floor. I scan it: the scene where Romeo and Juliet meet. It's awkward reading a love scene with my teacher, but that's theatre for you.

"Now, this excerpt doesn't mean I'm considering you for Juliet," Mr. Harrison says. "I know you know this, but I like to remind people it's just to see how you read in scene, and for me to get a feel for where I might cast you, whether for your chosen part or not." He looks at his clipboard. "You're trying out for Lady Capulet, yes?"

I nod.

"Start from 'Romeo, Romeo,' and we'll go from there to Romeo's line 'I would adventure for such merchandise.'"

I take a deep breath, and begin.

"O Romeo, Romeo! wherefore art thou Romeo? Deny thy father and refuse thy name; or, if thou wilt not, be but sworn my love, and I'll no longer be a Capulet." I'm acting with my

8

voice, but I don't feel the words in my chest, the way I some-times can when I really get into character. I know what Mr. Harrison just said about cold reads, but still, I'm not much of a Juliet. I'm sure he can see that. I'm not Olivia with her sweet smile. And I'm not much for the Nurse role either; I'm not Olivia's best friend Courtney with her wisecracks. I'm me: tall, skinny, white, less outgoing than Courtney, more outspo-ken than Olivia. I'm the only girl in theatre—if I even am a girl—with short hair. I'm wearing my red Converse, the heart on one toe where Zoe drew it this summer. Thinking of her makes me smile, and I try to channel it into my read.

The scene goes okay. I carry it off well enough with my expressiveness, even if I'm not in character.

"All right," Mr. Harrison says, taking the scene excerpt back from me. "Are you ready for your monologue?"

"Yeah." I close my eyes, wiggling my fingers to get the shakes out. I'm not actually nervous; I know I'm a good actor. It's just the high stakes. Will he cast me as Lady Capulet? And if not, where else would he put me? I try not to think about the possibility that I might not get cast at all. That's happened to seniors in the past.

I look up. Mr. Harrison is watching me. "Whenever you're ready."

I nod once, and then I launch into the monologue.

"What say you? Can you love the gentleman?" I ask, draw-ing my eyebrows together, pleading, pretending Mr. Harrison is Juliet. The monologue is in act one, scene three, before Romeo and Juliet have met, before the party, before the deaths. Lady

Capulet asks Juliet if she's thought about marriage, and Juliet hasn't. Relatable. I mean, she's supposed to be what, like fourteen? Of course she's not thinking about marriage. But Lady Capulet presses on. This is what makes me think I can do this: She reminds me of my mom. Always pushing, always telling her kid what she wants and never asking Juliet what Juliet wants.

I sweep out my arms, extolling the delights of married love. "This precious book of love, this unbound lover, to beautify him only lacks a cover!" I'm halfway through the monologue and I'm flying. I'm the most ridiculous version of my mother I can be, pleading one moment, swooning the next, never really listening. Mr. Harrison is smiling and chuckling.

I lower my voice as I approach the last line. I'm earnest, my hands clasped over my heart, dreaming of my daughter's future. "So shall you share all that he doth possess, by having him, making yourself no less."

I can kind of get on board with that part. I think it means that being with someone makes you better, like you become both part of them and more of yourself. I think. It's hard to tell with all the Shakespearean language. But that's how I feel when I'm with Zoe: like I can be more of myself, like everything she is—smart, beautiful, funny, sweet, driven—lifts me up, makes me better. She's the girlfriend I always dreamed of having, all the way back to when I first realized I could date girls.

I grin at Mr. Harrison and bend into a deep bow, then straighten up. He claps. "Excellent work!"

"Thanks."

"I should have the cast list up soon. It'll be outside the

theatre on the board, like usual." He looks at me over his glasses. "Any questions?"

I shake my head.

"Wonderful. Send Olivia in on your way out, please."

"You got it." I shoot him finger-guns and trot out of the classroom.

When I step outside the school, the early-September warmth wraps me up like a blanket. The classroom was cold, but out here, summer in Seattle is still hanging on, the last gasp before ritual death-by-drowning in fall rain. The first week of school is almost over. One down, so many more to go.

"How'd it go?" Ronnie hops down from his perch on the bike rack. In the sunlight, his pink shirt glows bright against his warm black skin, the Oxford collar buttoned to the top. He promised me he'd stick around for post-audition moral support.

I'm still jazzed, riding high on performance adrenaline. "So good, dude. I was like, in it. And I made him laugh!"

"Nice!" He falls into step beside me. "Who'd you read for?"

I tell him. He raises an eyebrow. "And you want to play her?" He's heard me complain about the lack of good female roles in theatre before.

I shrug. "I don't really have much of a choice, right? Besides, I got into the monologue a little bit. I think it could be fun. I'm gonna channel my mom."

He snorts. We walk away from the school, toward the busy road along the neighborhood's edge. I'm starting to sweat in my hoodie, but I don't want to take it off. I'm more comfortable when I have an extra layer between me and the world.

"Besides, I don't really care what the role is as long as it's big," I say, looking over at him. "A lead for senior year will look so good on college applications."

On NYU's application. Because that's where I'm going. I'm applying other places, but . . .

I *have* to go to NYU. They have the best acting school in the country. Theatre isn't just an elective to me like it is for other kids. The rush of being on stage, of being someone else, escaping my head, escaping my body—that moment when everything hits right and the scene becomes real, the lines aren't just words but live wires connecting me to my scene partners—it's magic. It makes me feel alive. I want to do it forever. I want it to be a real career. And to do that, I need to go to the best school for it.

"You'll get in," Ronnie says.

"Did you start yours for Parsons yet?" We slow down at my bus stop.

"Opened the Common App last night," he says. "Just don't tell my dad." He grimaces.

We're all applying Early Decision: Ronnie for fashion design at Parsons New School, me and Zoe at NYU. New York City, baby. That's been the plan since Zoe and I started dating last year. I'm not even thinking about not getting in. Not getting in isn't an option.

The bus rolls up, we fist-bump, and I get on.

CHAPTER THREE

How many YouTube videos do you have to watch before you know for sure you're trans? It's not like I tried to pee standing up when I was a kid or refused to play with dolls or whatever. I know I don't fit some of the stereotypes of trans guys. But when I watch videos, when I scroll through trans guy hashtags on Instagram?

I feel something.

I don't know what that something is, but it feels right. It feels like recognition, and sometimes like jealousy.

Most of the time, being myself feels more like acting than theatre does, like I'm perched somewhere far back in my brain, pulling the levers that make my body move: Do this, say that, feel this emotion. Like every other girl got a manual of how to be a girl and I didn't, like I'm fumbling around trying to figure it out and whenever I think I'm getting close, it all gets fucked up again. Kind of like when your headphones are tangled up and you pull on the end but they just get more tangled. Maybe my gender is tangled-up headphones. Someone should tell the guys at school. Maybe then they'll stop making stupid jokes about how they identify.

I spend all weekend after auditions on YouTube. One of the guys whose channel I follow just got top surgery. In the video, he's all broad smiles, the barely healed scars raw and red. His breasts are gone. Even though his chest is still swollen, I can see the shape of it, the pecs like every other bare-chested guy's pecs.

I touch my own chest, flattening it with both hands, and blur my eyes when I look down, trying to see the shape of what my body could be. Seven months ago, I thought most girls didn't like having boobs. But seven months ago, everything changed.

It was the beginning of February, a few weeks after Zoe and I started dating. "Movie night at my place tonight?" she asked, tilting her head with a smile. Uh, yes please.

She said something about watching *Boys Don't Cry*. The title sounded familiar, and I nodded, but all I could think about on the bus ride to her apartment was her lips on mine, her body pressed against me. Watching a movie? More like making out every time her mom left the room.

At her apartment, I sat back on the couch, watching her pull up the movie on Netflix. The opening credits rolled and she settled beside me, then scooted closer, and I put my arm around her. Her hip touched my hip. Her shoulder nestled under my armpit. Her arm laid a trail of fire across my stomach. Every place our bodies touched lit up my nerve endings like fireworks. In the kitchen, pots clanged on the stovetop as her mom, Sheena, cooked dinner.

What seemed like hours later, Zoe's gentle kiss on my neck startled me, pulling me away from the movie. "Dean?" She looked up at me. I glanced around, blinking. Sheena was gone. The living room and adjoining kitchen was dark. "She's been in her room for a while," Zoe whispered.

I looked back at the screen, watching the main character. He was a trans man. Brandon Teena. I knew that trans women existed, but I didn't know there were also trans men. When I looked at him, a wordless echo sounded in my head. I couldn't look away.

After that night, I got online whenever I could, searching through Instagram, YouTube, personal blogs. I wanted to know more about trans men, how they felt, why they chose to transition. And in every post I saw myself. I knew I was supposed to be a girl, but I'd always failed at it, never feminine enough, always so uncomfortable with the latest fashions, perpetually confused or annoyed by the expectations people seemed to have for me. But it ran deeper than that, like my body was never quite right, like my face wasn't really me. I'd noticed that as soon as I was tall enough to look in mirrors. So I usually avoided mirrors.

I read more, and the wordless echo became a siren wail. Everything made sense now: Why I always wished I could play male roles in theatre. Why I wanted everyone to call me Dean instead of my full name. Why clothes made for girls never felt right, no matter how boyish they were. I tried to stop looking at the websites, but every few weeks I found myself on my laptop, watching videos in the private browser. I still watch all the trans guys I follow on YouTube, almost every night.

I think I want to transition.

But I have to come out first.

I just don't know how.

When I get to school on Monday, Ronnie and Zoe are standing at my locker. Ronnie's flinging his hands around, which means he's excited about something.

"What's up?" I say, and they both jerk their heads like I caught them doing something wrong.

"Hey you," Zoe says, brushing a long strand of wavy teal hair out of her face. Her skin is milky-white, black eyeliner sweeping in wings away from her eyes. Her striped dress highlights the curve of her wide hips.

I smile before I even realize I'm smiling. She does that to me.

She stands up on her tiptoes, my hands finding her waist, the fabric of her dress soft under my fingers. We kiss, ignoring Ronnie's coo. Her lips are soft and taste like her coconut lip balm.

"So." I look at both of them. "What are you plotting?"

"Whatever do you mean?" Ronnie puts a hand to his heart.

"I saw your hands flying." I spin my combination lock. "What's going on?"

They exchange a look. "You haven't seen yet?" Ronnie asks.

I stop mid-spin.

"The casting decisions." Ronnie looks at Zoe again, and back to me. "They're up."

"Oh." I go back to spinning.

Zoe grabs the lock with her hand and stops me. "You need to go see."

"Why?" I let go.

"Oh my god." Ronnie rolls his eyes and grabs my arm. He marches away and I stumble after him, under the giant construction paper arch still screaming WELCOME, SENIORS. Down the hall, weaving through the crowd, people laughing, running, huddling with their friends, until we're rounding the corner of the hallway where Mr. Harrison's classroom sits and beyond that, the theatre, its double doors shut tight. There's a bulletin board to the right of the doors.

There's a list pinned to the bulletin board.

I stop before I'm close enough to read it, yanking out of Ronnie's grasp, and just stand there. Back here, the noise of the halls is a distant hum. Back here, it's just me and Ronnie, standing side by side in front of the board. Posters of past productions line the walls: *The Crucible, Rumors, Grease*. I want to look at the list, but at the same time I just want to walk away. I don't want to play a girl again. I don't know why Ronnie is so excited. Am I Juliet?

The thought makes me want to vomit. Just a little bit.

Okay, deep breaths. You can do this. I step forward, run my finger down the list. *Foster, Dean.* Thank you, Mr. Harrison, for always using my nickname. I follow the line over to the role.

I read it again.

I look at Ronnie and he throws a hand to his forehead. "Romeo, O Romeo!"

I look at the list. There's my name, and there's the role on the same line as my name: *Romeo Montague.*

Is this allowed?

Maybe Mr. Harrison made a mistake, mixed up the names or the roles. I look up and down the list, but all the female roles are assigned to girls.

"Hey." I turn and it's Blake. I step back from the list as he looks for his name and finds it. "Benvolio?" His shoulders fall.

Ronnie elbows me. Blake always tries out for the lead role, and Mr. Harrison always casts him as the sidekick.

And this time he's mine.

If the list is right.

I feel like I'm floating. Over Blake's shoulder, I can still see my name, right there, with Romeo's beside it. He turns.

"You're Romeo?" he asks.

I nod.

No one speaks. He stares at me, and I can't take my eyes off the list.

"Congrats," he says finally, voice flat.

"Thanks," I say. I can tell he doesn't mean it, but I don't really care.

I'm Romeo.

He fades out of the hallway and it's just me and Ronnie again.

"You got a lead role," Ronnie says, right behind me. "Holy fucking shit. You're Romeo."

"I'm Romeo," I say slowly, the words sticking on my tongue like a new language. I turn and grin at him, and he claps his hands, and then I see Zoe behind him right before she grabs me in a tight hug, Then we're all jumping up and down, yelling and shrieking in the middle of the hallway, chanting the name over and over:

"Romeo! Romeo! Romeo!"

The bell's shrill buzz startles us into quiet.

"This is going to be a good year," Ronnie says, wiggling his shoulders.

Zoe grabs my hand and we head to class. Ronnie chatters about costume design, the aesthetic he wants, the fabrics he's imagining, but I'm only half listening, their voices like music in another room. This is happening. No more dresses, no more Mom cooing over how pretty I look on stage. Just me, under the lights.

CHAPTER FOUR

My house sits in North Seattle, a short bus ride or a long walk from school, on a hill where we could see the Olympic Mountains and the Puget Sound if all the pine trees and the other houses weren't in the way. By the time I get home that day, gray clouds and rain have swept away the sunny afternoon. I turn on the furnace and curl up on the couch to study my lines.

But I can't focus. I'm too excited. I'm finally playing a lead role at Jefferson.

And not just any lead role. Romeo Montague, one of the most well-known male roles of all time.

A male role. When everyone thinks I'm a girl.

Have there ever been people cast across genders at school? I can't remember anyone else in the years I've been at Jefferson. Maybe a few henchmen, bit parts here and there, the law of supply and demand dictating roles be filled somehow, but never this. Never a lead.

This isn't my first lead role, of course—I played Rosalind in *As You Like It* the summer before high school, during the Act Up in the Park workshop I'd been doing since I was a kid. Another Shakespeare play, but in that one I wasn't playing a boy, just a girl who disguises herself as one. It was the first time I'd really gotten into character. Acting was always fun before that, but with Rosalind it was different. On opening night—or rather, opening afternoon, with the sun flooding Volunteer Park—I felt myself submerge into her until I wasn't acting anymore, just reacting. She was me, or I was her, and I felt everyone around me rise to meet the Rosalind speaking through me. We hit every joke, and the audience laughed and laughed. It was electric.

I spent most of the play as Ganymede, Rosalind's male alias, and every time I was him I felt lighter, like I could breathe easy in a way I never had, like I wasn't guarding my every move and word.

How will it feel to play a boy for real?

I keep seeing the list flash in front of my eyes, and every time it's like a door opening, like I'm breathing in fresh air from another world. Like I'm standing on the edge of a cliff, like this picture I saw online once of a suspension bridge high above a canyon. The view was beautiful and terrifying at the same time. I didn't understand how people could make themselves cross that bridge.

I'm still on the couch when our car pulls into the driveway, disappearing up the side of the house toward the garage. Footsteps, jingle of keys, back door opening.

Mom calls out my full name. Ugh. She knows I hate it, but that doesn't stop her from using it. *It's a beautiful name,* she always says. *Your aunt's name.* Like, just because I'm named after her sister, who died before I was born, means I'm supposed to be cool with it.

I'm not cool with it. But it's not worth arguing over. I never get anywhere when I do.

"Living room!" I call.

Her heels click across the kitchen floor, and she appears in the arched doorway, bag of groceries in her arms, blond bangs matted to her forehead. Her eyes flick to the script in my hands. A head tilt, then a smile, recognition blooming in her eyes. She shifts the bag to her hip.

"What part did you get, honey?"

"I'm Romeo."

Her smile flattens. Back to the kitchen, refrigerator door opening, clink of jars. "That's wonderful," she calls out. "You're finally playing the lead."

I wait.

"Mr. Harrison is quite the maverick, isn't he?"

There it is.

"What do you mean?" I close the script and go to the doorway. She's separating fruits and vegetables neatly into the bottom bins of the fridge.

"Casting you as Romeo." She laughs. "Is this a lesbian version of *Romeo and Juliet,* or is Juliet gender-swapped too?"

"Neither. I'm playing Romeo as a dude."

She lines up eggs, milk, and yogurt neatly on the right side of the fridge, her back to me. I look at the family photo in the breakfast nook, hanging crooked on its nail.

"I'm really excited, Mom. It's a great acting challenge."

"I'm sure that's true, but I don't understand why your teacher cast you in a male role." She straightens, shuts the fridge, stuffs the now-empty bag into the bag drawer.

"Probably because I'll be good at it."

She looks at me finally, at my hoodie and thrift-store polo, my skinny black jeans, my red Converse, and shakes her head. "You'd be just as good as Juliet. If you dressed differently—"

I turn and beeline for the back hallway, open the basement door, and slam it with all my strength. I thump down the stairs to the basement, stomping as hard as I can on each step. My skin crawls as if her gaze, her disgust, is still sweeping over me like a laser beam. There's nothing I can say that she'll hear, no line I can memorize to get her off my back. In eighth grade, every boy I was friends with became a possible boyfriend, until I shouted at her one night that I was gay. She cried. Dad sat with her on the couch while I stood there, staring at both of them, waiting for her to say something. She just kept crying. Later, in my bedroom, I could still hear her. I wanted her to understand. I wanted her to see me, thought maybe if I said the right thing or showed enough emotion, she would stop trying to live through me and start letting me live.

But she didn't. When I cut all my hair off freshman year, she lost it, asking me why I wanted to look like a boy, if I was trying to embarrass her. She loved my long hair, strawberry blond and wavy like her mother's, how it framed my face, brought out the heart shape of my chin and cheekbones. She always says I have delicate features. I hate that phrase.

The temperature drops as I descend, and I bang into my room, flopping onto the bed. The ceiling hangs close and cracked, the white plaster stained in nebulous shapes. From the giant poster on the wall beside my bed, David Bowie stares down, face glowing in the dim light from the small window, one white hand pressed against his heart, the other upturned, like he's tipping an invisible hat. He's different and he knows it, but he revels in it. Me, I'm the opposite. He's a star, and I'm a black hole, the real me trapped by gravity. When I listen to his music, I close my eyes and I am him, on the stage, bursting with confidence, with shine, different and unapologetic.

"Ziggy Stardust isn't real," Mom told me once. "It's a persona."

As if I didn't know.

As if it mattered.

My whole life is a persona, I wanted to tell her. *Ziggy Stardust is more real than I am.*

Allison is facedown on her desk in first-period English the next morning. I sit down behind her and poke her with a pencil. No response. I poke her again. "You alive?"

"Nope," she groans, straight black hair draped over her face and across the desk. She's in her typical uniform, like she just stepped out of the nineties: oversized flannel, ripped blue jeans, Doc Marten boots.

"Must be hard being Instagram-famous," I say, smirking.

She sits upright, glaring at me. "Running a webcomic isn't about the fame. It's my work. I have fans. They expect things."

"Of course." I wave my hands in apology.

"And now that Mom's onto me I have to stay up late," she says. "The only time I can work without her watching my every move is when she's sleeping."

Ronnie slides in behind me, a red fedora on his head, a speckled feather in the leather band. Allison wolf-whistles. I frame my fingers and snap a photo. Ronnie pulls off the hat with a flourish, revealing a fresh fade on his short-cropped Afro.

"Thank you, thank you," he says, hand on his chest. "My first try making a hat."

"Your first try." Allison snorts. "Jesus, Ronnie. How are you so talented?"

"Good morning to you too, A-Naka," he says. A-Naka is Allison's webcomic pseudonym: her first initial, and part of her last name, Nakamura. "How's Third-Date Troy?"

"Third-Date Troy is now No-Date Troy," she says. "I'm done with men."

Ronnie looks around, frowning. "Do you feel that, Dean?"

"What?" I side-eye him.

He puts out a hand, clutching my arm. "Déjà vu."

We burst out laughing, covering our heads as Allison swats at us. "I'm serious this time! This is the year I finally get a girlfriend."

"A girlfriend for you and a boyfriend for me," Ronnie says, pointing at her.

"Make it so," I say in my best Captain Picard voice.

The day slides by, the promise of rehearsal glittering in the distance beyond a blur of classrooms. After English: History, morning break, Spanish, Biology, lunch, Calculus. And then the bell rings, my summons, my renewal: sixth-period Theatre. I bolt out of Calc, through the school, and into the auditorium.

The silence stops me when I enter. From the top of the center aisle, I can see the whole place: the black backdrop, the red velvet curtain faded to pale rose from years under the hot lights, pulled back on either side of the wide sweep of the stage, the wood dark and rich, tape marking the places where we stand in each scene still stuck there from plays past.

The theatre is empty. I drop my backpack in the front row and vault onto the stage. A few lights are on above me, the rows of seats disappearing into darkness toward the doors. The carpet is faded, the stage is scuffed, but it's mine. Well, not really. But part of me lives here. I imagine the seats are full, that I'm on stage in costume. I don't want the audience to see a girl in boy's clothes. I don't want them to see a lesbian version of the play. I want them to see Romeo.

The house lights go up, dimming the shine of the stage lights. Mr. Harrison stands at the top of the center aisle, smiling at me. "I'd tell you to picture them all in their underwear, but that never works."

"I don't get nervous anymore," I say, grinning.

He strolls down the aisle, taking the steps on stage left. "Better watch out. The moment you get cocky is the moment you forget a line." The double doors at the top of the aisle open and Blake comes in, holding hands with Olivia. She's too nice to date him, but here we are.

"Hello, Juliet!" Mr. Harrison says as she joins us on stage. Blake sits in the front row, fiddling with his phone. I remember last year, how hard he tried to get Zoe to date him. And now his current girlfriend is playing my onstage star-crossed lover. Part of me feels like I've won something.

The rest of the cast and crew arrives, circling up as Mr. Harrison calls us to order. People hug, high-five, and chatter as he raises his voice to be heard. Ronnie slides in beside me and we elbow back and forth. I love this part, the beginning of the year, all of us back together on the stage. It feels like the start of something big and important.

"Hey dudes," someone says behind us, and Jared appears on Ronnie's other side. His dirty-blond hair is up in a bun, skin still tan from the summer, and he's in black from head to toe: a Jurassic 5 shirt, jeans, and Vans.

"You back on set crew?" I ask, and he nods. The set crew is mostly guys and a few girls, a mix of skaters, punks, and other kids most likely to have unusual hair colors.

"Now that Harvey's graduated, I'm hoping it won't be such a shitshow," he says, naming the senior guy who ran the crew last year. Harvey had been voted Funniest Guy in the senior polls. The category would have been more accurate if they'd called it Most Likely to Make a Sexist Joke.

On the other side of the circle, Mr. Harrison claps his hands. Everyone quiets down as he claps again, until finally only a few whispers remain, drifting through the air with the dust motes.

"This is an ambitious play," Mr. Harrison says into the lull. "It involves elements we have not dealt with in previous productions—stage combat, for instance." A murmur sweeps the group. "A local combat instructor and colleague of mine has agreed to help us." His gaze rests on me briefly. "And I took a chance with some of my casting decisions. But good theatre requires an open mind and an unorthodox method. I trust you will all be up to the task."

Kids nod, and a few exchange raised eyebrows. Across the circle, Courtney whispers something in Olivia's ear.

"Unorthodox method?" Ronnie nudges me. "Is he talking about you?"

I shrug. We stand up for a game to open class, rounds of Zip Zap Zop that go faster and faster until we're all laughing, people shouting the words as they point at someone in the ring, trying to get their friends out. I mess up early and stand outside the circle with the others as the game whittles down to two people. Without the game to distract me, Mr. Harrison's words keep flashing in my mind. He took a chance. Is that chance me?

It has to be.

What does that mean?

The game ends—Jared wins, pumping his fist in the air—and Ronnie heads for the costume closet, the props and set-crew kids for their own work areas. The cast stays behind, people sitting or sprawling on the stage for the read-through. I know people are staring at me, but whenever I sneak a glance, everyone is focused on their scripts, waiting to speak.

When I say Romeo's lines, and Olivia answers as Juliet, someone giggles. Mr. Harrison clears his throat and silence reigns again, but I stumble over my speech, blinking back tears. My high voice sounds stupid next to the deep ones of the boys playing Benvolio, Mercutio, and the other male characters. I'm the odd one out, like always.

When I found out people could be something other than straight, I thought I'd discovered the reason why I never fit in, why being a girl felt more like something I had to figure out than something that came naturally. But now I know there's more to it than that. Has Mr. Harrison guessed? Is that why he gave me this role?

I want to be Romeo. But sitting here, silence hardening like concrete in all the empty space, I'm not sure I can do it.

I've been looking forward to this moment all month, looking forward to being back on stage, reading lines, playing games, never wanting class to end. But instead, for the first time in my life, the end of rehearsal is a relief.

Mom actually believes me when I tell her I have no homework that weekend. I can only lie so many times; after the first month of the school year is over, she gets suspicious. But

I'll take the literal and figurative open door for now. Goodbye, textbooks; hello, date with Zoe at Carkeek Park.

The bus drops me at the south entrance, across from the grocery store. Zoe comes walking across the parking lot a few minutes later, earbuds in. When she sees me, she rips them out, stretching a hand toward me.

"My dearest!" I shriek. She clutches her chest. The street is clear and we slow-motion run toward each other like we're in a cheesy romantic movie, mouths wide, arms thrown back. We meet in the middle of the street and she grabs the front of my shirt, pulling me in for a kiss. A car horn blares. We jerk apart, sprint back to the sidewalk, giggling wildly as the driver yells after us.

The path into the park is muddy, sunlight filtering through the tall pines along the stream to our left. As we near the park, the Puget Sound glimmers through the trees. The playground is busy: kids screaming, parents talking and ignoring the kids, dogs running across the playfield. Across the bridge, over the train tracks, and down the steep metal stairs is the beach, a thin strip of sand and rocks cut in half by a stream. An anonymous fort-maker has been here: small structures made out of driftwood stand smooth and silent in muted shades of brown and gray, glowing in the sun. We lean back against a log, looking out at the Olympic Mountains rearing up across the sound.

"Remember our first date here?" Zoe asks.

"The first date that almost wasn't?" I say. "The first hangout with a girl I thought was probably straight?"

She pushes my shoulder. "I knew you thought that."

"When you said your mom was having a hard time accepting you were gay, I was so happy." She raises an eyebrow and I clarify. "Because then I knew you were gay. Not because your mom was being an asshole."

Zoe laughs, shaking her head. "She was. That sucked." The waves lap at the sand, gliding almost to the tips of our toes and then out again. "But she loves you. Now I think she's actually into me being gay. Like it gives her some good-mom cred with her friends." She rolls her eyes. "How was rehearsal this week?"

Sand crumbles away from our feet as the waves wash out. We get up, jumping from log to log across the stony beach, and I fill her in on Mr. Harrison's comment about casting. "So now I don't know if he cast me for an avant-garde cross-gender thing or because he thinks I would make a good Romeo. My mom even asked if he was trying for a lesbian version of the play."

Zoe balances on the end of a giant tree trunk, like a pirate queen surveying the sea. "Typical."

"I know." The mountains are blue-white teeth across the water, small sailboats dotting the shoreline. "But what if that's really what he wants?"

"Is that bad? I think that would be cool."

"Yeah, but I want to play Romeo as a guy, not a girl."

Zoe splashes into the stream. "So talk to him."

"Yeah," I say. Agreeing is easier than explaining why talking to him isn't as simple as she thinks it is. I can't even explain it to myself. I just see it in my mind: Me, standing in front of Mr.

Harrison, no words coming out. Me, walking away. Me, the lesbian Romeo. *Stop it, brain.* I follow her into the creek and she turns, flinging water at me. I yell and it's on, a full-blown battle, water flying in all directions, her running for the other side, me following, kicking huge sprays after her.

She takes refuge on the sand, far enough away so I can't splash her.

"Truce!" she gasps, laughing.

I stalk along the streambank, eyeing her as she giggles, and then nod like the gentleman I am. When I climb out of the creek, I pounce: arms wrapping around her, fully soaked body pressed against her dry clothes. She shrieks, laughing and writhing, until I let her go.

We find another log, far away from the incoming tide, and sit down, letting the sun warm us. "Did you start writing your personal statement yet?" I ask.

She talks and I watch her face, her legs warm on top of mine. Her pale skin glows in the afternoon light. When I look at her, my heart is the sound of the waves breaking on the beach, the words always there in the back of my mind. I can't say them yet. I'm not worthy of saying them, of feeling the way I do. She knows who she is, what she wants from life. I'm Romeo: *But, soft! What light through yonder window breaks? It is the east, and Juliet is the sun.* Romeo lives for nothing in life but women and parties, until he meets Juliet, and I'm living for the moment when I can be on stage, or holding Zoe. She is a whole person and I am a ghost in her light.

CHAPTER FIVE

On Sunday night, I open the Common App for the first time and have a minor freak-out. After I've stopped pacing and my heart has slowed down, I sit on my bed, staring at my laptop. I know I want this. But my fingers won't move and my brain seems to have calcified into a wall I can't get over.

I click over to YouTube and put a video on in the background, one of the guys I follow talking about starting testosterone for the first time, and open another browser tab. Search term: *acting monologues women*. I know there are literally twenty other things I could do right now for my NYU application, all of them higher priority than figuring out which monologue I'm going to audition with, but whatever. I have to pick one eventually. Might as well do it now.

Hermia, from *A Midsummer Night's Dream*? Throwback. I was cast as Hermia in sixth grade, opposite Ronnie as

Lysander. It took all of one rehearsal for us to come out to each other; we were already friends in class and the play solidified it. Playing Hermia was strange then and it might be easy now, but still weird. Lovesick straight girls? Can't relate.

Well, maybe the lovesick part.

I scroll through way too many Shakespeare monologues before adding a search term: *contemporary*.

Something from *The Vagina Monologues*? I try to imagine reciting an ode to my genitals in front of someone in charge of letting me into college. Nope.

Maybe Tony Kushner. I went through a phase after Zoe and I watched *Angels in America* and read a few of his other plays. Something political, edgy, obscure, something that will make me stand out. Annabella Gotchling, the working-class artist from *A Bright Room Called Day*?

But the monologue reads flat, like I'm trying too hard to be something I'm not.

I click back to the video. The YouTuber is listing the effects of testosterone. He calls it T, like most trans people do. Voice drop, muscle gain, fat redistribution. Or, not redistribution, exactly; the fat you already have won't magically move to another part of your body. But you'll gain fat in different places, places that cis men have fat. I squeeze my hips, try to imagine fat accumulating at my middle instead, erasing the curve I can't stand. That would be boss.

"And holy ass hair, Batman," the guy on the screen says, widening his eyes. "Sorry for the TMI, but it's a jungle down there." I fall over laughing.

Dad's heavy steps thump down the basement stairs. I close the tab and click back to the Common App.

He knocks on the door and when I answer, opens it. "Dinnertime, Dee-dee."

"Dad." I glare at him. "Don't call me that."

"Sorry, kiddo. How's life as the leading man?"

I give him a double thumbs-up. *The leading man.* I like that.

He scratches his dark beard. "I bet you're great in that role."

"Mom doesn't seem to think so."

"Your mom loves you. She's just adjusting."

"She's been adjusting since I was thirteen." I close the laptop.

"Come on, let's not argue. I made your favorite tonight—chili mac and cheese." He wiggles his eyebrows. I sigh and follow him upstairs to the dining room.

"My two favorite people in the world!" Mom says as we sit down. "How was your day, sweetie?"

I shrug. "Fine."

Mom frowns, but I avoid her stare, reaching for the Parmesan. With a sigh, she looks at Dad. "How about you, Leon?"

He shakes his head, says something about his boss at the city planning office. I tune out, thinking about Zoe, about us alone together. Sheena checks on us every thirty minutes when we're at their apartment. Here, we can't even hang out in my bedroom. Not that I have Zoe over much anyway; Mom's fake niceness is too weird. But Sheena was out of town a few weeks ago, and for the first time, Zoe and I went further than making out. When I kissed her neck, I thought of the tulips that grow outside our house every spring, their petals smooth and soft. She was shaking as she took off her shirt, and so was I, but when we started kissing again, the shaking stopped.

"How's Zoe doing?"

I jerk my head up.

Dad chuckles. "Welcome back to Earth."

The blush spreads hot across my face. "She's fine."

"We haven't seen her in a while," Mom says. "I was starting to wonder if you were still together."

"We're great," I say. "She's working on college applications right now."

Mom eyes me. "Speaking of which . . ."

"It's under control." I take a bite. The last of the sunlight through the window is fading, and Dad reaches over to the wall and flips on the light above the table.

"I suppose that's all I'm going to get out of you on that subject," Mom says.

"Yep."

Dad clears his throat. "Did I tell you two about the new guy at the office?"

I half listen, pushing the macaroni noodles around my plate, stacking them into a tiny wall. Zoe fills my mind again, the soft roundness of her arms stretched above her head, the sounds she made as I kissed my way down her body. Naked in her bedroom, I was conscious of all my body parts moving, but when I touched her, I could push it away for a while.

Normally, I'd go back online after dinner, but right now I want to FaceTime Zoe instead. Sometimes if I read about transition for too long, my insides shrink and my mind drifts like I'm floating away from my body and trapped inside it at the same time. I want to hear her voice. I need her to anchor me.

We start blocking the play on Monday afternoon. The read-through wrapped up last week, and now it's time to decide how we'll enter and exit, where we'll stand on stage, where we'll move as we talk to each other. Mr. Harrison skips through the fight scene that opens the play, saying we'll come back to it when we start stage combat.

"But that doesn't mean you get to relax," he says to the boys playing the Capulet and Montague henchmen. "You should be running lines. As should everyone who is not on stage or waiting for their cue," he adds, scanning the room.

We begin from the fight's aftermath: Montague and his lady talking to Benvolio about the fight, asking him where Romeo is. I wait in the wings, watching Mr. Harrison roam around the three actors, trying different configurations, asking their input. After the first day of the read-through, no one laughed at me again. Maybe everything will be fine.

I thumb through the script; I've already highlighted all my lines. I like memorizing as soon as possible, and this time it's even more urgent. If I'm off-book, no one will have any reason to doubt why I should be in the role. Not even Blake. I could tell he was disappointed when he found out he was Benvolio. He probably thought he had Romeo on lockdown.

"Dean!"

I jerk my head up. Mr. Harrison motions me forward. The kids playing Montague and Lady Montague are gone. Blake is standing behind Mr. Harrison, and he shakes his head, rolling his eyes. Shit. I missed my cue. I hustle on stage, trying not to show how embarrassed I am.

"So," Mr. Harrison says. "I'm thinking here I want you to wander on. You're in your head, thinking about the girl you're pining over. You don't even see Benvolio; his greeting brings you back to Earth. How does that sound?"

"Great." I don't look at Blake. I don't want to see him make a face again.

"Wonderful." Mr. Harrison claps his hands once. "Let's take it from the top."

By the end of rehearsal, we've moved on from my first scene with Blake, but the face he made keeps flashing in my head. I can't believe I missed my first cue. A rookie mistake.

"We still on for studying?" Ronnie asks as we pack up. I nod.

As we ride the bus, Ronnie scrolls through Instagram while I study my lines, trying to push past my doubts. Mr. Harrison said he made unorthodox choices, which means he picked me for a reason. But that also means he knows that choice was out of the norm, which makes it risky. What if I can't live up to what he was hoping for when he cast me? What was he hoping for, anyway? The page I'm staring at blurs, my thoughts pinging off each other like flies against glass.

Ronnie's house is a small brick bungalow in a neighborhood the opposite direction from mine, the lawn and garden maintained by his mom, Arlene. A few bright blooms still hang from the rosebushes, and the hedges are freshly trimmed into dark green rectangles. Ronnie grabs the hidden key from the fake rock beside the porch and lets us in.

"Mom? Dad?" Ronnie's voice echoes into the silent house. His parents aren't home from work yet; Jamal, his dad, works for Boeing as an engineer, and Arlene is a school counselor at a high school in South Seattle.

We spread out on the living room couch, books and school laptops on the cushions around us, chips and salsa on the glass coffee table. Ronnie turns on a studying playlist from Spotify, all wordless ambient electronic music.

"So." He crunches a chip. "What are we doing first? I have Math homework and a response to write for History."

I click through the assignments listed in my student portal. Ronnie and I are in different class periods, but we have the same World History teacher. "I have to do that response too."

"Draft and then trade?"

"Sure."

We settle in, the music washing around us. The baseboard heaters come on with a click and a whoosh, warm air filtering into the room. Ronnie types away. I stare out the front window. I need to find a way to care about the relationship between the British monarchy and the church, but all I can think about is the play.

Fifteen minutes later, I still haven't written a single word.

"Done!" Ronnie announces, striking a last key and looking up at me.

I grimace. He tilts his head. I turn my laptop around to show him my blank page and he laughs.

"I just can't focus," I say, shutting the laptop. "Why are we learning about old dead white guys again?"

"Right?" He pops another chip in his mouth. "I miss Ms. Maldonado." Ms. M was our junior year History teacher, for American Government, and she taught the topic through an overview of social justice movements. We'd watched a documentary on the Black Panthers and one about the representation of women in media. History had seemed interesting for once, like it was actually relevant to our lives instead of the musty words of our racist Founding Fathers.

Ronnie snaps his laptop shut. "Wanna run some lines?"

"That would be good," I say, digging out my script. "Then Blake can stop making faces at me."

"What?"

I tell him what happened in rehearsal, and then suddenly I'm spilling out everything I've been thinking about, how I'm afraid Mr. Harrison made the wrong choice, how I don't know which way he wants me to play Romeo, even what my mom said.

"Damn." Ronnie shakes his head. "I'm sorry."

"Thanks." I stare down at the script.

"Blake is an asshole," Ronnie says. "You got that role because you deserve it."

I smile in spite of myself. "I guess."

"You know what would make you feel better?" Ronnie asks.

"What?"

He grins. "Getting your ass kicked at Mario Kart."

"Shut the fuck up! I beat you last time!"

He leaps away from my swatting hand, laughing. "That was pure luck." He turns on the TV and tosses me a controller. "Get ready to be destroyed."

We chase each other down the Rainbow Road, shrieking when we fall off, stuffing chips in our mouths as we careen around track after track. I lose myself in the game, and after a while, Blake's face fades away. Ronnie's right. I can do this.

CHAPTER SIX

Over the weekend, we hit the thrift store and help Ronnie look for costumes. He's going with a fifties theme for the play, all sharp suits for the male roles, floral or pastel dresses for the female ones.

For the first time, I have a reason to go in the men's section. I know it's okay for me to be here. I'm helping Ronnie. But I swear the other guys in the section are staring at us, at me, and I avoid looking at them. I focus on the racks, flipping through shirts, searching for something flamboyant enough for Mercutio's costume.

Allison and Zoe appear from the dressing rooms in poofy formal dresses. I laugh as Ronnie takes their picture, and they all squeeze together for a selfie. I shake my head when they try to get me to join. I want to be in the photos, but I never like the way I look.

"Check this out!" Jared rolls up on his wheeled sneakers, waving a dark red button-up shirt with a gold collar.

"That's wassup!" Ronnie snatches it from him, looks at the label. "My size too."

Jared grabs the shirt back, and they tug-of-war for a moment, laughing, before Ronnie gives up.

"Trying out a new look?" I ask Jared.

He shrugs, draping the shirt over his shoulder. "I guess. I'm just tired of the same old same old."

I nod. We separate again, drifting through the aisles. I'm sifting through T-shirts when Ronnie's squeal makes me look up.

He turns, holding up a suit for me to see across the racks. It's a slim-cut two piece in silvery gray, and the jacket has black velvet lapels. "A white shirt," he says, gesturing at his chest. "And a blue pocket square?"

I stare at the suit. "Who is it for?"

"You, obviously."

I put my hands to my cheeks. "Oh my god. Ronnie. It's perfect."

He grins. "I thought you'd like it."

Once Zoe and Allison change back into their own clothes, we head for the registers. Zoe links her arm through mine. "Did you start your NYU application yet?"

I nod. "I opened it, anyway."

"Do you want to work on our applications together? Maybe, like, next weekend?"

I smile down at her. "Sure."

Ronnie sweeps his costume finds into a huge tote bag and we each take a strap, lugging it out of the store to his family's van.

"So what happened this time?" I ask him as we buckle up. I know there's only one reason why his dad would let him use their car: guilt.

He rolls down the windows, turns up the radio. "We had a fight. The usual." He hits the gas and we zoom across oncoming traffic into the middle lane. "Making clothes is a hobby, not a career," he says, dropping his voice into a perfect bass imitation of his dad.

"Damn." The baseball bobblehead on the dash shakes back and forth. In the backseat, Jared, Allison, and Zoe rock out to the music. "What about your mom?"

"I hear them talking about it sometimes. Dad hasn't changed his mind though." He hangs a right through a yellow light toward Zoe's neighborhood. "Whatever." He looks at me, arching an eyebrow. "We are going to New York City."

I pump my fist and turn the music up louder.

Ronnie drops me and Zoe off at her apartment, Jared scrambling into the front seat as the car careens away from the curb. Inside, on the kitchen table, we find a note from Sheena: *Gone for the afternoon, at the spa with friends. Leftover casserole in the fridge!*

We heat up the food in the microwave and eat on the couch, sharing from one huge plate.

"So I'm thinking about declaring a History major," Zoe

says through a mouthful of food. "I figure I can start there and specialize in Women's Studies in grad school."

"Grad school?" I raise my eyebrows.

"I have to go to grad school to be a professor," she says with a shrug.

"Wow."

"What?"

"You're just so . . ." I spear a chunk of vegetables with my fork. "Prepared."

"And you're not?"

"I don't know." I shrug. "I know I want to keep acting, and I want to go to NYU. But I haven't thought about anything besides that."

"I mean, the path for an actor is different than a professor," she says. "You don't need grad school, you can just start acting."

I nod.

She tilts her head. "Are you okay?"

"What do you mean?" I half laugh.

"You seem . . ." She twists her mouth around. "I don't know. Off?"

"I'm fine." I reach out and poke her with my fork.

She bats it away, and I keep trying to poke her until she's laughing, until she grabs the fork from my hand. When she smiles, it spreads across her whole face, like a sunrise. Sometimes I can't believe she's with me.

"You're so beautiful," I say.

"Oh, is that all I am?" She puts her hands on her hips.

"No. You're also perfect."

She arches an eyebrow. "I'm definitely not."

"You're smart, hot, funny, and cool. That's basically the definition of perfect."

She shakes her head, rolling her eyes, and gets up, taking the plate to the sink. I watch her rinse it off, smiling.

We sprawl out on the couch and read through lines, her prompting me every time I miss one. I'm almost memorized, but not quite. A few pages in, I close my eyes, make her wait while I try and remember.

When I open my eyes, she's peeking at me over the script. "So, my mom won't be back for a while . . ."

Instant grin. My stomach does a happy-nervous flutter. She tosses the script onto the table and I follow her out of the living room, down the narrow hall to the apartment's two bedrooms, and into hers. The door closes behind us with a faint click and we're pressed together, lips meeting, warm and gentle at first and then rougher, mouths opening, teeth catching bottom lips until she pulls me to the bed, breathless and laughing, and I lay her down, kissing the soft inch of her stomach between shirt hem and belt. She pulls me up and kisses me hard, our hands moving on each other's bodies like ocean waves into tide pools. Last time, I was too self-conscious to let her touch me, but not today. I want her to touch me, help me remember what it's like to be in this body, remember that it's good, that I can stay the shape she likes. I have to. The static in my head retreats and all I hear is our breathing, heavier and heavier, yet high and light as the cool breeze through her window. I love touching her, love kissing her, love the softness of her skin against mine. Love her body, her thick thighs and waist; love who she is—I love everything about her.

I almost say it right then. *I love you, Zoe.* But I press my lips against her neck instead. Sometimes my heart feels like a weight in constant danger of pulling everything off-center if I say or do the wrong thing. I want to keep everything the way it is, in perfect balance.

Even though I want to let it go, that moment with Blake haunts me. I can't seem to get comfortable as we practice our blocking, still reading from scripts. I can tell he's judging my every move, wondering why I'm Romeo. I say a line and he responds with an edge of sarcasm, the kind teachers never notice, or mistake for sincerity. Mr. Harrison thinks he's embodying Benvolio as a boisterous joker, but I know better.

I think. Sometimes I wonder if I'm making it up.

"Just ignore him," Ronnie says in the library one afternoon. We're studying for English with Allison, marking up the reading. We've been in the same English classes since freshman year, when we were assigned a group project together: make a short film out of one act of *King Lear*. Allison filmed and Ronnie and I played all the roles. Sometimes multiple roles in the same scene. A technically brilliant move. Our teacher gave us a C.

"I literally cannot ignore Blake," I say, laying my head on the table. "There would be no play if I ignored him. Or no me. Mr. Harrison would replace me." I sigh. "Maybe he should."

"Are you still thinking about why he cast you?" Ronnie claps his book shut. "For the love of Gay Jesus, talk to him already."

A giggle from Allison. I glare and she props her chin on one hand, blinking at me innocently.

A faint ding from the bell on the librarian's desk makes me look up. Blake is standing there, handing over cash for his fines.

"Oh my god." Ronnie grabs my arm. "The man, the myth, the legend."

"He's gonna hear you!" I pull away.

Blake turns. Our eyes meet. Too late to pretend I don't see him.

"Hey," I call out, and Allison kicks me under the table. I widen my eyes at her and kick back.

Blake comes over. "What's up?"

I shrug.

"You memorized yet?" He doesn't look at Allison and Ronnie.

"Getting there," I say. He's wearing a shirt with an advertisement on it, some shitty light beer, the kind we always have at cast parties. Technically, alcohol logos aren't allowed in our dress code, but of course no one has made him change. I've noticed us white kids tend to get away with breaking those rules.

"Getting there, huh? So basically you're already off-book?" He grins and I smile back. "Later," he says, and leaves.

Allison eyes me.

"What?" I flip through my reading, avoiding her stare.

"I will never understand how you're cool with him," she says.

"It's just easier that way."

Ronnie snorts. "That's so you."

I pull back, staring at him. "What does that mean?"

"Nothing. I just meant . . . I don't know." He sighs. "You're just too nice sometimes, Dean."

I want to be offended, but he's not saying anything mean. I look across the table at Allison, who gives me a half smile, lips pressed together. A lump swells in my throat and I swallow it down. I know Blake is an asshole. I've heard him say things. But I don't know what to do when he does that. My mind goes blank and my heart beats like bird wings and I wait for the moment to pass, for the teacher to say something stern and meaningless that will ultimately change nothing.

Ronnie nudges me. "Are you mad at me?"

"I'm fine," I say. "I'm just not like you. I have to act with Blake every day. I can't avoid him."

"Okay," Ronnie says. We keep studying, the silence like armor, thick and heavy on my shoulders.

CHAPTER SEVEN

"From Romeo's entrance!" Mr. Harrison calls again. I've lost count of how many times we've started this part of the first scene over.

Blake sighs and strides back to his mark. I run back to the side of the stage.

On Monday, to groans and protests, Mr. Harrison announced we were moving off-book. He would hold a script and prompt us if we forgot a line, but he wanted us to start practicing without ours.

I'm mostly memorized. But I can't relax. I still need to ask him how he wants me to play Romeo. And what he meant by his comments.

Unorthodox method.

Am I just an experiment?

Across the stage, Blake lifts his eyebrows at me. I missed my cue again. He repeats the line, and I walk on stage.

"Dean, hands out of pockets," Mr. Harrison says. I yank them out, but then I have to decide where they're supposed to go. At my sides? Arms crossed? I clasp them behind my back. Maybe a military pose will make me look more masculine.

"Good morrow, cousin," Blake says.

"Is the day so young?" I put my hand on my hip. No. Stand up straight. Blake is at ease, arms hanging loose on either side of his broad chest. We trade lines, and then it's time for my monologue, my mooning over Rosaline, the girl who doesn't return my affections.

"Feather of lead, cold smoke, bright fire—"

"Bright smoke, cold fire!" Mr. Harrison calls out.

"Feather of lead, bright smoke, cold fire, sick health!" I can do this. Come on. "Still-waking sleep is not what—that feel not what—" Blake is staring at me, his back to Mr. Harrison. His jawline meets his ear in a perfect square, the buzz-cut completing the look along his forehead. He's a guy, like Romeo. He's a guy, and I'm not. Why am I Romeo, and not him? Out in the audience, people are laughing, running up and down the aisle. Rehearsal is going longer than usual, and it's my fault.

Blake exhales loudly, turning away. Mr. Harrison stares down at the script, then claps it closed and sets it on the stage.

"Let's take a break," he says. "Then let's run this bit once all the way through. I know you two can do it."

"I'm not the one messing up my lines," Blake mumbles, but Mr. Harrison is already looking out into the theatre, voice raised to rein in the aisle-racers.

Blake jumps off the stage and grabs one of his friends in a headlock, then pounds fists with another guy. He says something and they all laugh, glancing over at me. My face burns.

I take refuge in the wings, flopping down on the ratty couch shoved against the back wall. The teal vinyl is cool on my skin. I stare up into the dark rafters, wishing I was just a henchman, a two-line bit part. I probably look ridiculous on stage next to Blake. He's as confident as a quarterback, cool in his fake-vintage T-shirts and dark blue jeans. Everything Romeo is and I will never be.

"You OK?" Ronnie's tall frame moves into my periphery. He sits down at the end of the couch. I can hear people giggling on the other side of the stage.

"I hate messing up my lines," I say.

"Want to run them later?"

"No. I have them. I just . . ." The words dry up. Dust hangs high in the air, hovering around the glow of the stage lights.

"If you wanna talk about anything . . ." Ronnie trails off.

"It's fine." I sit up, giving him a half smile.

His eyebrows crinkle, but he nods. "If you say so."

The silence stretches like a rubber band. I want to tell Ronnie everything, how I can't stop comparing myself to Blake, how I want to be Romeo but I know I'm not good enough, how my own body is betraying me on stage every day. How every night, I scroll through pictures wishing my body looked like the ones on the screen. I close my eyes, arrange the words in my mind.

Mr. Harrison calls my name. I squash the words back down and walk out of the wings without looking at Ronnie.

Five tries later, we make it through the scene. "Finally!" someone yells from the auditorium, laughter following like hyenas on the hunt. Mr. Harrison frowns, but releases us.

I take my time, waiting for people to leave, waving Ronnie away. My chest tightens. I have to know, now, what Mr. Harrison sees in me.

He's sitting on the edge of the stage, flipping through the stack of character sheets we handed in at the beginning of class. When I step forward out of the aisle, he looks up.

"Why did you cast me as Romeo?" I ask.

"Everyone has a rough rehearsal at some point, Dean."

"It's not that. I just want to know . . ."

He waits. The lights on the stage are bright, but here in the audience, I'm out of their golden reach. The floor is dingy under the weak house lights. "Do you want me to play Romeo as a boy or . . . ?" I can't bring myself to finish the sentence.

He hums, nodding slowly. His bow tie today is red with black polka dots. "You're the actor, Dean. How do you want to play Romeo?"

I open my mouth, then close it, biting my lower lip. I don't know what he wants to hear, whether he'll still want me to play Romeo if I tell him. I think of Mom, laughing at the thought of a lesbian version of the play. As if I can never play any role other than the one I've been playing off stage.

"I want to play Romeo—" I stop. My heart is rattling out of my chest, like continuous thunder in my ears, adrenaline flash flooding my veins. *Come on. You can do this.* "I want to play Romeo as a guy."

His eyebrows raise once. If I move, I'll faint, or my knees will give out. *Wham.* Flat on my face in front of Mr. Harrison. Breathe.

"I do admit that when I picked you for the role, I hoped we could turn some of the expectations people have of this play on their head," Mr. Harrison says finally. "Cross-gender casting isn't unusual in theatre, but it doesn't often happen at the high school level."

My heart deflates. Mom was right.

"However," he adds, "directing is a collaboration. If you want to play Romeo as a boy, then show me who he is. Right now, I see you're still working on lines. But who is Romeo to you? How will you show that? Make those decisions."

"You told the cast you'd taken a chance on casting. That they should keep an open mind."

"Ah, that." He smiles, shaking his head slightly. "I'm sorry if I made you feel singled out. You have it much easier here than I did as a young gay man in London. But if there's one thing I've learned, it is that there are no guarantees. I only meant to acknowledge and forestall any negative reactions."

"Thanks," I say quietly, shifting my feet. I'm already thinking about the questions he just asked: about who Romeo is, how he walks, his gestures, his facial expressions. I want to go home and read the play again, write down everything I can find about Romeo in the text.

He inclines his head. "I'll see you at rehearsal tomorrow, Dean."

I grab my stuff and leave the auditorium into the crisp afternoon. So Mr. Harrison hasn't guessed my secret. Maybe he just wanted to mess with audience expectations. Whatever. I can live with that. What matters is I can play Romeo the way I want. The sun warms my face all the way to the bus stop.

Friday night, I stare at the Common App's personal statement options for a full hour, trying to get past the wall in my mind. I can talk about a meaningful aspect of my identity, or a time I faced obstacles, or a belief I questioned, or or or—is it just me, or are there too many prompts?

I shut my laptop and close my eyes. Five weeks until the application is due. Six weeks until auditions for Tisch, NYU's acting school.

I don't know how to do this.

I open the laptop again and search monologues. I read through blog after blog promising Great Monologues for Teens and 5 Perfect Comedic Monologues for Actresses and 20 Classic Audition Monologues for Women until a lump swells in my throat. I can't do this. I don't want to.

I mean. I want to go to Tisch. But none of these monologues fit me.

Because they're all for women.

I toss the laptop aside and go to the bathroom. Afterward, washing my hands, I stare at myself in the mirror. I don't see a Lady Capulet, or a Hermia, or a Vagina Monologuer, or any female role I can think of. Even if there was a play featuring tomboy lesbians, I wouldn't pick a monologue from it, because I'm not a tomboy lesbian.

And I don't want the Tisch admissions reviewers to see me that way either. Not that there's anything wrong with that. But it's not me.

I ruffle my hair out of place and smooth it back again. It's starting to grow out from my short summer cut, the sides shaggy, the top beginning to curl. My under-eye circles look dark against my skin, its golden summer glow faded into pinkish-white again. I don't look like a girl to me.

But I don't look like what I want to see. The admissions officers will probably laugh me off the screen if I try a male character's monologue for my digital audition.

I sigh and go back to my room.

The weather this weekend is perfect: sunny and cool, and most importantly, dry. That won't last long.

"You read my mind," Jared says when I call him. We meet at the skate park an hour later.

"Mr. Harrison is gonna kill you if you break your leg again," he says, nodding at the board in my hand. Last year, I sprained my ankle right before opening weekend.

I laugh. "Flats only." Looking down at my toes, I rock back and forth on the board. "No bowl. No ollies. What Mr. Harrison doesn't know won't hurt him."

He shrugs, drops his board, and rolls to the edge of the bowl, then tips down with a clack, zooming to the bottom, wheels a metallic whir echoing up to me. I zip around the sides, zigzagging back and forth, enjoying the scrape of the board underneath my shoes. I do a wide circle around the park, dodging benches, gliding down the smooth walkway to the far end and back, while Jared bursts from the bowl again and again, board caught in one hand, arm flung high into the air. My mind is as clean as the sky.

As soon as I notice that, though, the thoughts come back. Monologues, auditions, the application. I skate faster, wishing I could jump just one curb. But I don't want to bust an ankle—or worse—again. Especially now that I'm playing a lead. Mr. Harrison was angry enough last year, when I was just a secondary character.

After a while, Jared sails up to the top and sits on the edge of the bowl, unwraps a candy bar, and offers me a piece. We eat together, looking across the bowl to the green playfield beyond.

"It's been a while," he says.

"Yeah." I lie back onto the warm concrete, staring up at the blue sky. "Your skater bros aren't really my people."

"I know."

"I noticed you've been hanging with us more," I say, putting a hand to my face and squinting over at him.

"Yeah." He pulls his knees up, clasping his hands. "I'm just tired of the bullshit. It's constant. And whenever I say something, *I'm the problem.* I can't take a joke, or I'm a pussy, or something. Sorry," he adds, glancing down at me.

I grimace. "You're just repeating what they're saying. It's not you saying it."

"I guess."

I sit up, watching a group of guys skate into the park at the other end. Behind them, swallows dip and sail across the field.

"I just don't want to hear that stuff," he says. "I want to stop it. But nothing I do makes a difference."

"I'm sorry," I reply, because I don't know what else to say. I stopped hanging out with Jared's skater friends for the same reason he's avoiding them. All the stupid, gross stuff they said about women, things they said because they didn't seem to realize I was there. Or because I was there and they didn't see me as a girl.

Which made me feel good, and then immediately like a horrible person for not standing up to them.

"Whatever," he says.

"It's not just skaters," I say, even though I know he knows that.

"Yeah, you've gotta deal with Blake every day." He rolls his eyes. "The heir to Harvey's asshole kingdom."

I snort. "I can just tell he thinks he should be Romeo."

"Fuck him," Jared says. "You were made for that role."

"What?" I lean back, staring at him, a smile tugging at the corner of my mouth.

"Dude. You've got that swagger."

"Shut up," I say.

He shrugs, grinning. "It's true."

"I just feel like it's weird," I say. The guys across from us clank down into the bowl one by one, looping around the bottom, avoiding the section of the lip where we sit.

"Why?"

I side-eye him. "Because Romeo is a guy. And I'm . . ."

"You're kinda like a guy to me," he says. Darts his eyes at me. "Sorry if that's offensive."

I look away, grinning. "Nah." I start laughing, and he quirks his eyebrows, his smile hesitant. "Not at all."

"Cool," he says, and we keep sitting there, legs dangling off the edge, watching the skaters and the swallows fly.

CHAPTER EIGHT

At the beginning of the week, we walk into rehearsal and there
they are: a costume for each character, hung on a long rolling
rack at center stage. I find the hanger labeled *Romeo* and smile.
The suit from our thrift store run is just as sleek and silver
as I remember, the black velvet lapels on the jacket soft, the
dress shirt crisp and white, a silky blue handkerchief folded
up and peeking out of the breast pocket. No shoes; we'll all
be wearing the black leather character shoes from the back of
the costume closet. They look nice, but they smell like twenty
years of sweaty feet.

We circle up, clutching our costumes, admiring others.
Olivia holds her dress against her, showing it off to me with a
smile; it's peach, with a Peter Pan collar, pearl buttons all the
way down to the cinched waist.

"Today is an exciting day!" Mr. Harrison says to us. "As you all know, since you have undoubtedly memorized our entire rehearsal schedule, dress rehearsals don't start until the beginning of December. But Ronnie has put together the signature costume for each person, so today, you'll be taking that costume home. I want you to try it on, wear it around, carry it with you, even sleep in it if you must." One of the guys lets out a loud fake snore and we laugh. The corners of Mr. Harrison's mouth twitch upward. "Get to know the clothes and how they fit with your character. At the end of this week, I expect a short write-up about what you experienced."

Rehearsal flies by, all of us floating on the excitement of costumes. When we're done, I slip the suit into its garment bag and head out.

The suit is beautiful. I want it to fit me, but I know Ronnie will have to alter it. My chest and hips aren't much, but they're enough to ruin a suit. I try to stay above my circling thoughts, running lines and stage directions in my head to distract myself, but I keep getting stuck halfway through the first scene.

Enter Romeo. He tells Benvolio that he's pining for a girl named Rosaline. He starts to leave and Benvolio tries to come along. Romeo shakes his head. *I have lost myself; I am not here; This is not Romeo, he's some other where.* What's next? *This is not Romeo, he's some other where.*

At home, in my room, I strip down to my underwear, stare at the garment bag draped over my bed. The clothes make the man, or so people say. I'm an astronaut charting the void, no map, surrounded by darkness. The idea of wearing men's clothes seems wrong, like I'm breaking some unwritten rule. I try to imagine wearing it tomorrow. It's tradition—everyone in the cast wears their signature costume to the first rehearsal after we get the clothes.

I reach out, unzip the bag, touch the soft lapels of the jacket. This is it; this is the moment when someone appears out of nowhere, demands to know what I'm doing with clothes for the wrong gender.

I zip up the bag, hang it on the back of my door, and go upstairs for a snack.

At school the next day, I pass Olivia, Courtney, and the other theatre girls. Garment bags hang off their shoulders, costumes ready to wear for rehearsal. Olivia catches my eye and waves, but I make like I have to rush to class, mouthing a sorry and dodging around the corner. I don't want her to ask me about this. I don't want to do this at all.

I leave my suit folded up carefully in my locker. Everyone is going to wear their costume. I'll be the odd one out. Me, the star of the show. *Good plan, Dean.*

All through lunch, I pretend I'm listening to my friends. I smile and nod, laugh and say the right things in the right places, but I'm Robot Dean. Real Dean is thinking about the suit. At the end of lunch, I walk Zoe to class, kiss her, and head to Calculus.

And then my legs are taking me to my locker instead, hands turning the combination lock, arms bundling out the garment bag. I speed walk to the auditorium, keeping an eye out for the security guard. I don't want to get caught skipping class. My heart isn't pounding. I am calm, far away from my body, as if I'm not in control. My body moves without me, making this happen.

The theatre is empty and dark. I feel my way up the steps onto the stage and behind the curtain to the girls' dressing room. Inside, I turn on the lights around one of the mirrors and hang the garment bag on the rack.

Now I'm back in my own head again, in charge of my own movements. I strip down to my underwear and stare at the bag, then reach out and unzip it. First the pants, then the shirt. They actually fit all right. A little baggy, but that's okay. *Nice one, Ronnie.* I button up the shirt and turn to the mirror, shift side to side. I can see the curve of my chest. I pick at the front of the shirt, trying to get it to drape just right so it conceals my breasts.

I take off the shirt and stare at myself. My summer tan is gone, skin pale again, white sports bra gleaming in the dim light. How do I bind without a binder? I think of the posts I've read online. *Never use tape or Ace bandages,* one guy had written on Reddit.

Sorry, Internet Trans Guy. I don't have a lot of options. I know it's dangerous, I know I shouldn't do it, but it's just this once. Only for a minute. I won't even wear it for rehearsal. I just want to see how it could look.

I glance around. What I need isn't in this room. I go to the door and listen.

Nothing. I open the door and tiptoe out into the darkness, to the tool closet. I feel around on each shelf, finding boxes of nails, the thick shape of a screwdriver. My ears strain for any sound.

There it is. I grab the duct tape.

Back to the dressing room. I close the door and shove a chair under the knob, like people do in movies to keep doors shut. It does absolutely nothing. Fine. Whatever. I move it back. Then I tear one end of the tape away from the roll and press it to the bottom band of the bra, in the middle of my chest. I wrap the roll around and around myself, squashing my breasts outward and upward, as flat as I can, as fast as I can. Around and around, up and up, until I tear the other end of the tape from the roll and press it to the top of my bra. It's tight and uncomfortable. I can't even take a full breath.

Then the shirt again. I button it up, the sheath of tape disappearing behind crisp white fabric. I tuck the shirt into the pants, then pull on the suit jacket. I look down.

It's flat.

I look up.

I turn sideways.

This time, my chest looks right.

The front of my jacket lies flat. I face front again. In the mirror, it's me. Not a girl with short hair, in jeans, T-shirt, big hoodie to hide her chest.

It's me. In a gray suit, the black velvet lapels forming a perfect V to the center button of the white shirt, my chest flat, hips hidden under the bottom hem of the jacket.

I look like a boy.

I am a boy.

I press my hands to my chest, touch my face, comb the curling ends of my hair to the side. I thought I wanted to transition. And now I know for sure.

I need this. This suit, this body.

I need to go to NYU as a boy. No matter what the admissions people think.

I need to be Zoe's boyfriend, not her girlfriend.

I need to be a boy forever, not just for now.

Tears blur my vision and I blink. When my eyes are clear, I look at myself again. The boy is gone, the girl is back. I look the same as ever, but I feel different. She is not me.

The boy is me.

I hear voices in the auditorium, a burst of chatter and laughter. Heat jolts through my body. The rest of the cast is here for rehearsal. Footsteps on the stage. No time to undress and take off the tape. The door swings open.

"Oh my god!" Olivia presses a hand to her chest. She smiles. "You scared the shit out of me, Dean." She squeezes behind me with her costume, the girls following, Courtney eyeing me up and down in the mirror with a raised eyebrow.

I scuttle out of the room before anyone can say anything or notice my chest. Out in the theatre, the cast and crew arrive, Ronnie waving to me on his way to the costume closet. I wave back, sweat gathering in my armpits despite the frozen-tundra air of the auditorium.

I'm Robot Dean again, in my head, watching myself through the opening game. Then, rehearsal. Every line leaves my head, a few holding on like rotten teeth, the rest gone. The tape cuts into the flesh on my chest, keeping me from drawing a full breath. Any minute now. Any minute now someone will figure out I'm binding, will understand what that means, will howl it to the whole group.

No one else is fully memorized either, but I know my mistakes throw everyone else off. I know everyone is staring, whispering when I'm not looking. Every giggle off stage is a dagger in my heart, a hand around my throat.

Finally, Mr. Harrison heaves a sigh. Early dismissal, study your lines tonight, please. Emphasis on the *please*.

He does not look at me.

I loiter backstage, scrolling through Instagram on my phone until I'm sure all the girls have left the dressing room. Then I go in, undress as fast as I can, and tear off the tape. I hate seeing my chest curvy again, but it's a relief to be able to breathe right. I need to get a binder soon, so I can do it right and hopefully avoid rashes, back pain, breathing problems, even rib damage—I've read some horror stories online about injuries from incorrect binding. I hang the suit alongside the other costumes, grab my backpack, and leave out the door at the back of the theatre.

On the walk home, I remember Mom wrestling me into dresses as a kid, how I always wanted to play with the boys, how Mom and Dad took me to see *West Side Story* at the 5th Avenue Theatre when I was ten. I was already in love with performing, thanks to summer acting camp, and I totally fell for Tony, the leading man of *West Side Story*.

No. I remember his gentle strength, his deep voice belting out those songs, how he wooed Maria, the sister of the rival gang leader. I didn't want to be with him. I wanted to *be* him.

"I wanted to be Tony," I whisper.

And I'd told Mom so, but she shook her head, and then she said it: "You can't be Tony, honey. Tony's a boy, and you're a girl. Girls play girl characters and boys play boys."

She was wrong. People play roles across gender all the time in theatre. And I wasn't a girl, then or now.

Wait. Mr. Harrison's assignment.

My heart shrivels. What am I supposed to say? *This costume made me realize I want to transition?* Right. That will go over well. A-plus for sure.

But I don't want to make something up. Not for Mr. Harrison's class.

I could come out.

No. Bad thought, bad idea. It's already uncomfortable enough being gay. At least there are other gay kids at school. If I come out as trans, I'll be alone. The only one. In my mind, I hear Blake, and the things he could say. The things I've read online, the words I don't even want to repeat in my own head. And the things that happen to kids like me. Brandon Teena's murder flashes into my mind, and my stomach boils, breath coming short and sharp. I stop on the sidewalk, staring down the road lined with trees, their leaves aflame in orange and yellow.

I could be Romeo. I could play him every night, bind my chest, wear the costume. I could be a boy.

And then, the end. Last show. Last cast party. Back to life as Dean Foster, the girl.

I can't do this.

I can't do this.

My throat constricts and the tears well up and I let them slide silently down my cheeks all the way home.

ACT TWO

"Can I go forward when my heart is here?"

—ROMEO

Romeo and Juliet, act 2, scene 1

CHAPTER NINE

"Here's what I don't get," Ronnie says the next day at lunch. We're eating in the senior hallway, sprawled out against the wall of windows. "Why are we reading Hemingway? I don't give a fuck about Hemingway." He bites a carrot in half.

"It's a classic, dude. *The Old Man and the Sea*? It's man's eternal battle with nature," Jared says, leaning back on his arms. Ronnie arches an eyebrow and looks at us.

"Ronnie's right," Zoe says. "There are so many other amazing writers we could be reading who aren't old white straight people."

"I know, right? And all this bullshit about symbolism? Please. He's just an old man who can't catch a fish." Ronnie shakes his head. I summon a smile to match everyone else's.

When the bell rings, I get my things and head to class. Halfway down the hall, Ronnie calls my name and catches up to me.

"You looked good as hell in that suit yesterday," he says. "I want to take it in a little bit but it's almost perfect."

I nod, not looking at him.

"I mean, I knew as soon as I saw it that it was Romeo's suit. That silver, and the velvet? Yes. I think I'm going to include the design for the play as part of my portfolio for Parsons."

"Cool," I say. I want to be excited, want to talk about it with him, but if I do, I'll cry, and then it will all come out.

"Are you okay?" he asks.

The tears well up without my permission and I shake my head. We're almost at my classroom and we stop, me looking at the lockers. I can feel his eyes on me. My brain is buzzing, my chest tight like all my emotions are filling me up, pressing against my rib cage until I explode.

"What's going on?" His voice is soft and warm now.

The late bell splits the noise of the hallway.

"Shit," he says, looking down the hall and back at me.

"Later?" I say.

He nods and starts to turn, then pivots and wraps me in a tight hug before I can move. He steps back and disappears into the crowd.

I'm in a daze the rest of the day. Rehearsal's focus is on other characters, so I run lines with people in the seats and spend the rest of the period doing homework until the bell rings. My heart pounds as I walk to my locker. I don't know what to tell Ronnie. How much I should say. How much I can say without having to say all of it.

I leave a few books in my locker and grab others. My phone buzzes with a text from Ronnie.

Wanna come over?

I stare at the text.

And I leave school without replying.

At home that night, I can't focus. I try the same math problem over and over, but I keep slipping away, into my head, the week replaying like the world's worst movie. Ronnie sends me a few more texts, asking if I got his, if I'm okay, that I know where to find him if I want to talk. I still haven't replied. Every time I start to type, my hands get shaky and my chest tightens and I have to put the phone down.

My chest presses against the bed. I wish it was gone. I wish I wasn't in this body, wasn't in this life. My limbs are electric, like I could punch through a wall and keep swinging.

I want to come out. I want to transition. But when I try to picture it, there's a black hole in my mind, between present me and future me. There's me now, in the most boyish clothes I can find in the girls' section, my face betraying me every time I look in the mirror. And then there's future me, like breath on the glass, fuzzy at the edges but there: smiling, square-jawed, broad. Wearing the right clothes. Flat-chested without a binder.

In between, there's nothing, just a void sucking up all the pieces I could use to build a bridge. If I jump, I might fall. I might never see the me on the other side.

I shove the homework onto the floor and roll over onto my back.

Bowie's there on the wall, staring off into the distance. Next to him, above the head of my bed, is my collage: printed photos of my friends, places I've been, concert tickets, programs from past plays tacked up on the wall. The picture in the center is a selfie, me and Ronnie at our first Pride Parade last year, smiles huge, sun blazing down as we pose in front of the Seattle Center fountain on full blast. He's shirtless and covered in glitter; I'm in a black sports bra, rainbow beads around my neck. Behind us, thousands of dancing people, frozen mid-dash toward the water, or stumbling out drenched and grinning. There's a man in the far background in a gold bodysuit, two girls kissing right beside him. I close my eyes. I smell pizza, hear bass thumping, feel the sun hot on my shoulders.

"Race you," Ronnie said, socked me in the arm, and took off down toward the water. I shrieked and ran after him, and then we were right up against the fountain, spread-eagled against the metal sculpture as cold water soaked us to the skin, huge sprays arcing above us, rainbows glittering in the air.

When Ronnie and I came out to each other, it was just a formality. We knew. We saw each other and knew we were family.

My room is cold. I grab my blanket, pulling it around me, curling up. Hot tears slide down my cheeks. I need Ronnie. I need to talk.

The next morning, I text him before I can think about it too much: Sorry I ditched u, meet at smokers alley after school?

He texts back a thumbs-up.

Smokers Alley is really a staircase, the one at the far end of the sports fields that goes down to the main street. After the last bell, another Romeo-less rehearsal setting me free early, I grab my stuff and head out.

The sky is gray, a fine October mist speckling my hoodie and face as I cross the baseball diamond. Ronnie is sitting on the top step with his back to me, staring down at his phone. No one else is there, just him and a few cigarette butts littering the top step. He turns and stands up as I approach.

"Wanna go to my house?" he asks, and I nod.

On the bus ride there, we make small talk about classes, theatre, more of his costume ideas. Ronnie gets me. He knows I don't want to break down in public.

At his house, we kick off our shoes and head to the kitchen for snacks. I sit down at the table in the breakfast nook and he plops down across from me, dropping a box of cookies between us.

His brown eyes catch mine. "What's up?"

I look at the kitchen, small but neat, every inch used for a purpose. There are pictures on the fridge of family barbecues, uncles and aunts at holidays, cards for every season. The appliances are old but clean.

"It's the play," I say into the stillness. "I don't know if I can do it."

He's quiet, watching me. At least, that's what it looks like out of the corner of my eye. I stare at the spice rack.

"I'm just not ready for this role." The silence is growing, sitting on my shoulders, pressing me into the chair. "That suit." My throat is closing up. I swallow. "It's so perfect. But it made me realize things. I can't do the costume assignment."

"What do you mean?" Ronnie's voice is gentle.

Tears burn my eyes and I press my hands against them. "I never could have played Lady Capulet."

"Nah. I can't see you as any of the women in that play."

"Because I'm not one."

The old analog clock over the doorway ticks. Outside, the mist turns to rain tapping the window.

"You're not one?" Ronnie asks. "You're not a woman?"

"I'm transgender," I say, and as I breathe out I start sobbing.

A moment later he's beside me, arms around me, muttering *oh wow oh wow* and *it's okay, you're cool* and *I got you* into my ear, over and over, but I can't stop crying. My body shakes and he hugs me tighter until I collapse against him, face pressed against his soft golden sweater. When I finally straighten up, wiping my face, he runs to the bathroom and returns with a cold washcloth. I press it to my eyes. A box of tissues is sitting in front of me when I look again.

"Does that mean you feel like a guy?" he asks.

I nod.

"Okay. Okay." He nods. "This makes sense."

I let out a half sob, half laugh. "It does?"

He puts a fist up to his mouth. "Oh my god. Do you remember when we first met?"

I smile. "You thought I was a guy."

"And then the teacher said your name and I was like—what?"

We both laugh. Ronnie's round eleven-year-old face pops into my mind, his eyes widening as the teacher walked away, right after we bonded over our mutual hatred of sports. *That name doesn't fit you at all,* he said. *I'm gonna call you Dean.* It was a shortened version of my given name, but it felt way better, like the name I should have had all along. I nodded, grinning, and that was it. By high school, I started asking everyone to call me Dean, even teachers. At first I'd thought of it as a nickname, and so did everyone else, but now I know—it's my real name.

He stares at me, brown eyes serious. "Tell me you're not trying to quit the play."

I put my head down on my arms. "I don't know."

"Dean."

I look at him. He arches an eyebrow.

"Okay, no. I'm not quitting the play." I sigh. "I just don't know what to do. We have to turn in our assignment to Mr. Harrison tomorrow. About how our costume made us feel. I don't want to just lie about it, but I can't tell him the truth."

"Why not?" Ronnie leans his chin on his fist.

"What if he's not cool with it?"

"He's gay," Ronnie says.

"That doesn't guarantee anything," I say.

"He cast you," Ronnie says. "That means he saw something in you. Whether he originally wanted to gender-swap it or whatever, there was still something that made him do it. You really think he'll be that surprised?"

I shrug.

"You don't have to tell everyone," Ronnie says. "It's just Mr. Harrison."

"I guess." I sit up, plucking a cookie from the box. The tightness in my chest is easing, the heaviness of the silence is lighter. Maybe I can do this. It's not like the whole world will know.

"Have you told Zoe?" Ronnie asks.

I slump down. "No."

"Are you going to?"

"I don't know." I munch on the cookie. "I've been following a lot of trans stuff online. When someone in a couple transitions . . ." I shrug. "It doesn't always work out."

"It's Zoe," Ronnie says. "She loves you."

I cut my eyes at him. "She does not."

"Dean. Are you that oblivious?"

"She hasn't said anything."

He looks at me, shaking his head, and laughs. "She doesn't have to."

I stay up late that night writing my response for Mr. Harrison. We only have to write one page, and I say it as plainly as I can:

I've been thinking about gender transition for a while, and this costume made me realize that I want to. I'm a trans guy.

It feels good to write down, and even better to hold in my hands and read once I print it. Good, and terrifying. I stuff it into my backpack and brush my teeth, thoughts carrying me away into the next day: Me handing it to Mr. Harrison. Him leaving it out where someone sees it, and it gets out to the whole school. Zoe finding out and breaking up with me.

I shake my head, trying to get rid of the images. In bed, I lie on my back, staring up at the dark ceiling. I want to believe Ronnie. The idea that Zoe might love me as well is almost too good to imagine. I never thought I would find a girl like her. I've dated girls before—okay, one girl, freshman year—but it didn't last long. After a few months, the stares and jokes were too much for her. Ronnie kept me stocked with chocolate after that breakup, but when I look back, I can't remember why I was so sad. The way I feel about Zoe is so much bigger, the sun instead of the moon, a source of light instead of a reflection. Eight months and counting. I hope it never ends.

CHAPTER TEN

"Guess what?"

"Gah!" I almost drop my History textbook as Ronnie appears beside me the next morning.

"I found something," he says, leaning against the lockers next to mine. "A support group."

"What?"

"For trans teenagers," he says. "There's a support group. It meets every Monday evening on Capitol Hill."

Capitol Hill. The gay neighborhood, or so legend has it. I've never been there. There are probably rainbow flags in every storefront, happy gay couples holding hands on the street, nobody staring or making weird comments. Sounds like heaven. Or just better than here.

He holds up his phone. The browser is open to a website for someplace called Lambert House. I take the phone and scroll through. It's a queer youth center. They have a bunch of different support groups. And one of the groups is for trans youth.

"I thought you might want to talk with people who get it," he says.

"I can't." I hand the phone back. "I have rehearsal."

"It's not until seven," he says. "Rehearsal's done at what, four? Five? That's plenty of time to get to the Hill."

"I'm okay," I say. "I have you to talk to."

"Yeah, but I'm not trans," Ronnie says.

"Do you not want to talk about it?" My chest tightens. Maybe I made a mistake. Maybe this is too weird for Ronnie.

"No, no!" He waves his hands. "Oh my god. It's not that. It's just . . ." He sighs. "Look, I don't talk to you about all of *my* gay feelings."

"You don't?"

"No, because you're white, Dean."

"Oh." I close the locker and click the combination lock into place. I know what he means. We've talked about this before, the way the world treats me as a white kid versus the way it treats him. How even though I'm queer, I still get the benefit of the doubt in any situation because I'm white. And how he doesn't. Adults, white adults anyway, act like it's so hard just to acknowledge this, but it's not. I see it. Sometimes literally. Like that time Ronnie and I hung out at the mall in freshman year, and the security guards at one of the big department stores followed us until Ronnie went to go find the bathroom. And then they left me alone and followed him.

So yeah. Part of me wants us to talk about everything, but it makes sense why Ronnie doesn't always want to, and that's okay.

I look up and his eyes are fixed on my face, mouth slightly open, teeth clenched together like he's waiting.

"Yeah," I say, and his face relaxes, just a little. "I understand. Or, I mean, I don't, because I'm not you, but I know what you're talking about."

"Yeah," he says. He turns, leaning his back against the lockers, legs straight out in front of him. His gold sneakers shine. "Sometimes I just want to talk to my uncle, or some of the gay kids in the club, because I know they really get it." He'd started going to the Black Student Union meetings last year. "I thought it might be like that for you."

"I don't know," I say. First bell rings, and Ronnie pushes off the lockers, walking beside me through the crowd. I chew on my bottom lip, thoughts swirling in my mind. "What if they tell me I don't belong there?"

"What?" Ronnie pulls his head back. "Of course you belong."

"But like, what if I'm not trans enough?" I know what I'm saying is silly, but it's there anyway. So many trans guys online talk about how they always knew, and that's not me. I knew I was different, but I didn't know being transgender was a thing until high school. All I know is that I feel better, more me, more at peace when I imagine myself as a guy, but is that the same as always knowing? Does it matter?

"You're more trans than I am," Ronnie says. "I think that qualifies."

I snort, shaking my head.

"Just think about it," he says.

That afternoon, I wait until the end of rehearsal, when Mr. Harrison makes a last call for assignments, and I take mine up to him.

"Excellent," he says as he adds it to the stack. "I'm very much looking forward to reading this."

I force a smile, my sweaty hands balled up inside the pockets of my hoodie.

"How are your lines coming?" he asks.

I shrug. "I'm almost off-book."

"That's good to hear. You seemed to struggle a bit this week."

"Yeah." I fiddle with the hoodie's zipper, pulling it up and down and back up. "It's just a lot."

"Lead roles are a challenge," he says. "But that's why I cast you. You can do this."

I nod. My smile is starting to feel more like a death-grimace. I back away as someone else hands him a paper and escape up the center aisle.

"Do you think any of this even matters?" Allison asks me and Zoe on Sunday. The three of us are in a coffee shop in Zoe's neighborhood, working on our college applications.

Zoe and I look up from our screens as Allison pushes her laptop away, sliding down in her chair. She wraps her brown bomber jacket closer and crosses her arms. Soft eighties music—sad, deep-voiced singers over dark guitars—plays overhead, and people pass outside the windows in the constant rain.

"Of course," Zoe says.

"Why, though? So we can graduate and go into a boring career and marry someone we hate and die?" Allison makes a puking noise.

"That escalated quickly," I say. "What's up?"

Allison sighs, tilting her head back over the seat until all we can see is the bottom of her chin. "I don't want to go to college."

"What?" Zoe says. I elbow her. *What*, she mouths. I widen my eyes.

Allison sits back up and takes a long swig from her iced coffee, glaring at her laptop. "Mom has all these ideas. Like, I could be a CEO! Or a congresswoman! Or a journalist!"

"Does she know you?" I ask.

"Right?" Allison flings out her hands. "I would pretty much always rather be in my room drawing comics than literally anything else. I don't want to go to a fancy college like she and Dad did. I don't want to run a business, and I definitely don't want to become a senator." She shudders. "It's like Ms. Maldonado always said, anyway. 'Real change happens from the ground up.'" She air-quotes the phrase.

"What about art school?" Zoe asks.

Allison shakes her head. "I don't need anyone to teach me how to draw. I'd rather teach myself."

Zoe and I exchange glances. "I'm sorry," I say.

Allison shrugs. "Maybe I'll just get a job and move out once I turn eighteen."

"You could come to New York City with us," Zoe says.

Allison arches an eyebrow.

"Seriously." Zoe tilts her screen down, leaning forward. "New York City is where all the publishing houses are. Where all the artists go. You could keep working on your art, find an agent, put a book of your comics together."

"What she said." I jerk my thumb at Zoe and she grins at me. Her cheeks are pink, a few strands of hair escaping her bun. The teal is fading now, a lighter blue-green, her dark roots showing.

I smile at her and she leans over for a kiss.

"Ugh, could you two stop being cute for one second?" Allison asks, but she's smiling too.

"Not possible," I say. "I mean, have you seen Zoe?" I Vanna White my hands in her direction, like I'm displaying an amazing painting.

Zoe rolls her eyes. "Oh, stop."

"Goals," Allison says, circling her hand at us. "Please never break up."

"Done," I say.

"Great. Great." Allison leans back, putting her hands behind her head.

Zoe laughs, staring at her screen, cheeks turning pink.

"Even your laugh is perfect," I say.

"Oh my god." Zoe covers her face with her hands. "It is not."

I grin at her. She sticks her tongue out at me.

"Anywaaaaay," Allison says, raising her eyebrows. "For real, though. NYC. That's not a bad idea."

"It's a great idea," Zoe says. "Besides, how will I survive in NYC without my best friend?"

Allison rolls her eyes. "You'd be fine. You'd forget about me."

"Never."

I smirk. "Should I be jealous?"

Zoe smacks my arm lightly and Allison bursts out laughing. "That ship sailed a long time ago," she says. I hold up my hands to show I'm joking.

"This is fun," Zoe says. "Just the girls hanging out. I'm kind of glad Ronnie and Jared couldn't make it."

Her words stab me in the chest. *The girls.* Allison nods, and I bob my head like a wooden doll, but I'm out of my body now, hovering somewhere, watching us all interact. They're smiling and laughing. They don't notice how I've gone quiet. I mumble something about the bathroom and get up from the table, weaving through the cafe to the back hallway. The restroom is single-stall and gender-neutral, like most coffee shop restrooms in Seattle, and I lock the door behind me.

I lean against the door, avoiding the mirror. In here, the music is louder, piped straight in without the chatter of people to cover it. I recognize the singer's voice. Debbie Harry, the lead singer of Blondie. One of Zoe's favorite bands. Zoe loves any band that has a girl in it, even better if it's all girls, and especially old rock bands. She and Allison are similar like that, though Allison likes weirder stuff like FKA Twigs and Grimes.

Debbie's singing about a heart of glass, and her voice pierces me like Zoe's words did. I close my eyes and try to take deep breaths, willing myself not to cry. It's not Zoe's fault. She doesn't know I'm trans. She doesn't know what she said hurts me. If she knew, she wouldn't say that.

If she knew.

I want to tell her. I want to tell her so many things. Not just that I'm trans, but that I love her too. If what Ronnie says is the truth.

But what if she hates me? Or worse—doesn't believe me.

I stay in the bathroom for as long as I think I can get away with, and then I open the door and walk back to the table. They're quiet now, both focused on their screens. I can see Allison's as I approach: She's coloring in a panel of her comic, bit by bit, with her trackpad.

Zoe glances up and her gaze holds on me. "There you are," she says, smiling. Her eyes take me in, like she can see through my clothes, through my skin and bones and into my heart, see how it beats a little faster just because she's looking at me.

"Here I am," I say, sitting beside her.

I can do this.

I can tell her.

Just.

Not yet.

CHAPTER ELEVEN

"We're going to run lines today," Mr. Harrison says in sixth period on Monday. He hasn't looked at me since the brief nod he gave me as I came in. "At the end of class, I'll hand back your assignments." He names the scenes we'll be running in rehearsal, none of them mine, and then everyone moves to pair up.

"Without scripts!" he adds, and a few people groan.

I look around for someone to pair up with. Everyone's moving toward someone else.

"Dean," Mr. Harrison says behind me. I turn. His face is unreadable. "Could you come to my office for a moment?"

I nod, stomach clenching. As I follow him out of the theatre, Jared comes in, hammer in hand. He tilts his head as he passes me, eyebrows questioning.

"What'd you do?" he whispers.

I shrug, widening my eyes.

But I know what this is about.

The office is part of Mr. Harrison's classroom, a room within the larger room where we auditioned at the beginning of the year. His desk is stacked with assignments, a large framed map of the London subway behind him, a bookcase crammed with plays across from the door.

I sit in the small chair in front of his desk. There's a photo beside his laptop: a smiling, silver-haired man in a tweed jacket. His husband? Mr. Harrison never talks about his personal life with us.

He leans back in his rolling chair, hands folded in his lap. "I read your assignment."

I stare at him, waiting.

"I'm honored you trusted me," he says, and tears prick my eyes. I look down, blinking. He takes a deep breath, letting it out in a sigh. "I must admit, I'm out of my depth."

I look up at him. His beard is salt-and-pepper, as close-cropped as his hair, and he squints a little, as if he's trying to figure out what to say next. He scans my face for so long I shift in the chair. "I've been part of the gay community for most of my adult life, but I don't know any transgender people."

"Neither do I," I say.

He laughs and leans forward, elbows on his desk. "Are you out?" he asks.

"Ronnie knows." I look away from him. "I haven't told anyone else."

He nods, studies me longer. "Dean, how can I support you?"

I put my hands into my hoodie pockets and shrug.

"Have you thought about your bio for the play program?"

I blink and shake my head.

He hmmms. "Because I'm wondering now how you'll want to be referred to. After I read your assignment, I did a little reading. About proper terms, that sort of thing. It occurred to me that maybe you'd want to change your pronouns."

Pronouns. My bio. "Oh," I say.

"Yes." He looks at me. "I'm assigning the bio next week. I thought you might need some time to think."

Of course. My bio last year was all *she* and *her*. It grated on me like gravel against skin. But if I change my pronouns in the bio . . . ?

"Then, of course, my next question would be whether you want to come out to the cast before your bio does it for you," he says.

At my locker after rehearsal, I spin the lock in my robot haze, the conversation replaying in my mind. If I change my pronouns in my bio, then I'll have to come out to the cast. And if I'm going to come out to the cast, I need to come out to Zoe first.

I don't know how to do this.

Another trans person would understand. They'd know what to do. I've thought of myself as the only one for so long.

I know I'm not. It just feels that way.

Outside, the sky is a flat gray, the air damp, like rain is coming, or just finished. I'm spaced out, staring at the stop across the intersection from mine, when a bus pulls up to it. The screen on the side reads CAPITOL HILL in orange digital letters.

The support group at Lambert House. It's tonight.

The walk sign at the intersection is on. I look at the bus. At the sign. And run to the corner, across the street, waving at the bus as the doors close and then open again to let me in, breathless. I scan my fare card and head for the empty seats at the back.

We rattle south, over the potholed roads, through the University District and up to Capitol Hill. The bus driver glances back at me in the mirror, but I avoid his eyes, staring out the window. The ship canal unfolds under the Eastlake Bridge, a ribbon of cold gray water rolling onward underneath the I-5 bridge, toward Lake Union and the Puget Sound. I close my eyes and see the bus from above, me sitting warm inside, the water below me, the Olympic Mountains to my right, Cascade Range to my left. I am safe in between.

When I open my eyes, we're curving to the left down Broadway, the main street through Capitol Hill. At the corner of Broadway and Pine, I step off the bus. Here, the clouds are darker. I flip up the hood of my raincoat and head up Pine Street.

There's a park on my left, guys skating on makeshift jumps inside the tennis court, people kicking around a soccer ball on the field. To my right, an old brick building draws itself up, sitting in state on the corner. I cross the street and walk alongside it, looking in the windows of the businesses. There are people on the streets, everyone walking like they're going somewhere on purpose.

The next street over is Pike, lined with bars, shiny storefronts, cafes, a music venue. Rainbow flags hang in windows just like I imagined, a flash of color, like I've landed in Oz after a flight from Kansas.

There's a coffee shop among the bars. I walk inside; it's quiet, a few people at tables to my right, the walls dark, turning the place into a warm cave. I sit by the window with a scone and tea, gazing out at the street. I remember Ronnie grabbing my shoulders backstage at school last year, telling me in an excited whisper about his first kiss—and first makeout session—somewhere on the Hill, in the bathroom of an all-ages club.

The tea is hot, the mint calming me as I sip it. An older woman reads in the corner, her black boots propped up on a chair, gray buzzcut catching the glow from the overhead lights. Two large and bearded men talk quietly over another window table, giggling every so often. My thoughts drift away from the support group to the play, to my classmates on stage, all of them perfect and comfortable in the bodies they were born in. Not that I hate my body. There are just parts of it that aren't what they should be.

It's not fair that they don't have to think about any of this. They carry on as if they're the normal ones, the ones by whom everyone else is measured and found not good enough. Olivia and Courtney and their long hair, the curves they seem to love. Blake, his muscular shoulders, his deep voice. He always acts nice when people are watching, but I know who he really is. The images flash in my mind: Me, sitting on the stage with everyone else. Me, coming out. His face across the circle.

I squeeze the cup in my hands, trying to focus on its warmth.

The evening rolls in, bringing a misty rain. Lambert House is an old Victorian on the east side of the neighborhood, away from downtown. When I walk up, all the lights are on inside, and the front door creaks as I push it open.

The person at the desk inside smiles at me. "What can I do for you?"

"I'm here for the, um, the group?" My voice comes out way too high. But I keep my face calm, put down my name and my email address on the sign-in sheet, and write my name on a blank sticker.

"Don't forget to write your pronouns."

I look up. A girl stands framed in the doorway behind me, tall and curvy, skin dark brown and glowing, long beaded braids swaying around her shoulders. Tiny blue and green flowers spiral all over her black dress, lime-green heels planted firmly on the floor. She lifts one hand in a small wave. "I'm Jade. My pronouns are *she* and *her*. What're yours?"

I stare at her. "I, um . . . I don't know." *He* and *him*, I want to say, but the words are stuck in my throat.

She smiles. "That's okay. Sometimes it takes time."

I nod. I don't know what to say. She's so pretty, and I'm so awkward.

"Come on," she says, walking around me. "We don't bite."

I follow her up the stairs to a small room lined with bookshelves. People sit in a circle inside, the tall lamp in the corner casting a warm glow over their faces. Jade motions me after her as she walks around to an empty chair, and I take the one beside her. The girl on her other side gives her a hug, then smiles at me.

"I'm Nina," the girl says. I mumble my name. Nina looks super-cool in an orange hoodie and paint-stained jeans, bright purple hair flowing from under her black beanie, a nose ring sparkling against her golden-brown skin.

"Dean," the facilitator says, reading my name tag. He's a short, broad-framed white guy. "Welcome. I'm Isaac. *He* and *him*."

Everyone introduces themselves with their name and pronoun. When it's my turn, I say my name, then stop.

"Dean hasn't picked pronouns yet," Jade offers before I can speak.

"No problem." Isaac smiles. "You have options. *He? She? They?*"

"Um." I shrug, wishing everyone would stop looking at me. "You can use *he*." My heart beats faster, I wait for someone to scoff and tell me I can't use that pronoun, but people just smile and nod.

The other kids have a lot to catch up on. Jade talks about how she moved out after graduating last year; her parents were still trying to get her to move back in, even though she had found her own place and was going to community college. "They only love me as their baby boy," she says matter-of-factly. "No way am I going back in that closet." Nina grabs her hand.

"I'm really scared about that," I say. "Coming out, I mean." Everyone in the group looks at me. "My mom is still weird about me being a lesbian. I don't know how she's going to react to me being—" I stop. It's still hard to say out loud. "Not a girl," I finish quietly. "I haven't even told my girlfriend." The tears well up and I look down at the carpet.

Isaac breaks the silence. "Can anyone else share their coming-out story?"

One person's parents are fine with it. Some live at home still, but their families are in denial, or hostile. Others are homeless. I'm quiet, imagining life without my home, my room, without Dad's cooking every night, sleeping next to strangers, not knowing where my next meal is coming from. I can't picture it. But then again, I've never had to before.

I sneak a look at Jade. She's listening to the nonbinary kid who's talking now, nodding at what they're saying. I wonder how long she's been coming here. She seems so settled, so confident in who she is. I want that confidence too.

CHAPTER TWELVE

In the morning, I'm at my locker, and Zoe's talking to me about something. But my mind is on the support group from the night before, on Jade, who told me I should come back next week. On pronouns. *She* is a barb stuck in my heart; it's been there so long the pain has dulled to an ache I hardly notice. Except now, when I have to think about it. My mind slides away from *he*. Even though that's what I want, I can't touch it. When I do, I get this electric-fence shock, like I've remembered something embarrassing I did forever ago.

Maybe *he* isn't the right pronoun. No one had a chance to call me *he* last night, and I still don't know how it would feel to actually hear it.

"Dean?" I look down at Zoe. She's frowning. "Are you listening?"

"Yeah. Yes. I'm sorry." I throw my backpack over my shoulder and shut the locker.

"Is everything okay?"

"Um." I weave ahead of her through the hall. "Yeah! Of course."

She reaches out and grabs my arm. I face her, people diverting around us in their rush to class. "Are you sure? You're not, like, annoyed at me or something?"

"What?" I blink at her. "Definitely not. Why would you think that?"

She shrugs, biting her lower lip. "I don't know. I was kind of going on and on back there."

"No, no." I shake my head. "You're fine. I was just in my head about stuff."

"What's going on?"

We start walking again, slower. What do I say? I smile down at her. "I'm just stressed about the NYU application." That's not a total lie, even if it wasn't what I was thinking about.

Her face relaxes. "Oh my god, same." We walk on toward class. "I swear my personal statement gets shittier every time I revise it."

"I haven't even started mine," I say.

"You're kidding." Her eyes widen.

"I know." I stare straight ahead. "I haven't picked a monologue either."

"Let's work on it together. Soon. This weekend?"

"Okay."

Saturday morning, I take the bus to Ronnie's house to hang out. The rain is heavy, soaking my shoes as I walk up the hill from the stop to his place. I knock on the front door. No answer. After a few moments of cold wind whipping rain into my face, I jump off the porch, find their hidden key in the usual spot, and let myself in.

"Ronnie, I just don't think that school is a good option." Jamal's voice drifts out from the kitchen.

"But I'm almost done with the application," Ronnie says.

"Do you have a plan to pay for it?" Jamal asks. Silence. I stand in the hallway, water dripping off my jacket onto the floor. Should I go back outside? Pretend I didn't hear anything?

"That account we opened," Ronnie says.

"Your college fund? There's some in there, but not enough."

"Then I'll get scholarships, take out loans, I don't care!"

"Ronnie," Jamal says. Ronnie doesn't reply, and after a moment Jamal continues. "I know you want this, but is fashion design going to keep a roof over your head? It's a long road to success in that field. How many people from all those seasons of *Project Runway* are rich and famous now?"

"I'm not doing this for the fame," Ronnie says.

"I know. You've got a talent. But you need a backup plan. I can't sign off on a loan knowing I'm setting you up for a lifetime of debt."

Ronnie strides out of the kitchen and stops dead in his tracks, staring at me. I grimace, holding up the key.

Jamal appears behind him, bald head almost brushing the top of the doorway. His concerned frown shifts into a stiff smile. "Hello, Dean. I forgot you were coming over today."

I nod and bend to untie my shoes, staring down at the laces. "We can talk later, son," Jamal says softly. His footsteps recede to the kitchen.

I follow Ronnie into his room. "This is so stupid," he says, slumping onto the bed and putting his head in his hands. "All he cares about is job security."

I sit next to him, putting my arm around his shoulders, and he leans against me, letting out a heavy sigh.

"I don't want a backup plan," he says. "I want to make costumes on Broadway."

I look at the poster above his dresser, a muscled Anthony Mackie as the Falcon in *Captain America: The Winter Soldier.* "What if you could get a bunch of scholarships?"

"Where am I going to find time for that?"

"I'll help you," I say. "I'm going to need them too if I get into NYU."

"I guess."

"You guess?" I tickle his ribs.

"Okay." He straightens up, pushing me away, but he's smiling, the tears drying on his cheeks.

"You got this," I say.

He gets up, crossing the room to turn on the old radio we found at a thrift store. The pounding beat of some pop song fills the room and he moonwalks across the hardwood floor in his stocking feet.

I watch him. "I went to the support group."

He stops dead.

"And I told them I use *he* and *him* pronouns."

"How was that?"

"Well, I haven't actually heard anyone use them yet."

"What if we try it out?"

"What do you mean?"

He starts moonwalking again, sashaying around the foot of the bed. "You'll see." He grabs a raincoat from his closet and twirls to face me. "Let's take the real Dean out on the town."

We catch the bus over to Capitol Hill. I beg, I plead, I threaten, but he just shakes his head, refusing to tell me what he's planning, a smirk on his face the whole way. When we get off the bus, he takes me straight to Caffe Vita, the coffee shop where I sat the other night before Lambert House. Inside, he waltzes up to the counter, beaming at the slight young man behind it.

"I'll have a tall latte, please. He'll have a chai." He flips his wrist to point at me, and the barista grins. The pronoun echoes in my mind, not the stab of *she*, but something softer, an embrace. Ronnie pays before I can protest.

"So. Was that good for you?" Ronnie deepens his voice, batting his eyelashes.

"Shut up." I land a light smack on his shoulder as he dodges away. I smile. "It was fine."

"Fine?" He crosses his arms. "Guess we'll have to keep trying."

The barista sets our cups on the counter. "Here you go, boys." His smile is wide and gap-toothed, and my heart flutters as the words spill out of his mouth. *Boys.*

"Here, let me." Ronnie grabs both cups and smiles at the barista, jerking his head in my direction. "He always spills it." The barista giggles.

We sit in the same seat by the window as my first visit, snagging the table just as someone gets up to leave. The cafe is crowded, people chatting with friends, or reading, or working with papers spread around them.

"Well?" Ronnie arches an eyebrow, sipping his latte.

I look out the window, smiling. I let the pronoun sink in, filling my whole body, and my smile expands until I'm laughing. Ronnie starts laughing too, and then we're contagious, the laughter rolling back and forth between us until we slow to chuckles, and then silence, grinning at each other. I know people are looking at us, but I don't care.

"That felt good," I say. "That felt good."

We sip our drinks, the warmth filling me up. He's here.

No.

I'm here.

"Maybe I should try the twelve-egg omelet." Zoe taps a finger against her lower lip, scanning the menu.

"You say that every time." I grin at her over the top of mine.

The twelve-egg omelets at Beth's Cafe are legendary. None of us has ever eaten an entire one alone, though Jared and Ronnie and I once finished one together. Outside, cars zip by on Aurora Avenue, past Green Lake and onward to downtown Seattle. People pack the place, crowding every booth, pinballs from the back-room arcade thwacking over the jukebox. Someone has put in enough coins to run the Cure's entire discography. It's Sunday, but according to the jukebox, it's Friday and we're in love.

I watch Zoe a little longer. I wish I was brave enough to tell her how I feel.

In the end, I order my usual pancakes with peanut butter, Zoe gets the six-egg omelet, and we split our meals, eating from each other's plates. Through a mouthful of food, Zoe ticks off what she's completed on her application and what she has left to do. She's way ahead of me.

I look up at the crayon drawings papering the wall across from us, above us, all around us—evidence of a year's worth of people eating their fill in the ripped vinyl seats. There's a drawing of the Space Needle, two sets of initials in a heart beside it.

"So, what are you thinking for your monologue?" she asks finally.

I grimace. "I don't know. Nothing seems right. All of them are so . . . girly."

She frowns. "Is there something wrong with that?"

"No! No." I shake my head. "It's just not me. I mean, come on." I gesture at myself.

"Yeah." She stares off into space for a moment, fork still in her mouth. "Yeah, I see what you mean." She looks at me, her eyes soft. "I'm sorry, babe. Theatre needs better roles for people like us."

Who do you mean? I want to ask her. *Who is us?*

Instead, I nod, cutting my pancakes into smaller and smaller pieces.

She puts her fork down. "Dean . . ."

I look up. She toys with her eggs, pushing them around her plate, chewing on her bottom lip. I reach across the table and poke her with my fork.

She looks at me, but her mouth is turned down. "Are you sure you're okay?"

"I was about to ask you the same thing," I say, trying to sound gentle, but my heart is beating faster. And not in a good way.

She twists her mouth around. "I'm serious."

"I'm sorry. I'm sorry. I didn't mean it as a joke."

"You just . . ." She lets out a heavy sigh and sits back, hands in her lap. "You've seemed really . . . I don't know. Distant lately."

"Oh." I watch her. The noise of the cafe fades around us, like we're in our own world, in a glass bowl on the verge of breaking. Maybe she's already figured it out. Maybe she's already decided we're done.

"Not all the time," she adds. "Sometimes I feel like you're really there with me. But sometimes it seems like you're in your own world. Like you don't really see me—"

"That's not true," I say. "I do see you. You're amazing, Zoe."

"Dean . . ." She trails off. "I mean, that's part of it too."

I wait.

"You're always telling me I'm perfect. Amazing. Beautiful. Smart." She puts up a finger with each word. "And like. That's nice to hear, and I like the way I look, and I do think I'm smart, but I'm not perfect. You telling me I am just makes me feel like, if I make one mistake, you'll leave me."

"What?" My voice cracks. "I'm not going to leave you."

Tears glitter in her eyes. She swallows. "But how do I know, though? I mean, my dad promised us a thousand times that he wouldn't leave, that he was back for good, he was over his problem now, blah fucking blah, and now it's been three years since I've talked to him."

I stay quiet. Zoe hasn't told me a lot of details about her dad. I know he gambled away everything when she was a kid: their house, their car, their whole bank account. I know she hasn't seen him in a long time. But three years? How can a parent just abandon their kid like that?

"I always thought . . ." Her voice is ragged now. "I was kind of a handful when I was a kid. I acted out a lot. And sometimes I wonder if I'd been, I don't know . . . better, maybe he wouldn't have left us."

"Oh my god. Zoe." I breathe the words, reaching across the table.

She grabs my hands, holding tight. She looks up at the ceiling, blinking fast, then down at her hands. "I think I'm falling in love with you."

My eyes widen.

"And if I'm falling in love with you, I need to know you feel the same. But for real. Not just with the image you have of me."

She's falling.

In love. With me?

Those words. The ones I've wanted to say and haven't known how. My mouth opens and closes, my whole body a sunrise, light speeding through all my limbs.

"Zoe. I love you already," I say.

She looks up at me, the closed door of her face starting to open.

"What your dad did—it's not your fault. You were a little kid. And I'm sorry. For whatever I've said that made you feel like you had to be perfect." The words are scattered. I can hardly think. For a moment I was falling, and not in the good way. But now I'm falling, and it's the kind of falling that feels like flying. "I've just never felt this way before about anyone. I know you're not perfect. I guess I just mean . . . you're perfect for me."

She smiles. "I feel that way about you."

"Really?" My voice goes high.

She laughs. "I love you, Dean." She slides out of her side of the booth and into mine, throwing her arms around me, her lips on mine almost too hard, but I don't care, I want her teeth, I want her too-muchness, I want her everything. She loves me. She. Loves. Me.

She pulls back, laughing. I tickle her and she squirms away from me in the booth and then we're kissing again, her mouth opening to mine.

Eventually, she pulls away, leaning her head on her hand. On the table, our fingers lace together. "When did you know?" she asks.

I rub her thumb with mine and shrug, smiling. "I don't know. It just happened." I poke her. "Same question."

"The first time we did stuff. When my mom was out of town." The corner of her mouth lifts. "You actually cared about me enjoying it. No dude ever cared."

Her words sting, sweet and painful at the same time. I keep the smile on my face and look at our hands. I don't know what my eyes are saying and I don't want her to know. Shit, I don't even know. I should be happy. That I made her feel good. That I'm not like the guys she dated before she came out.

But I can hear it in her voice. She's glad I'm not a guy.

"And who you are," she says. "I love everything about you. I want . . ." Her voice is almost a whisper. "I want to know everything about you."

I meet her eyes then. She looks small and unsure. We lock eyes for so long that she starts giggling. I lean over and kiss her, quick, and she squeaks, laughing against my mouth, then kisses me back.

"I love you," I whisper into her mouth, and she buries her face in my neck. The words feel so good to say out loud, like I've been holding my breath for years, living underwater, and now I'm breaking the surface. Love is a home I can live in. Even if it's meant for the girl she thinks I am. Maybe someday it won't be. Maybe someday the real me can live there too.

If she really does want to know everything.

CHAPTER THIRTEEN

I know that nothing has really changed on Monday morning when I walk into school, but I feel different. Zoe's words are echoing in my head, and I'm looking around, trying to catch a flash of her teal hair in the crowd, this electric current running from my chest to wherever she is, waiting to see her and spark again.

When the sea of swirling people parts at my locker and she's standing there, the voltage of her smile shocks me into my own.

"Hi," she says, blushing, as I stop in front of her.

"Hey." We grin at each other, like our smiles are saying everything we can't.

"I love you," she whispers.

"I love you back," I say, and she giggles, throwing her arms around me, pressing her face against my chest.

When she pulls back, we kiss, soft and warm, for a long moment.

She watches me while I open my locker. "How was the rest of your weekend?"

"After my amazing girlfriend told me she loves me? Fucking fantastic," I say, and she bursts out laughing. My cheeks hurt, I'm smiling so hard. I find the book I need and stuff it into my backpack.

"So what I told you . . ." She looks up at me. "It wasn't too much?"

"No way." I put my hands on her cheeks, holding her face. "I'm glad that you told me."

She smiles and pulls me down for another kiss, this one fiercer, making my heart race.

"Do you want to hang out tonight?" she asks as we wind through the halls toward my English class.

"Hell yeah," I say.

"Sweet. I was thinking we could maybe—" And then the rest of her words are blurring to a soft fuzz in my ears because I've just remembered something.

Lambert House.

The group meets tonight.

Shit. I want to hang out with Zoe, but I want to go to the group too. The minute I remember it, I see the faces of the kids in the circle, see Jade's and Nina's smiles. Now that I've tried out my pronouns in real life, introductions will be different; I'll be able to say my pronouns with my whole chest. I want to claim that in front of everyone, be back in that space with kids like me. Kids who understand what I'm going through.

Ronnie was right. It does make a difference.

"Dean?" I blink. Zoe's hand is waving in front of my face. We're approaching my classroom.

"Sorry," I say.

"Did you hear anything I just said?" She's frowning.

"No," I say, grimacing. "I'm so sorry. I just realized—I forgot I have a thing tonight. After rehearsal."

"Oh." Her face falls. "What are you doing?"

"Um." I think fast. "Uh. Dentist appointment."

"At night?"

"Yeah, they're open late." I shrug, doing my best rueful smile.

"Okay." We stand in front of the classroom door, kids flooding around us. "Well, some other time, then?"

"Yeah, definitely."

She stands on her tiptoes to kiss me, and then darts away before I can say anything else. Before I have to lie again.

Lie. To my girlfriend, to the person I just said I'm in love with. I know why I did it, but I still feel awful. I need to tell her. Soon.

I get to Lambert House a few minutes after seven and take the stairs two at a time to the top. When I walk in, Isaac beams. When Jade and I make eye contact, she waves from across the circle. Nina smiles at me, and I squeeze around the outside of the circle to the only empty chair, right next to her. I try not to think about the fact that Zoe thinks I'm at the dentist right now. What if she asks me how it went? How long will I have to stretch the truth? I push the thoughts away and take a deep breath.

The group is smaller than last time. We start again with names and pronouns. When it's my turn, I say my name, and after a few moments, I add my pronouns. *He* and *him*.

It's easier this time. It feels good. I think of Ronnie, and the coffee shop, and smile to myself.

One of the other kids in the group cries when it's his turn to speak. His parents haven't kicked him out, but they won't refer to him as a boy or use the name he's chosen. I think of Mom refusing to call me Dean. What will she say when she finds out it's not just a nickname to me?

When it's my turn to share, I tell them about how Zoe and I finally said I love you. I don't tell them about my lie.

"Be careful with your girl," Jade says when I'm done. "Love's a big word to say when you don't know how she'll react to you being trans."

Nina murmurs in agreement.

I stiffen, crossing my arms. "You don't know Zoe," I say.

Jade half smiles, shrugging. "I'm just speaking from experience."

"Tell me more about that," Isaac says, before I can say anything.

"I mean, y'all know what I'm talking about," Jade says, looking around the circle. "Some people don't wanna date trans girls because they think we aren't real women. Just because of whatever body parts we have or don't have."

A few of the other girls nod.

"That's happened to me too," says a kid whose name I can't remember. "Well, not the exact same thing, but sometimes people treat me like my gender isn't real just because I'm non-binary. Or they think because I have certain body parts, that means I'm really the gender I was assigned at birth."

"Exactly," Jade says. "I was dating this girl for a minute last month—" She stops, shakes her head. "I don't even want to repeat what she said when I told her." Her voice cracks, goes watery, like she's trying not to cry. "It just hurts. People get so hung up on that shit, and they don't even see the person in front of them."

Isaac nods. Nina threads her arm through Jade's, and Jade grabs her hand, holds it tight. I want to reach out too, but I'm too far away, and I don't know Jade well enough—maybe she wouldn't want that from me.

The other kids murmur empathetic words. The discussion continues, and I listen. My brain feels like putty, like it's stretching, expanding, filling my skull. Everything they're saying, it's not exactly stuff I've heard before, but it makes sense, as if it could have been in any one of the articles Zoe has sent me about fat acceptance or queer rights or anti-racism. Jade and Nina aren't any less women, just like I'm not any less of a guy.

I want Zoe to see me as a guy, and like me as a guy. What if I tell her, and she says she's okay with me, but it's only because somewhere in her mind she still sees me as kind of a girl, just because of my body? The thought makes me feel like I'm choking.

At the end of the hour, I sit there for a moment as everyone gathers their things. Jade and Nina are talking with another girl, and I watch them as I put on my coat. I want to talk to them. I take a deep breath and stand up as the girl leaves.

"I liked what you said," I say. Nina glances over at me, eyebrows twitching in a confused frown.

She puts a hand on Jade's arm. "Sorry, what?"

"What you said." My knees are locked. I shift my feet as they stare at me. "I liked it."

Smooth, Dean.

"What did you like about it?" Jade asks, smiling.

My face heats up. "What you said about how people don't see you as a real woman. Just because of your body parts. It's fucked up that people think our bodies dictate who we are." I look from Nina to Jade. "I'm sorry that girl said whatever she said."

Nina nods, a small smile on her face. Her hair is dyed dark today, hanging shaggy around her face.

Jade shrugs. "I mean, when you think about it, all that shit is made up. Gender, sex, whatever. Someone just decided a penis means man and a vagina means woman."

"Yeah!" I grin. "I never thought about it that way before."

Jade smiles, pulling on her long, bright pink peacoat.

"I was wondering, do you all want to hang out before group sometime? Like next week?" I'm not sure where my words are coming from, but now that I'm talking, I can't seem to stop.

"I have to work next week," Nina says. "But maybe the week after?" She looks at Jade, who shrugs again.

"Sure," she says, smiling. I take out my phone, she gives me her number, and I text her mine.

"Cool," I say, trying not to show how excited I am. "I'll text you."

"Not if I text you first," she says with a wink, and sweeps out, Nina following her with a wave.

The library is empty. I replay the conversation over and over in my mind, my gaze unseeing at the shelves of books. I'm shaky for some reason, but not in fear. I realize I'm smiling, and then the room comes back into focus. I look at the rainbow of spines in front of me, and a title jumps out: TRANSGENDER WARRIORS. I step forward and pull the book out, looking at the back cover. An entire book about people like me.

"Oh, Dean!" I start and look over at Isaac, smiling at me from the doorway. "You're still here."

"Can I borrow this?" I hold up the book.

"Please do." He stands aside as I cross to the door. "See you later."

I smile and nod. The words, coming from his mouth, sound like a promise, like safety. Outside, on the front steps, I stuff the book into my backpack and breathe in the night air, the scent of pine on the breeze. The rain is gone, the sky clear and dark and scattered with stars.

See you later.

Yes, you will.

Every day the rest of the week is sunny, the sky a blue so bright it hurts. The sun falls through the banks of windows down the Jefferson halls, making perfect squares of light. Zoe doesn't ask me about the dentist, and I relax as the week goes on, the moment fading to a small, guilty shape in the back of my mind.

I'm on my way to my locker on Thursday morning when I hear my name. Olivia weaves through the hall toward me. We trade the required *hi how are you i'm so tired senior year is killing me* until we're standing at my locker and I'm opening it.

"I was wondering," she starts. She looks around at the flood of people passing us. "Do you want to run lines together later?"

"Sure," I say. "I mean, we are the leads. I hear that's, like, important or something?"

She smiles. "Maybe the theatre? At lunch?"

"Sounds good."

"Great." She flips her hair over her shoulder and disappears into the crowd.

After fourth period, I bust my ass to the cafeteria, getting in line when it's still only a few kids deep. I snake through the kitchen, grabbing a bag of chips and a bowl of mashed potatoes, and dropping something that looks like a veggie patty on top. I'm not sure. It doesn't taste like meat, anyway, as I stuff it in my mouth on the way to the theatre.

Olivia and I haven't had much rehearsal time yet. We've run a few scenes, but neither of us was fully memorized, and most of last week was spent on stage combat.

"My first priority is that none of you die," the instructor had said after Mr. Harrison had introduced him. He was a short man with an upper body that looked like it could bench-press five of me. Someone in the back had snickered, but he hadn't so much as twitched. Just stared at us, his mouth a straight line under a bushy mustache.

He held the stare until the room was silent.

No one laughed after that.

"Dean, Dean! Sign my backpack!" Olivia mock-swoons as I enter, grinning at me from the stage.

"Oh my god. Is that—it can't be. The famous Olivia Greene?" I gasp.

She twirls her hair, pretending to pose for a camera. We've never been close, but I remember her in sixth grade, how quiet she was. She's still quiet, but now it's a confident quiet, like theatre brought her out of her shell, the same way it did for me.

"Okay," she says when I'm on the stage. "I was thinking we could run the lines for the balcony scene. There's just so many and I've never made it all the way through without checking the script."

The set pieces for the scene are still half-constructed back-stage, so we find the tape marking where it will eventually sit, and from there, our blocking: where we'll start in the scene.

Olivia struggles a little bit through her opening lines, pausing for a long moment on one, but she finds it and finishes. I move from the shadows at the side of the stage, as if drawn by her voice. I've decided Romeo is a flirt, a bit melodramatic, and so I usually move with a strut, stance wide, gestures sweeping and assured. But here in the garden, Romeo's a little more uncertain at first, still in the haze of his chance meeting with Juliet at the party, not sure if he should make himself known to her.

It's easier now to find Romeo, to sink into my body and feel it become his body. When I'm Romeo, I'm the kind of guy I've imagined I could be. Maybe without the arrogance. But Romeo isn't just an entitled nobleman. He's romantic, bold, witty. I want to be that person.

We make it through the scene, only stopping a few times to check lines. Olivia finishes her final speech perfectly, and when we close the scene, she high-fives me.

A slow clap sounds from the audience. We turn, squinting into the lights, and see Blake standing at the bottom of the center aisle.

"Hey you," Olivia says with a smile. "What are you doing here?"

"I can't come to the theatre?" he asks, his voice light, but his arms are crossed.

"Of course you can!" Olivia says quickly.

"Courtney told me you were here," he says. "Don't let me interrupt." His eyes shift to me. "Wouldn't want to disturb the star-crossed lovers."

"Blake," Olivia says, with a little laugh.

He sits down in the second row, puts his feet up on the back of a seat. I look at her and shrug. The stage lights are hot, and I'm starting to sweat.

"I'm good for now," I say. "Want to practice another time?"

"Sure," she says.

I grab the rest of my food and leave, avoiding Blake's stare, but I see his head turn as I pass. I can feel his eyes on my back all the way up the aisle, but I don't look over my shoulder.

"Why are you being this way?" I hear Olivia say as I push open the double doors, and then they close behind me.

The moment replays in my mind all through the next period, all through the quiz I'm supposed to be taking. I stay after the bell to finish the last problem, which makes me late to sixth period. When I arrive at the theatre, the cast is already circled up on stage, mid-game. I join them, slipping in between two of the girls, my eyes catching Blake's across the circle. His head jerks back slightly and he frowns, then flinches as the person beside him elbows him. He looks over, opening his arms wide, staggering slightly as he pretends to shape them around a giant ball—invisible, of course. We've all played this warm-up game a thousand times: each person uses their hands to shape a ball of any size and weight, then makes eye contact with another person and throws the imaginary ball to them. That person then reshapes the ball and passes it on, until everyone has a turn. Mr. Harrison loves games that make us use our imaginations and our bodies at the same time.

"Character isn't just in your head, it's in your actions too," he always says, someone mouthing it behind him while we all nod solemnly, as if we've never heard him say it before.

Olivia turns the ball into a tiny pea, feather-light, and wafts it over to me. I catch it on a fingertip and use my other hand to pull it large and oblong, then pass it on. I glance back at Blake. He's staring at me, face set. I nod like I've seen guys nod to each other: a quick jerk of the chin, just an acknowledgment.

Blake looks away.

CHAPTER FOURTEEN

"Homework!" Mr. Harrison calls out Friday afternoon as we're packing up our stuff for the end of class. "We have homework this weekend." He passes a stack of worksheets to Courtney, who's wearing the pillbox hat Ronnie found for her role as Juliet's nurse.

I grab a worksheet when they come to me. Name, grade, character, previous roles, how we got started in theatre, a fun fact.

"Your bios," Mr. Harrison says. "Fill in the blanks, then put them together into a coherent paragraph. You've all written bios for our programs before, so this should be easy." His eyes meet mine and move on around the group. "Questions?"

Silence. Feet shuffle on the stage, and then the bell rings and we're all stampeding for the door.

"Due Monday!" Mr. Harrison shouts behind us, over the din, and then I'm out the door into the hall, our current joining the river of students heading to lockers, school buses, sports practices.

On the bus home, I fill out the paper. Name and grade: Dean Foster, senior. Mr. Harrison has never questioned my nickname, unlike some of the other teachers; the only place I ever see my full name for his class is on the student roster, where he can't change it.

Character: Romeo Montague. Previous roles: Chorus roles in *Seussical* and *The Wizard of Oz*, before I realized I hated musicals. One of the Puritan girls in *The Crucible*, sophomore year. I had to wear a horrible dress for that one, and I hated every minute of it. Even the rush of being on stage hadn't made up for that. Playing Sylvie last year was better: pants instead of dresses, a brassy character who smoked cigarettes on stage. I'd had fun with those, the fake kind you blew into, the powder inside making a puff of smoke come out the other end.

My start in theatre: summer acting camp, before *West Side Story*, before *boys play boy characters*, before Ronnie. I was Flotsam, one of the eels in *The Little Mermaid*, and I hated the singing but loved the acting.

The stage was a raised wooden platform on the long, green lawn behind the camp's main building. No lights, no darkness, just a curtain strung up behind the platform to hide the performers. Backstage, I waited for my cue, stomach aching with nerves. I could hear the scene on stage, but as if from the other side of a thick wall instead of thin fabric, all the words a muffled, distant murmur. I peeked around the curtain, my eyes focused on the tape marking the stage. That was my spot, where I would stand when I entered.

All I remember after that are two distinct moments: the tape on the stage, and standing on stage at the end, hands clasped on either side by other kids, the crowd cheering in front of me. My stomachache was gone. I wasn't the star, or even close to a lead, but the applause roared in my ears as if it was all for me. As if the audience was hundreds of people in a grand theatre instead of twenty parents clapping on a lawn.

Flotsam. In the show, a boy eel.

I smile. So Romeo isn't my first male role.

At the next fill-in-the-blank, I stop.

Fun fact: I'm transgender.

I shake my head at the page. I'm not writing that.

When I get home, I blast Bowie out of my laptop speakers. He sings about changes. Correction: ch-ch-changes. I type the bio up, and then I stare at it.

Dean Foster is a senior at Jefferson High School, playing Romeo Montague. She got her start at Act Up in the Park when she was ten, as Flotsam in The Little Mermaid. *At Jefferson, she has previously appeared as Sylvie in* The Odd Couple, *a Puritan girl in* The Crucible, *and in the chorus for* Seussical *and* The Wizard of Oz. *But her proudest moment was eating an entire habanero pepper raw and living to tell the tale.*

I close my eyes. Every *she*, every *her*, clangs in my mind, the echo of someone else's voice in my head: the girl I never was, the girl everyone wanted me to be. Well, not everyone. Even as a girl, I've never been the right kind for Mom.

I stare at the screen, see myself reflected in it, see myself handing the bio in to Mr. Harrison. See myself, standing in front of the cast, telling them who I am. Who I've wanted to be. Who I've always been, underneath all the expectations, the definitions of who I should be, what my body means.

I move the cursor and delete every letter that doesn't belong, add the ones that do.

I read the bio again.

Dean Foster is a senior at Jefferson High School, playing Romeo Montague. He got his start at Act Up in the Park when he was ten, as Flotsam in The Little Mermaid. *At Jefferson, he has previously appeared as Sylvie in* The Odd Couple, *a Puritan girl in* The Crucible, *and in the chorus for* Seussical *and* The Wizard of Oz. *But his proudest moment was eating an entire habanero pepper raw and living to tell the tale.*

I know the roles I've listed will make people think twice, but I don't care. The bio finally sounds right in my head, the pronouns a soft sigh letting go of everything I never wanted to hold in the first place.

This is how it should have been. How it should always be.

With my bio written, I know what I have to do this weekend.

Hang out tomorrow? I text Zoe Saturday night.

Yes please, heart-eyes emoji.

We meet at Beth's again and share the same brunch. We talk, and each moment is heavy, important. *This is the last time we'll talk about backstage drama before she knows*, and *this is the last time I'll make her laugh with a silly joke before she knows*, and *this is the last time she'll do her feminist analysis of our new favorite TV show before she knows.*

"*Steven Universe* is the only perfect show," she says finally.

"We should dress up as the characters for Halloween," I say. "You'd look so cute as Pearl." I can already see her in Pearl's adorable sleeveless top and silk ballet skirt. Pearl is sweet, always taking responsibility and caring about everyone around her.

"No way. I'm definitely more of an Amethyst," she says. "Her purple hair is so badass! And she's so fun and independent." She smiles. "You'd make a cute Steven."

I grin. That's exactly what I imagined.

We finish the last bites of our food. Is now the moment? My heart kick-starts like a motorcycle. We walk up to pay, and then we're standing outside in the gray afternoon. The sun is gone, but it's not raining, just cloudy, the air damp and thick with the smell of pine trees.

We end up walking around the lake across the street from the diner. She looks out at the water, at a lone duck paddling along the edge. The pressure in my brain is building: *Tell her. Tell her. Tell her tell her tell her tell her tell her tell her—*

"Um," I say. My voice cracks, and I clear my throat.

She glances up at me.

Shit. I have no idea how to begin.

"I like that you think I'd be Steven," I say.

She raises her eyebrows, smiling. "I'm glad?"

Internal face-palm. "Because he's a boy character." I stop on the walking path. "Can we sit down?"

"Sure." She follows me to a bench, and we sit facing each other. She's frowning now. "What's up?"

"Nothing bad," I say, and her forehead smooths out, but she still looks confused. "I just have something I need to tell you. I've been holding this in for a while. I wasn't sure how you'd react." I take a deep breath.

She reaches out, grabbing my hand. "I love you, Dean."

Tears prick my eyes at the words. "I love you too." I clear my throat. "You remember how I wanted to play Romeo as a guy?"

She nods.

"That's because. Because I am one."

She tilts her head.

"I'm transgender. I want to transition. I feel like a guy, and I want people to see me that way."

Her mouth opens slightly, her eyebrows raising, and she says a silent *oh* into the cold air.

"Ronnie knows, and so does Mr. Harrison, and I'm planning to come out to the cast next week because I'm going to use *he* and *him* pronouns in my bio for the program. I'm sorry I didn't tell you sooner," I say. "I was just nervous." I swallow. The tears are threatening to fall now. She still hasn't said anything. "Are you mad at me? Please don't be mad at me."

"I'm not mad," she says. She turns my hand over in hers, tracing the lines of my palm. "Why were you scared to tell me?"

"You're gay," I say. "I'm a guy. I've been going to this support group, and reading stuff online about what happens to couples when someone transitions, and a lot of times . . ." I don't finish.

"But I love you," she says. Shakes her head. "You're still Dean."

"You're really not upset?"

"No?" She looks up at me like a deer on the edge of a forest, like she's ready to bolt. "I mean, I wish you told me earlier. I don't really understand what this means for you. But I still want to be with you." She takes a deep breath. "You still want to be with me, right?"

My eyes widen. "Of course!"

She slides across the bench into my arms, holding me tight, my face in her hair, the sharp citrus scent of her all around me. She's warm and soft and I want every inch of my body against hers. My hand is in her hair and her face is in my neck and I don't want to let go. I can't. My heart pounds, my limbs are watery. I did it.

"You said you were going to a support group?" she asks a little bit later. We're still on the bench watching the water, her legs over mine, her head on my chest. I'm getting cold, but I don't mind.

"Yeah. It's a group for trans teenagers. It meets every Monday night at Lambert House."

"Oh." She's quiet for a second, and sits up a little. "Monday nights? So that time you went to the dentist . . ."

I grimace. "I was actually at Lambert House. I'm sorry. I just wasn't ready to tell you. I shouldn't have lied to you."

She nods slowly, looking out at the water. "No . . . no. I understand why you did it."

"Are you sure?"

"Yeah. It's kinda weird that you didn't tell me the truth, but I know you weren't trying to hurt me."

"I would never," I say, pulling her close, and she snuggles into me.

"When are you going to tell the cast?"

"Not sure. We turn in our bios tomorrow," I say.

"Wow." She picks at the pilling on her purple tights. "How do you think people will take it?"

I shrug. "No idea."

She pulls back, looking up at me. "Do you think it'll be okay? What if people freak out?"

I shift, sitting up straighter, and she moves her legs off my lap. "I mean. I really don't know, babe. There's never been a trans person at school before. That I know of, anyway." I take a deep breath and smile at her. "If people freak out, they freak out. That's not my problem."

She nods. Looks at the people passing out on the path. "I'm cold. I should probably get home."

I walk her out to her bus stop. We're quiet until it arrives, and I watch it go, touching my lips where the warmth of hers still lingers.

I did it. And we're okay.

At home that night, I open up the NYU application again. I still haven't started my personal statement, but that's not what I care about right now. Even though the application is due in two weeks. November first. Early Decision.

I go to the search box and type: *audition monologues*.

And after a pause, I add: *for men*.

The results populate and a smile takes over my face. No one can stop me from doing this. I can pick any monologue here and it will actually be what I want.

Look out, NYU. I'm coming for you.

CHAPTER FIFTEEN

"How was your weekend?" Allison asks as we walk to Spanish together on Monday.

I shrug. "Oh, you know, just trying to figure out how to package my life into a single essay."

She snorts, adjusting her patch-covered messenger bag. "Personal statements are such bullshit."

"How's yours going?"

She arches an eyebrow up at me. "It's not."

"What do you mean?"

"I'm not applying anywhere," she says, darting ahead of me into the classroom. Ms. Rodriguez is busy writing the warm-up on the board, people still trickling in from break.

We sit down, and I turn to face her. She pulls out her textbook and unfolds her sketchbook inside it. "I'm going to get a job as soon as I can and move to New York City with you all in September," she says.

"Do your parents know?"

She shakes her head.

I let out a breath. "Damn, Allison."

She smiles. "It's my life, right?"

I nod.

"Anyway. I'm not the only one with secrets." Her pen circles on the page, the outline of a face.

"Oh yeah?" I lean my elbows on her desk.

"Zoe told me," she says.

Adrenaline hits me like a train. She knows. She knows.

"Don't worry, I don't care," she says. "I mean. It's important to you, so I care about that, obviously. But I don't have a problem with it."

I watch her draw, words stuck in my throat. I spent so much time building myself up to tell Zoe, and I did that, and now suddenly Allison knows too. Without me even having to think about how to tell her. Without me getting to decide.

On her sketchpad, a hairline appears, and then a jawline. The person she's drawing looks familiar, but they're upside down. I have to say something. "Thanks."

She waves her other hand. "Don't thank me. I'm just doing the bare minimum."

At the front of the room, Ms. Rodriguez claps her hands, and I face front. About half the class pays attention. The other half is whispering, or on their phones under their desks, or they're Blake, who's drawing a border of tiny dicks around the edge of his desk. From the desk on his other side, Jared catches my gaze and rolls his eyes. I smirk and shake my head, but my heart starts pounding again. Now that Allison knows, I have to tell Jared too. This is all happening so fast.

"Have you come out to your parents yet?" Allison whispers behind me.

I half turn, my feet in the aisle, so I look like I'm listening to Ms. Rodriguez, and shake my head.

She exhales. "Good luck. I was so worried when I came out as bi. I was going to this horrible all-white private school and kids were always asking me stupid stuff about being Japanese. The idea of also not being straight . . ." She shakes her head.

I glance down at her sketchbook. The character's hair is fully shaded, and she's working on the face. "How's Operation Get a Girlfriend?"

She makes a noise of disgust. "All of the girls at this school are either straight or they just want to experiment with me behind their boyfriend's back."

"I'm sorry."

She shrugs. "Whatever. At least my parents will be happy."

"Were they not cool about it?"

"They were fine. They didn't disown me. But I think they're still hoping I'll just fall for boys so they don't have to actually deal with it."

I roll my eyes in sympathy and turn to the front again. Ms.

Rodriguez is talking about verb conjugation, calling on different people. I pretend to listen and replay the conversation in my head. Allison is cool with me. In fact, it barely seems to matter to her at all.

Maybe this is okay. I don't have to go through the whole big explanation with yet another person. And Allison and Zoe are best friends. I guess I should have expected this. It's not like I told Zoe not to tell anyone.

But still. She could have asked me. She *should* have asked me.

My hands are still shaking from the rush of Allison's words, and I clasp them in front of me on the desk, staring at my knuckles. I tighten my fingers until the joints turn white and then release them. It's fine. This is fine. Zoe meant well.

I glance over at Jared. He stares up at Ms. Rodriguez, his hair down today, flowing over his shoulders. For a moment, his eyelids flutter shut and his chin slips, but he catches himself and sits up straight.

I look away before he can catch me staring. It's going to be fine. I hope.

At lunch, I get to the usual spot in the senior hallway first. Zoe walks up a moment later.

When she sits down, she smiles at me for a little too long. "What's up?" I ask.

"Nothing." She brushes some hair out of my eyes. "I'm just happy to see you."

Ronnie and Allison join us, and then Jared rolls up on his wheeled sneakers.

"Okay!" Zoe claps her hands. "I want to talk about something."

Oh no.

"Now that we all know, I was wondering what we should do about pronouns." She smiles at me, dropping her voice on the last word.

Oh. No.

"Pronouns?" Jared looks from her to me. His eyebrows furrow.

Well, shit. I guess we're doing this.

"Zoe." I close my eyes tight, as if I can open them and this moment will be different. "Jared doesn't know." I look at her and her mouth opens, but no sound comes out.

"Awkward," Allison says.

"It's fine." I want to smile, pretend everything is okay, but I can't. My chest feels like it's going to explode. "Uh, Jared. I'm trans."

"Oh." He's silent for a moment. "Okay. Uh. So you're a guy?"

"Yeah." I watch him.

"Okay." He nods. "Yeah. That makes sense."

"Oh my god," Ronnie says, pressing fingertips to his forehead. "Zoe, maybe check next time before you assume?"

She covers her mouth and looks at me, eyes a little too

bright, like she's about to cry. "I'm sorry. I'm sorry. I wasn't thinking."

I shake my head, my cheeks hot. Part of me wants to snap at her, but she's already upset and I don't want to be a jerk. "It's okay," I say as she starts to talk again. "It's really fine. Just. Don't tell anyone else?"

She shakes her head. "I promise." Reaching out, she takes my hand and squeezes it, and I finally force a grin. She gives me a small smile back.

We decide the group will call me "he" when no one else is near, at least until Friday. That's when I'm planning on coming out to the cast.

After that? I don't know what will happen, and I don't want to think about it.

Zoe doesn't say anything else about me being trans for the rest of lunch. She acts like nothing happened, and I do too, but it's like everything I say and do is an echo, a little behind everyone else. No one notices. I joke, and laugh, but it's Robot Dean doing it. Robot Dean looks good, like he has everything together, but inside is me, a mess of tangled wires and short circuits. I didn't think about whether I wanted to tell Allison and Jared, and now it's too late.

It's fine. I would have told them eventually.

I just.

I wanted to be the one to do it.

When I turn the bio in to Mr. Harrison, and tell him my plan, something shifts inside me, like I've set the imaginary sphere from his game loose and it's rolling and I can't stop it.

Even though I don't want to hold on to it.

I wanted to let it go, but now that I have, I keep imagining every way this could go wrong, like the sphere is blazing a trail of destruction instead of freedom. By fifth period on Friday, I'm in another world, watching the one around me go by. I know everyone was fine with it up until now. Ronnie, Allison, Zoe, Jared, Mr. Harrison: Everyone was fine. But the list of names isn't enough. Nothing is.

The bell rings. I stand, walk out, head toward the theatre like it's a magnet drawing me in. I'm not me. I'm in a movie and this is the slow-motion moment.

"Dean." Ronnie's hand on my shoulder jerks me back to the hallway. We're at the double doors. He looks me right in the eye. "You got this."

Jared appears behind him, jerks his chin in a nod. I take a deep breath, and we walk in together.

Mr. Harrison has us circle up, and I look around at everyone. Blake, playing with Olivia's hair. Courtney, whispering something to another girl. Blake's buddies, jostling each other; the set-crew kids with their black clothes, the props master with her oversized glasses. So many seniors; so many people I've been in this class with for three, four years even. And the juniors, hungry for their turn; the freshmen and sophomores, filling out the bit parts, helping out wherever they can, just to be part of it. This theatre is magic.

Will it still feel that way once everyone knows?

"Before we get started, I want everyone's attention. One of your fellow students has something important to share." Mr. Harrison stares at each person in turn, until everyone is quiet. He looks over at me and inclines his head.

Showtime.

"Hey, so." I don't know what I'm going to say, but I'm speaking. The words are there, like they've been waiting for this moment. "A while ago, I realized something. I thought about it for a long time, and when Mr. Harrison cast me as Romeo, I knew I didn't want to hide it anymore."

As I say it, I know it's true. It wasn't always, but it is now.

"You might notice something different in the program this year. Instead of referring to me as *she* and *her*, it'll say *he* and *him*."

My gaze finds Olivia's. She's starting to smile and nod. Courtney looks confused, Blake's face is blank. I hear whispers, but I focus on Olivia and the encouragement in her eyes. Beside me, Ronnie puts his hand on my knee and squeezes.

"I'd like everyone here to use those pronouns, and just call me Dean. I mean, you all do anyway. But yeah. I've realized that I've felt this way most of my life. I know everyone sees me as a girl, but I'm not a girl."

One more deep breath, out of habit, but my hands aren't shaking. I'm not Robot Dean.

I'm Real Dean.

And I say it to them, to myself, to the world. "I'm a trans guy."

ACT THREE

"I must be gone and live, or stay and die."

—ROMEO

Romeo and Juliet, act 3, scene 5

CHAPTER SIXTEEN

"So did you come out to your girlfriend yet?" Jade asks me after group on Monday. We're all putting chairs away, gathering our things. After missing last week's meeting, it's nice to be back.

I smile.

"He did!" Nina laughs.

"Not just her." I tell them about Allison, Jared, and the cast. Everyone was cool at rehearsal, or at least they pretended to be. Olivia high-fived me. Blake and his buddies didn't say anything, just left me alone. So far, so good.

"Ooh, girlfriend outed you?" Jade grimaces. "Not cool."

"She has a name," I say.

Jade waves her hand. "Yeah, okay. Zoe outed you. You're not mad?"

I shrug. "It worked out." Sure, every time I remember how Zoe's voice dropped when she said *pronouns*, like it was some dirty secret, I feel a little sick, but it's not the biggest deal. Not enough to confront her. It's not like she's being horribly transphobic.

Jade raises her eyebrows, but lets it go.

"We're going to Caffe Vita," Nina says. "You want to come?"

I check my phone. It's almost nine. "I have to get home. Ten o'clock curfew."

"Aww, curfew!" Jade grins. "Our little Dean-O."

"Shut up." I try to glare, but I can't help smiling. She pinches my cheeks and I bat her hand away.

"Next time." Nina smiles at me.

We end up walking the same way, me toward my bus stop, them to the cafe. It's the long way for me, but I don't tell them that.

"When did you know?" I ask them.

"Ah, the transgender origin story," Jade says. "It was a dark and stormy night . . ." The corny joke catches me off guard and I laugh. Jade shrugs. "I always wished I was a girl. I didn't know what that meant for the longest time and I learned quick I had to hide it. Nobody in my family ever talked about trans people unless they were mocking the women on Jerry Springer."

Nina snaps her fingers in agreement.

Jade zips up the front of her leather jacket as it starts to rain. "My first girlfriend was bi and we went to Pride together junior year of high school. Someone passed me this flyer about trans rights. I went home that night and looked up *transgender* online and here we are."

I tell them about seeing *West Side Story* when I was a kid and watching *Boys Don't Cry* with Zoe. "When Mom told me I couldn't play boy roles because I was a girl, I was kind of like, 'Oh, okay.' I was disappointed, but I thought the reason I felt different was because I was gay. I hated being seen as a girl, though."

"So you're a trans guy," Nina says.

I frown. "Yeah."

"And you're mad about it?" Jade asks. I look at her, ready for another joke, but her smile is kind, her eyes gentle.

I swallow. "I'm not mad. I'm just . . ." We turn right on Pine Street, walking down toward the park. "It's confusing. Every time someone calls me a girl, every time someone calls me *she*, I feel like shit. I hate my given name. I want my body to be different."

I'm saying these things out loud for the first time, and I realize they're true. I do want my body to be different. I want my body in Romeo's suit to look just like any other cis boy's body. But there's something else, something that makes me think none of it is real.

"The thing is, I don't want a penis."

They're both quiet, Jade's heels clicking on the pavement, Nina's sneakers lighting up with every step.

"The penis doesn't make the man," Jade says. "We talked about that, remember?" Her voice is light, playful.

"Yeah." I stare at the concrete passing under my Converse, the puddles catching the streetlights and the shadows of buildings.

"Gender is bullshit," Nina says. "You can make yours whatever you want." She brushes back her long hair, dyed a fresh hot pink. "Like, for me, I don't care about passing. Yeah, this world is scary, but I'm not femme like Jade. I'd break my ankle in heels. So it's up to you to decide how you want to look, what makes you feel like yourself."

I nod.

She smiles. "Plus, you might change your mind about the penis. I used to care a lot about passing as cis, but now I kinda think I might be nonbinary. Sometimes gender can change over time."

A few people stare at us as we cut over toward Pike. I pretend I don't notice. One man's eyes follow Jade and Nina down the entire block; he twists as we pass him, brow locked in a glare, lip curled back. My chest and limbs flood with shaky energy and I realize my fists are clenched around the straps of my backpack. I uncurl my hands, shoving them into my pockets as we leave the man behind.

"Did you see that guy?" I ask. We're approaching the coffee shop, its windows golden. Golden and safe.

Nina glances at me. Jade stares straight ahead.

"He was staring at us like . . ."

"Like he wanted to kill us?" Jade's voice is gravel scraping underfoot. "Get used to it."

The words dry up in my mouth, scenes playing over and over in my mind: the man glaring as we pass, the man getting up and yelling something at us, the man waiting for Jade and Nina when they leave the cafe, the man—

"Dean." Nina squeezes my arm. Her eyes are soft. "We're all okay."

I nod. I can't speak. If I speak, I'll cry.

"Didn't you have a bus to catch?" Jade asks.

"Oh." I've walked blocks away from where I'm supposed to be. "Yeah."

"You sure you don't want to come in?" She glances into the shop, then back at me.

"Uh." I'm torn for a second. "I really can't."

"Your loss," she says, but she's got that smile again, the one where her lips press together like she's holding in a secret.

"Walk safe," Nina says, and then they're gone, into the cafe.

I make the bus with minutes to spare. By the time it drops me off a few blocks away from home, I'm almost half an hour late. The lights are on inside the house when I walk up. Mom sits in the living room, reading. I walk up to the back door, turn the key in the lock as slowly and quietly as I can.

Mom calls out my given name. I make for the door to the basement and the safety of my room, but she appears in the kitchen.

"Where have you been? It's after ten."

"I was just hanging out with some friends and lost track of time," I say.

Her eyes flash. "I called Ronnie, Allison, Jared, and Zoe's houses and you weren't with any of them."

"Wow, Mom. Stalker much?"

She glares at me, lips pursed. "I have the right to know where you are."

"Yeah, well, that's not going to matter in April when I turn eighteen." I cross my arms.

Dad comes into the kitchen. "What's going on, girls?"

I want to scream, throw something, punch the wall. "Mom's just trying to control my every move, as usual," I say, my voice filling up the room.

"I am not trying to control you," she snaps. And then she says my given name like a slap, loud and hard.

"Stop calling me that!" I shout.

"That is your name!" she yells back. "Until you turn eighteen you are in my house and you will live by my rules! And if you're so impatient to be in control of your own life, then you are more than welcome to move out as soon as your birthday arrives!"

I stare at her, then at Dad. He's pale, mouth half-open, staring at both of us. I dash out of the kitchen, wrench open the basement door, slam it shut behind me, and run down to my room.

She doesn't come after me. Neither does Dad. I can hear the distant murmur of their voices through the ceiling. My limbs hum with rage and I punch my pillow again and again and again, mind blanking with the impact of fist on fabric, my breath coming hard and fast. I pick up the pillow and throw it across the room.

Move out as soon as your birthday arrives. Like I should be grateful she's not kicking me out right now. Fuck her. Why wait?

I get up and go to my closet, pull out my suitcase. Footsteps on the stairs. I stride to my door and lock it, stepping back. A knock.

"Dean. Can we talk?" It's Dad's voice, soft and low.

I stare at the door. I know I should say something, but I don't want to. I want him to wait, want him to agonize.

"Honey?" The pet names now. I clench my fists. *You can't get to me that way.* "Okay. Take some time, cool off. Whenever you're ready." His footsteps recede, plodding slow and heavy up the stairs again.

Like ice melting, all the rage goes out of my body and I collapse on the floor, curling into a ball. I cry the way I've learned how, face scrunched up, body shaking, mouth open. But silent. Always silent.

Ronnie's eyes widen when I come into class the next morning. Reaching forward, he smacks Allison's shoulder and she looks up.

I sit down.

"What's wrong?" Ronnie says.

I tell them. I cried all night, so my voice is low and ragged. I like the sound of it, and somewhere in my brain a dim chime rings. Will my voice sound like this on testosterone?

As I talk, Ronnie wraps his hand around my upper arm, squeezing. I fold my hand over his. I can't cry here. I tense my jaw and the tears stay put.

"That's so fucked." Allison gazes at me. "Do you think she really meant it?"

"I think she knows," I say. The bell rings. "On some level."

Ronnie pitches his voice high like Mom's. *"That is your name.* I cannot believe she said that."

The class quiets and we face front. Ms. Porter starts to say something, the chatter fading, but I zone out. If Mom is catching on, is Dad? Should I tell them? I don't know if I want to—if I'm ready.

But I have to. Mom and Dad always come to opening night, and Mom saves a copy of the program for every play I'm in, framing them with my school photo from each year.

I have to tell them before they see my bio.

Of course I put it off. There's only room for one thing in my brain this week: the deadline for NYU. On Sunday, the fated day, I stay up way too late putting the final touches on my personal statement. I chose a prompt last week: a meaningful aspect of my identity.

I wrote about being trans. The essay was hard to write, but easy too. I took the write-up I did for Mr. Harrison's costume assignment and reshaped it into the opening hook. *Get them with the anecdote,* Ms. Porter always tells us in English.

I hope it works. Because if I'm going to go to NYU, I'm doing it as me. Not Robot Dean, not girl Dean.

Real Dean. Real me.

I hit send a few minutes before the application closes. Next up, in two weeks: my audition. Since I'm not in New York City and there's no way my parents are dropping the dollars to fly me there, I'm doing it digitally.

SENT, Ronnie texts me and Zoe.

Same here omg I'm dying, she says.

I text a GIF of a boy tapping his fingers on a table, waiting. Then I toss my clothes in the corner and step into my PJ pants, taking my sports bra off underneath my shirt so I don't have to see my chest.

My eyelids were drooping when I sent the application, but the minute I lie down, I'm wide awake. Bowie's face is ghostly on the wall above me. My eyes unfocus. Mom's face materializes, the hardness of her voice during our fight, the way she crossed her arms like a wall, spit my name at me like a poison arrow.

I close my eyes. Sleep doesn't come. When I look at my phone, it's past one. I turn the lights on and tiptoe upstairs to make tea.

The kitchen is silent and dark, and I flip on the light over the stove, chasing the shadows into the corners. I fill a pot with water and wait for it to boil.

A creak from the living room. Dad shuffles into the kitchen, mug in hand. "Fancy meeting you here," he says.

I shrug. Tiny bubbles form at the bottom of the pot.

"Did you get your application in?" He selects another tea bag from the cabinet.

I nod.

"I'm proud of you."

"At least someone is." I stare at the water.

He leans against the counter. "I know your mom can be hard to reach. But she loves you."

"She doesn't love *me*. She loves who she wants me to be."

He sighs. "It's hard for her. She doesn't understand."

"You're fine with it. Why isn't she?" I turn to him. The kitchen glows dim and golden, the spotless tiled counter a soft blue. The refrigerator hums gently, rain lashing the windows.

"She was raised much more conservatively than I was. North Carolina is a long way from Berkeley." The water is bubbling. I turn off the stove and lift the pot, filling my cup. I pass the pot to him and he pours the rest of the water into his mug. "It hasn't always been easy for us to see eye to eye either. But we love each other, so we work it out."

I stir my tea, watching the water darken, the spicy scent drifting upward. I don't know why, but my heart is beating faster. I've never thought about Dad as his own person before. A few times, I've tried picturing coming out to my parents as trans, but at the center of every imagining is Mom. Mom, in shock. Mom, disowning me. Mom, telling me I'm disgusting. Or worse, telling me I'll always be her baby girl.

But when I came out as gay, Dad soothed Mom. I remember watching her cry on the couch as I stood before them. He rubbed her back and kept her from walking out.

The refrigerator's hum stops and we stand in the sudden quiet. My stomach growls and he chuckles. "Well, kiddo, I'm going to go read."

I nod, circling my hands around the mug, letting it warm my palms. He shuffles out to the living room and I stay in the kitchen, looking out at the dark street until my focus shifts and I see myself, pale and small, reflected in the window. I turn away and go back downstairs.

CHAPTER SEVENTEEN

"Look! That's her."

The half whisper rings in my ear as I pass a gaggle of freshman girls. I ignore them. I knew the news would make it around; some of the seniors in the cast have younger siblings at school, and those younger siblings have friends, and I don't have the energy to contain this anymore. I'm not going to make a grand coming-out post on Instagram or start campaigning with the Queer Alliance. I'm just going to live, and the haters can deal.

And now, almost two weeks after I came out to the cast, it seems they've finally caught up with me.

My phone pings. Hey Mr. D, It's Jade.

Oh hey, I text back.

What are you up to this weekend?

Nothing

Want to come to an open mic on Friday? It's mostly queer and trans, bring whoever you want. Even Zoe. An emoji sticking out its tongue. Which I think means she's joking. I think.

Queer. It seems like a stand-in for LGBT, but it's not. It rolls off the tongue like a sneer, something sly, a subversion of what everyone thinks is normal. I like it. And a whole open mic of queer and trans folks?

Yeah I'm down!

She texts me the address and time, and I get this rush, like my body's filling up with helium. My friends would love this.

What's everyone doing Friday night? I group-text the crew.

Avoiding my mother, Allison says

Fuck all, says Jared. Lol Allison

I tell them what's up.

OMG that's amazing, Zoe replies.

Yes please, Ronnie says.

Everyone responds. Everyone's in.

We work the scenes between Romeo and Juliet that week. It's just me and Olivia on stage for rehearsals after school, the crew behind us assembling the backdrop. On Thursday, Blake waits around for Olivia, playing on his phone in the second row. Sometimes I look out and he's staring at me, but I just give him a nod and keep going. I'm good at that nod now.

We begin again with Romeo's entrance into the garden under Juliet's window.

The scene rolls by, the words weaving us together on the stage. One of the set pieces is up already: a raised platform, the front painted in a pattern of gray stone blocks, a balcony jutting out, with a wall of canvas behind. The canvas is painted in the same pattern, broken only by a set of blue double doors with frosted glass, behind which is the rest of the platform. Olivia emerges through the doors onto the balcony and gazes around the stage. "Romeo, doff thy name, and for that name which is no part of thee, take all myself," she says with a sigh, and I answer, moving out of what will be the shadow of a tree trunk built by the crew. She draws back, a hand to her chest, and then I reveal myself as her new love, the handsome youth from her family's party just a short while before.

The lines become a dance, my vows of love and her uncertainty of my intentions, how I could feel so strongly so soon, whether I will prove false or true. We've both got our lines down cold. Mr. Harrison calls out the Nurse's interruptions, and at the end of the scene I retreat, watching Olivia as she disappears through the doors again. She smiles and gives me a thumbs-up from the small platform on the other side, hidden from the audience. Grinning, I bound over to Mr. Harrison.

"I can tell you've both worked hard," he says as Olivia comes down and joins us. "Dean, you're the picture of a young man infatuated. Olivia, your mix of reluctance and eagerness for love is palpable. Really nice work." After a few more notes, he releases us. I ignore Blake and run up the aisle to my stuff.

As I put on my coat, I watch the crew move a flat into place. The wooden frame is huge, the canvas stretched across it blank but ready to be painted. Blake and Olivia walk up the aisle toward me, holding hands.

I grab my backpack, glance up. From the stage, Jared flashes me a peace sign.

And then Blake shoulder-checks me, hard.

"Dude." I pivot as he passes, massaging my arm. "What the hell?"

"Sorry, man," he says, turning, the second word ringing a little too loud. A broad smile stretches his face, but there's no human behind it, just shark, coming for me. "How are those freak friends of yours?"

I stare at him. "What?"

"I saw you." He smirks. "On the Hill the other day."

My whole body stills, limbs pinned to my sides as if filled with lead. I remember now. Blake lives on Capitol Hill. His family's mansion is huge and old and sits in the neighborhood a few blocks away from Lambert House. I beat him once in beer pong at a cast party there.

"Have a nice day," he says, and adds my given name, the sound an arrow punching through my chest. Olivia drops his hand, stepping back, and he snorts, pushing through the double doors into the sun-filled lobby. The sudden light makes me blink, spots darting across my vision. Olivia catches the door before it shuts, but she just stands there, caught in the light, hair aglow. Her mouth is open, like she wants to say something but can't find the words. Then she's gone, the door closing with a thump.

Blake glares at me every time he sees me on Friday, but I ignore him. I don't have time for his bullshit. I'm going to a queer poetry night tonight.

"Bolo or no bolo?" Ronnie holds the tiny tie up to his neck, then away, then back at his neck. His house is right on a bus line to Capitol Hill, so we're all crowded into his room, watching him get dressed. Jared's sprawled on the bed, Allison's cross-legged on the floor.

"No bolo," Zoe says, touching up her eyeliner in the mirror over his dresser. The new Missy Elliott song blasts from Ronnie's phone. The beat makes me move my hips back and forth a little bit.

Ronnie stands beside her, buttons the collar of his white oxford shirt all the way up, and pulls on a plum-colored sweater. "Okay." He pats his chest. "I'm ready."

Watching him get dressed is fun, but it makes me anxious too. I like what I'm wearing: skinny black jeans, the Bowie T-shirt I screen-printed in art class, with my favorite hoodie and a denim jacket on top. But I fiddle with the zipper as we ride, pulling it up and down and up and down. I'm wearing my smallest, tightest sports bra, but my chest is still visible if someone looks close enough. I wish it was flat. I wish I had a binder. I don't want to play Romeo with my chest showing, but I'm not about to bind with tape again. I need to figure out how to get a real binder.

The open mic is at a small theatre attached to a coffee shop in Capitol Hill. Outside the theatre doors, people mill around the table at the entrance, talking and laughing. We each pay five dollars, and then we're in.

Rows of chairs lead up to a slightly elevated stage. An exposed brick wall is the backdrop, a red curtain drawn half-closed across it. People fill half the seats, and I scan the rows until I see Jade and Nina.

"You brought a posse," Jade says as we all file in.

We make introductions, Ronnie, Allison, and Jared sitting in the row in front of Jade, Nina, Zoe, and me. Jade stares at Zoe a little too long before she smiles in greeting.

"And you're all queer? This is adorable," Nina says.

"Except Jared," Allison says, slapping him on the back. "Our token straight boy."

Everyone laughs, Jared bending from the waist in a mock-bow.

Pretty soon we're all talking, Allison and Nina debating the merits of various digital illustration programs, Ronnie and Jared joking with me and Jade. Zoe's quiet beside me, sometimes laughing, sometimes squeezing my hand. Ronnie regales us with tales of costume closet shenanigans.

"I could put together the most fabulous drag outfits from that closet," he says.

Jade smiles. "I did theatre in high school too."

I sit up a little straighter. "What roles?"

She shrugs. "Minor ones. I was in jazz band too, so I didn't have a lot of time. But I do fringe theatre now, and me and some friends of mine are talking about starting a performance collective."

"That's so cool." I grin at her.

"Oh, stop." She waves a hand. "Maybe we can come see your play," she says, glancing at Nina engrossed in conversation with Allison, and back to me.

"You should," I say.

Jade smiles, her dark eyes meeting mine in the dim theatre. I wait for the snarky follow-up, but she doesn't say anything, just looks at me, her eyelids dusted with gold. A thread weaves through my chest like I'm back on stage under the spotlight.

"So Dean mentioned he met you at a support group?" Zoe asks.

Jade turns her gaze on Zoe. "Mm-hmm."

Zoe smiles, starts to say something, but the emcee steps up to the mic and the chatter around us fades. Zoe and Jade face front. All the seats are occupied now, and some couples share seats or sit in each other's laps. Still more people line the wall, standing or leaning or sitting on the floor. The doors close and the room darkens until only the stage is lit.

"Good evening, fam!" The emcee is short and round, curly hair cut as short as Ronnie's, gold studs in her earlobes. I watch her command the room, making everyone laugh, her hands moving in sure and jagged sweeps, like the conductor of a very queer orchestra.

She consults the sign-up sheet and calls up the first person on the list, who confidently takes the stage. Their words unfold into the room like vines, taking over every inch of space until we're all connected. Around me, the audience shifts, sighs, snaps their fingers. I sneak looks around the crowd, see a thin man in a flowing silk shirt entwine his fingers with the fingers of the man next to him, kissing his boyfriend's hand as if he doesn't know he's doing it, his pale blue eyes fixed on the speaker. I can't look away. It's the most beautiful thing I've ever seen, as if love has taken physical form.

Halfway through the night, a man takes the stage, clean-shaven and young, with round cheeks. He smiles at the crowd, who clap and whistle like they're all friends. Maybe they are. He waves a hand and takes the microphone off its stand.

"This is easier than making the stand short enough for me," he says, and everyone laughs.

He steps back, closing his eyes, his chest moving out in a deep breath. Then he looks out at us and speaks.

The poem is about testosterone. About him. How he agonized over starting hormones and how his life has changed since. I watch him move through the poem like it's a room he lives in, like he's completely at home in every word. It's not just what he's saying, but how he's saying it: the poem is truth. His body now is good and right, but he's lost pieces of who he was along the way, and he doesn't regret it but he still mourns the loss, the same way he misses the ex-girlfriend he doesn't want to be with anymore.

After the show, we hang around outside for a while. It's past ten, but I'm not worried. I told Dad I was spending the night at Ronnie's.

Which I am, technically. We just went to this show first.

Jade smiles at me. "What'd you think?"

"It was amazing," I say. I glance at Nina, who's talking to Allison, their phones out.

"See you on Monday?" Jade asks.

I smile at her. "I'll be there."

On Sunday I'm at Zoe's house, lying on the bed, listening to music. The door is closed and her mom isn't home, but we're not making out.

Not that I'm thinking about it.

"Oh my god. Look." Zoe tilts her phone to show me. It's Allison gushing over someone she's been talking to.

"Who is it?" I ask.

"It's Nina," Zoe says, widening her eyes. "They've been texting nonstop since the open mic on Friday."

"Oh shit." I grin. "That's perfect."

"Isn't it?" Zoe smiles at the phone. "Everyone should be as open-minded as Allison."

Open-minded? The word sinks into the pit of my stomach. Does Zoe think she's open-minded for being with me too?

The word makes it sound like she and Allison deserve praise for being attracted to trans people, as if we're so weird that dating us requires a special state of mind.

I want to say something, but I don't know where to start. After a moment, Zoe props herself on her side, looking at me. "That poem about testosterone was interesting."

I look at her. She's watching my face like she's waiting for something. "Yeah," I say.

She sits up and looks at me. "I did some research."

"What did you find out?"

"A lot of stuff. How hormones change your body. And what kind of surgeries people get." She chews her nail and I reach out, taking the hand away from her mouth and folding it in mine. Adrenaline pumps through my chest and into my limbs. She looks at me like a cat wary of coming too close. "Do you know what you want? Out of transition, I mean."

"I don't know."

She nods once. Twice.

I take a deep breath. "Are you sure you're okay with me being trans?" It's not exactly what I want to say, her words a moment ago still reeling through my mind, but it's the closest I can get.

Her eyes scan my face and I can hardly breathe. She smiles, slow and warm. "Yeah." I squeeze her hand and she squeezes back. "I mean, I'm not gonna lie, I'm still getting used to calling you *he* and seeing you as a guy. But I love you and I want to be with you, no matter what." She stretches out next to me again and we nestle into the bed, legs entwined. "I love you, Dean," she says, burrowing her head into my neck. My heartbeat is slowing, and I wait for happiness to bloom inside me. She wants to be with me, she's okay with who I am, so where is the glow in my chest? She just has to get used to it. That's what she said.

"I kind of freaked out for a second," she says. "When we were at the lake."

Above us, the tiny white lights strung around the edge of the ceiling glitter, the light dim and cold, like the moon. "Why?" I ask, keeping my voice as soft as possible.

"Just . . . for a minute I thought . . . I don't know." Her voice is watery now, and I wait. The song on the stereo ends, and the three seconds of silence crumble like a cliff under my feet. "I thought you were about to break up with me."

"Oh." The music starts up again and so does my brain. "Oh. No. Why did you think that?"

"Well, you'd been distant, and we talked about it and said *I love you* but then you were weird the next day, and I know that was because of the Lambert House thing, you didn't feel like you could tell me, but for a minute, right before you told me, I thought . . . I thought that was it."

"Oh my god. Zoe." I roll over, wrapping my arms around her, squeezing her so close she squeaks. I pull back and tilt up her chin, wipe the tears off her cheek. "I'm so sorry. I love you. I know I've been distant, but it's not going to be like that anymore." Tears well up in her eyes again and she kisses me, her face wet against mine.

"I just don't want to lose you," she says.

"You won't," I say.

She just looks at me, puts her hand to my cheek, smooths my hair back. I kiss her again and she hums into my mouth, pulling me on top of her. I put my lips on the corners of her mouth, down her jaw, onto her neck. I want to memorize her body, breathe the truth of my heart into her so she knows how much I love her. So she'll know who I am. So she'll keep loving me, the real me.

Her hands find my waist, slip under my shirt. When she slides under my sports bra, I flinch.

"Too cold?" Her voice is soft against my mouth, half words, half giggle.

"It's not that."

She pulls back a little. "What's up?" She tugs my shirt down, resting her hands on my waist. I roll away, onto my back, and she leans on an elbow, looking at me.

"It's just weird," I say. "When you touch this." I wave my hand over my torso. "It's a reminder. You know?" She tilts her head, brow wrinkling. I close my eyes. That part of my body grows in my mind and I want to fold my arms, cover it up. "My chest feels like it belongs to someone else. When you touch it, I remember it's mine. And that sucks."

She breathes a small *oh*. The apartment is still. I can hear the voices of people in the unit above us, the words nothing more than smudges, distant murmurs through the ceiling.

"I guess I kind of know what I want," I say. "I think I want to get a binder. At least for the play."

"You should," she says. I turn my head, look at her profile, the green of her hair almost all faded, revealing the yellow-blond of the bleach underneath.

"Are you okay with that?"

A short, surprised laugh leaps from her mouth. "It's your body, babe," she says. "You don't need my permission."

CHAPTER EIGHTEEN

I double-check my files before I hit upload. Acting résumé: check. Photo of me I don't hate, that looks halfway professional: check.

Send.

It's early afternoon and I'm missing rehearsal today for only one reason: my digital audition for Tisch. For NYU.

It's happening.

I enter the video conference, and one by one the other applicants who had signed up for this audition slot log in too. The evaluator plays us a short video about the department, and then we wait, one at a time, for our phone conversation and our live audition.

The evaluator seems nice, but she calls me by my given name. I hesitate a moment before telling her my pronouns and that I go by Dean, but she just says *great!* and we move on.

Faster than I'm ready for, I'm standing, setting the laptop on the kitchen table and backing up into my living room so they can see me while I perform my monologues.

I'm a little stiff at first. Acting to people on a screen, in an empty room, is awkward. But I hit my stride halfway through my first monologue, and when it's time for my second one, the comedic monologue, I'm golden. I even make her laugh a few times.

"Well, Dean! Do you have any questions?" she says finally, smiling at me through the screen.

I shake my head and thank her.

"You should hear back about your application around December fifteenth," she says. "Look for the email or check the application portal."

One month. I don't know how I'm going to make it.

We say goodbye, her image blinks out, and I close the browser. My knees are jelly. I sit down, and then flop all the way onto my back on the couch. I'm done.

Well.

Almost.

I'm not in yet.

I'm standing at my locker the next morning, fumbling with my backpack, when someone bumps into me from behind. My shoulder crashes into the open locker door, the clang echoing down the hall. I rub the sore spot and scan for the offender.

Blake is walking away from me. He doesn't look back.

"What the fuck was that?" Ronnie strolls up beside me, resplendent in a glittery gold suit jacket.

"Looking good, Sparkles." I grin at him.

"That the best you can do?" Ronnie rolls his eyes. "For real though. I saw that."

"Yeah." I stare after Blake as he rounds the corner. My heart is pounding, but I shrug. "Maybe it was an accident."

Ronnie eyes me. "Uh-huh. And I'm straight."

I shut the locker door. "Come on, we're going to be late to class."

Blake leaves me alone after the hallway incident. Well, sort of. In Spanish class, paper balls hit my desk. And my head. When I look at him, he's staring at the board, that smirk locked in place. His buddy looks me over, though, teeth showing in a sneer. I fix my gaze on the board. In sixth-period rehearsal, he's all professional, the kind and grounded Benvolio to my Romeo.

The same thing happens the next day. And the next. Ms. Rodriguez never sees it.

"Dude." Jared catches up to me after class on Thursday. "What's Blake's problem?"

"Me, apparently." I stare straight ahead.

"Want me to say something? I see him at the skate park sometimes."

"Nah. It's fine." I shrug. "I'm just gonna ignore him. He has to get bored eventually." I sound more chill than I feel, but I don't want Jared to see how freaked out I am. I know it won't help if he steps in. A cis guy fighting my battles for me? That will just give Blake even more reason to mock me.

By the end of the week I'm on edge, waiting for the next paper missile, the next shoulder-check. I scan every hall I walk through, looking for him, and change my route if I see him coming. Even if it means I'm late to class or can't go to my locker.

On Friday, I'm waiting for my turn in rehearsal, watching Courtney and Olivia run through one of their scenes. I need to pee, so I head out of the auditorium. I'm still using the girls' bathroom. I don't know what else to do. No one has told me not to, and there's no way I can use the boys' bathroom. Everyone knows who I am now.

Not that I could have gotten away with it before.

The bathrooms sit next to each other down the hall, the doorways separated by a bank of lockers. I'm almost there when someone steps out of the boys' room and my limbs do a slow freeze.

"What's up?" Blake's mouth is more sneer than smile when he says my given name.

"Don't call me that," I say, trying to pass him, but he steps in front of me. I back up a few steps. "What's your problem?"

"I'm just trying to help you." He sweeps an arm out to his right, toward the boys' bathroom. "If you want to be a man, you better start acting like one. Oh wait!" He drops his arm. "You already are, right? Except there's a lot more to being a guy than pretending to be one on stage."

"Good thing I'm better at both of those than you are," I say. I know I'm just playing into what Zoe calls toxic masculinity, tearing Blake's manhood down to make myself feel better, but right now I don't care.

His smile disappears. "You fucking freak," he says. He takes a few steps toward me and I back up, breath catching in my throat. He's the same height as me, but he's added muscle since the beginning of the year. He's even broader now, chest flat and hard under his T-shirt.

"What are you doing?"

We both look over. Olivia is standing there, eyes wide.

"We're just talking," Blake says before I can open my mouth. He brushes past me, and she watches him as he walks toward her. He goes to put his arm around her and she moves away.

"For real?" he says.

Her face twists into a frown. They stare at each other for a moment, and then he stomps away, back to the theatre.

She looks at me.

"Thanks," I say once he's vanished through the double doors.

"Are you okay?" she asks, moving toward me.

"Yeah, yeah." I let out a shaky breath. "He was just . . ."

"Oh, I heard him," she says, her face set.

The silence hangs between us. She's frowning at the lockers, and then she shakes her head.

"It's your turn to rehearse," she says. "Mr. Harrison sent me to look for you."

"Oh." I look at the bathroom.

She follows my gaze. "Oh." She looks over my shoulder, and then behind her. "Hey. I can guard the bathroom if you want."

I look at the bathroom doors again, the signs on the front like eyes watching me. The women's restroom is the easy choice. If easy means familiar. If easy means forgetting myself on purpose to make other people comfortable. It's only a few minutes.

But Olivia's here.

"Okay," I say. I look at the men's restroom, and then I step forward, place my hand on the door, and push it open.

The bathroom is empty. The tile is yellow-green, a couple urinals next to the sink, a stall on the opposite wall. I scuttle into the stall, adrenaline pumping through my body. On the toilet, I have to breathe deep and concentrate on releasing the muscles I've been clenching all day.

I stand up, zip my pants, buckle my belt, and then I'm out at the sink, shoulders hunched and head down. Even though I know Olivia's out there, I can't shake the sense that someone, some *guy*, might come in at any moment, see me, freak out like Blake did.

Or worse.

I catch water in my hands and splash it on my face, my heart racing. The water wakes me up, running down my neck into my shirt. I grab a paper towel, pat my cheeks and forehead, look at myself in the mirror. I'm here. I'm in the right bathroom. It's small, and dingy, and it smells like pee, but it's right.

I dart out the door.

"Yes!" Olivia claps her hands and we run back to the theatre.

No one saw. No one freaked out.

This time.

But still. Maybe one day I won't have to worry at all.

Mr. Harrison raises an eyebrow when we dash in. "Everything all right?"

I ignore Blake, but I can feel his eyes on me. "Yeah. I'm good."

At home that weekend, I try not to think about Blake, about whatever his problem is with me, about what might have happened if Olivia hadn't shown up. I don't know, and the not knowing is a black hole that reaches out to swallow me up if I get too close.

So I focus on a different problem. Coming out was just the beginning. Now that I'm out—well, mostly—I get to worry about everything that comes after.

Like testosterone. Which I think I maybe kind of probably want. Even though I told Zoe I didn't know. But I don't have the first clue how to start hormone therapy, and I cannot handle trying to figure it out.

So here I am, on my laptop, searching for binders in my private browser.

There are a lot of options. I comb trans Reddit, reading recommendation after recommendation. I already know my measurements, thanks to theatre, so I don't have to try and figure that out. I'm a small in every binder brand.

When I finally decide which binders I want to try, I put my plan into motion.

As far as I know, I have some money in the bank. Mom and Dad opened a checking account for me when I was eight, and they started teaching me how to manage money by paying me a dollar a week for my chores.

When Zoe found out, she thought it was wild. Her mom had never been able to do what my parents did. Once Sheena and Zoe's dad split, every dollar went into keeping the two of them afloat. Zoe's been working summers as a barista since sophomore year; she never had the choice to not do chores. With just the two of them, it was expected that she help out. I know Jared works part-time too—front counter at an auto shop on the weekends—and Allison was an assistant at an art camp for little kids last summer.

The money-for-chores racket stopped when I was twelve and bribery didn't work on me anymore. After that, the only money going into that account was the money my grandparents sent me at Christmas and my birthday. My parents let me spend half and made me save the rest.

Dad's parents are both dead now. Mom's are alive, I think. I haven't seen them since I was a kid, because they still live in North Carolina and Mom and Dad always say we can't afford to visit. I think it's really because Mom doesn't want to see them, but who am I to judge? Their money is about to fund Operation Flat Chest.

Or it will if I can get at it.

"Dad?" I lean through the doorway. Mom is out grocery shopping. It's the perfect time to crime.

A long pause. He's deep in a book, another thriller. I wait.

He looks up at me, blinking. "Yes?"

"Can I use the card for my account? I need to get something for the play."

"Oh. Sure." He gets up, book still in hand, and heads for their bedroom. I follow, a little behind. He rustles through the file cabinet in their closet, and then it's in my hand.

"What are you buying?" he asks as I head for the basement.

"Um. A costume piece."

He quirks an eyebrow. "Such as?"

"Clothes." I wave at my chest. "Under . . . stuff."

He holds up a hand. "Say no more."

I give him a thumbs-up and open the door. The stairs are right in front of me. I'm so close.

"Let me know how much it is, okay?"

"Okay!"

And I'm down the stairs, into my room, door locked behind me. I type in the card information and use Ronnie's house as the shipping address. There's no way I want Mom seeing the packages. If she sees them, she might open them, and I really don't want to have that conversation. The theatre excuse only goes so far.

I order three different binders. I'm not sure which one will fit the best and I don't want to take my chances. I've heard they can be really uncomfortable, and hey, more options is just more options, right? Plus, if I like all of them, so much the better.

I text Ronnie to let him know about the packages and he sends me a hand-clap emoji.

so excited for u! he says.

me too, I say. And add a David Bowie emoji plus a muscle arm, because that's exactly how I feel right now. Like a rock star. Like someone who can do anything. Handle anything. Someone who's strong as fuck.

That's me.

CHAPTER NINETEEN

When I get to sixth period on Monday, people are clumped in the middle of the stage, looking over each other's shoulders. The door thuds shut behind me and a few people raise their heads, elbow others, whisper something.

And then everyone is looking at me. The circle unfolds and there's my costume, my beautiful perfect gray suit lying on the floor, and oh my god.

It's in pieces.

"Dean!" Olivia's voice cuts the silence. We make eye contact. She tries to smile but it's more of a grimace. I just stare at her and back at the pile.

My legs start walking, but my head separates from my body, floating somewhere near the ceiling. I'm back in the movie of my life, watching it happen, and there's nothing I can do. I'm not involved. I just make the movements, hit my cues.

I walk up the steps of the stage toward the suit. There's a halo of heat around my face and tears in my eyes but I don't care. People separate in front of me.

This close, I can see someone has cut the suit jacket in half, up the back. The pants have gotten the same treatment, each leg lying by itself on the scratched stage.

"What the fuck?" Ronnie yells behind me.

He's there beside me, telling me *this is fucked up* and *it's not that bad but seriously fuck this* and *we can fix this we can fix this,* but his words wash over me. I am floating away and I don't know how to come back.

He bundles the pieces of the suit under one arm and grabs my hand, leading me away from everyone, off stage, toward the costume closet. Inside, he shuts the door, setting the suit down. I realize I'm breathing hard, almost hyperventilating, and then I fold up, sinking onto my knees, sobbing.

He drops beside me, wraps his arms around me, whispers *I'm sorry I'm sorry I'm sorry.* All around us, costumes hang from racks like curtains, the musty smell of years of theatre enveloping us. The light is dim from a single bare bulb overhead.

"I think I can mend it," he says when I'm quiet. I lean against his chest, his wool cardigan scratching my cheek. Outside the closet, I can hear people talking on the stage, the rhythms of a warm-up game.

"How?"

"I'll just sew up the cuts."

"It's not going to look the same."

He grabs my shoulders, pulls back to look at me. "Don't underestimate me." He's not grinning. His eyes are dark diamonds, hard and sparkling with a fire I've never seen before.

"Okay," I say.

He sits back and I pull up my knees to my chest, staring at the dusty linoleum floor.

"Who would do this?" Ronnie asks.

I look at him. "Who do you think?"

He lets out a sigh of disgust.

"We can't prove it," I say.

"I know."

A knock on the closet door startles us both. Ronnie rises to his knees as the door opens, but it's Jared.

"I'm so sorry, dude," he says, coming inside. "I just heard what happened."

"Does Mr. Harrison know?" I ask.

"I don't think so. Olivia told me backstage." He squats down. "What can we do?"

I put my forehead on my knees. "I don't know. I just want him to leave me alone."

"You should tell Mr. Harrison," Ronnie says.

"No."

"Come on."

"What the hell is Mr. Harrison going to do?" I ask. "Give him a detention? Great, then he'll have even more reason to hate me."

"He can't just get away with this," Jared says.

"I'm not telling anyone," I say. "I have to handle this myself."

"By doing what, exactly?" Ronnie says.

I don't have anything to say to that. So I get up and leave.

They don't stop me. Olivia and Courtney are rehearsing on stage, Mr. Harrison's back is to me, and I slip down the side stairs. I still have my backpack on; I never took it off. I forgot about it the moment I saw the costume.

The suit. My suit. I swipe at my eyes with the palm of my hand as I push out the theatre doors and speed walk down the hall. I need to get out of here.

The next morning, Zoe is waiting at my locker. She's got a cayenne chocolate bar in her hands, my favorite.

"Ronnie told me what happened," she says.

"Yeah." My voice cracks a little. I've been trying and failing to not think about it all morning. Every time I let my mind wander, I see the suit, separated from itself. Torn apart. Like me. Before transition, I could keep my emotions locked away if I wanted to, but now I can't anymore, and all the rage and sadness I've never truly felt is gathering in my chest, ready to explode.

"I'm so sorry," she says.

"Me too." I spin my lock on autopilot. Take books out. Put jacket in.

Her arms wrap around my waist, her head nestling under my armpit. Her touch is so warm and sudden, it shocks me, shakes something loose in my throat, and I start to cry. She squeezes tighter.

"Dean?"

I stop crying and look over. Olivia stands there, a few feet away, biting her lip.

"I just wanted to see how you were doing," she says. "After what happened yesterday. That was so messed up."

"You should tell that to your boyfriend," Zoe snaps, moving in front of me.

Olivia's face reddens. "He's not my boyfriend anymore," she says evenly.

"Well." Zoe crosses her arms. "Good."

"I'm sorry," I say to Olivia, because that's what you're supposed to say. Even though I'm not. Even though I hope Blake is feeling like the piece of shit he is right now.

She shrugs. "Anyway. I just wanted to say I'm sorry. I'll leave you alone now." She glances at Zoe, and then turns, weaving away through the crowded hall.

"I hate her," Zoe says.

"Seriously?"

"I mean. No." Zoe leans against the lockers, staring at the floor. "Kind of. She should have held Blake accountable."

"Wait, what?" I raise my eyebrows. "She did break up with him. And why is holding him accountable her job anyway?"

"Why are you defending her?" Zoe says.

I blink. Zoe seems angry now, out of nowhere. She's frowning at me, and I don't understand why, but I can't deal with this right now. "Please don't be mad at me," I say.

Her eyes turn sad. "I'm sorry." She sighs. "I'm just mad that this happened to you. I want to do something about it."

"Well, I just want my suit to not look like someone put it through a shredder," I say.

She nods. Moves closer. Looks up at me. "Can I hug you?"

I turn toward her and open my arms. She moves in, her body pressing against mine, but her warmth isn't comforting anymore. Instead of that perfect fit I'm used to, our embrace just feels like habit, and the sensation scares me. I pull her closer, trying to find whatever I've lost, and she hugs tighter, but nothing clicks. We're not Dean and Zoe. We're just two people standing in a hallway.

Blake resumes his paper-ball crusade that week. Paper balls, but with a twist: They're tiny and wet. One smacks against my cheek in Spanish that Friday and sticks. I pluck it off and look over to see him staring at me for once, a smirk twisting his face.

Fuck off, I mouth, and he gives me the finger back.

When class ends, I hustle for the door. I'm halfway down the hall when someone pushes me from behind, hard. I stumble forward into the guy in front of me, mumbling my sorries as he glares.

I turn, and Blake is right there, a few feet behind me.

"What gender do you feel like today?" he calls out.

I glare at him. "I already told everyone. I'm a guy."

"So what does being a guy feel like?" He stands there, hands in the pockets of his joggers. Behind him, his friends jostle and stare at me, the same smirks on their stupid faces.

"You tell me, Blake. You're a guy."

He puts a hand to his chest. "Are you assuming my gender?" His friends laugh. "You don't know how I feel inside." He emphasizes the last words in a high, nasal voice.

I charge toward him. "Shut the fuck up, Blake."

He closes the distance between us before I can think, his hands hitting my chest and sending me staggering backward, landing on my ass in the hallway. Shouts ring out, a crowd forming around us as Blake comes at me, a snarl ripping his face apart.

"Get up!" He kicks my shin and I curl up, clutching my leg. He kicks my side, catching my backpack with his foot. I scramble away, lurching to my feet against a classroom door.

"What are you doing?!" someone screams.

"You fucking dyke!" Blake shouts. He charges forward, grabs the front of my shirt, slams me back against the door. I kick wildly, catching his shin, and he punches me in the stomach. I heave, doubling over. He pushes me, face twisted in a grimace, all beast, no boy, like something is taking over. Or the real him is coming out.

I stagger forward into him, fists swinging, and he stumbles back, and then someone moves between us, their hands out but not pushing, blond hair swinging around their shoulders.

"Chill out, dude," Jared says, his whole body facing Blake.

"Get out of my way," Blake says.

"No."

"I'm telling you, man. Get. The fuck. Out. Of my way," Blake spits out.

Jared doesn't move.

"What the hell is going on?" All three of us look over. A teacher is in the doorway I crashed against, staring at the three of us, his face red.

"He fucking attacked me!" Yelling makes my stomach hurt, but I don't care. I'm done pretending things are okay when they aren't. Maybe it's guy code to say everything's fine, to keep quiet, to act like nothing hurts. But it's not my code.

Blake starts toward me.

"Stop right there!" The teacher booms, pointing a finger at Blake. "Fighting is unacceptable. Get to the principal's office, now!"

"I'm coming with you!" Mr. Harrison pushes out of the crowd, Olivia behind him.

I'm sorry, she mouths at me. Blake stares at her. She ignores him.

"Fine." The other teacher nods, glaring at us. "Move it. Everyone else, get back to your own business."

Olivia backs away as we pass and the hallway clears out, kids drifting away as they talk in low voices, watching us.

In the office, we wait in seats at opposite ends of the room, Mr. Harrison between us. The secretaries continue typing, sneaking a few glances at us over their computers. I don't look at anyone, just stare at the painting on the wall of small boats in a harbor. It's all blues, grays, and whites, probably something the office staff thought would be calming, but I want to rip it off the wall and smash the glass.

The principal, Mr. Carter, steps out of his doorway, hands in pockets and barrel chest thrown out, his face locked in a frown.

"Blake." And then a pause. "Dean." He sighs. "Come on back."

Mr. Harrison follows us. Mr. Carter doesn't say anything, just motions us to the chairs in front of his desk. Mr. Harrison takes the seat in the middle, Blake and me on either side. In his own chair, Mr. Carter leans forward, elbows on his desk, hands folded in front of him. Football trophies from the seventies line the shelf behind his desk. Under the lights, his bald head shines.

He looks at me, then at Blake.

"So. What happened?"

"He attacked me," I say. The tears are right there behind my eyes, my stomach still burning from Blake's punch.

Blake doesn't say anything.

Mr. Carter watches me. "For no reason?"

"Because he's an entitled asshole?"

"You didn't deserve that role," Blake says. "You only got it because you're his favorite." He jerks a thumb at Mr. Harrison.

"Blake, I understand you're upset, but that's not the case," Mr. Harrison says. "Dean got that role because he was right for the part."

Blake snorts. "He? Really?"

I look at Mr. Harrison. His eyes are fixed on Blake, forehead crinkled in a slight frown, eyes gentle. "Yes. He."

"She's not a guy!" Blake flings his arms out.

"Blake." Mr. Carter holds up a hand. Blake stares at him, jaw clenching. Mr. Carter closes his eyes for a moment, then looks at me. "You came out. As transgender, yes?"

I nod.

"Myself and the staff have been monitoring your situation," he says.

"Monitoring? Oh, please!" Mr. Harrison splutters. "You did nothing to protect her—I mean, him. Sorry, Dean."

I nod, barely hearing him. The *her* is a splinter. Carter's words are a sword right through my heart. They knew. They all knew, and no one said anything, no one helped me.

"It's impossible to predict how students will react to this kind of thing," Mr. Carter says. "We live in a progressive district. We thought it might just run its course and everything would be fine."

"As I said—you did nothing to protect Dean!" Mr. Harrison leans forward, pointing at the principal. "No school assembly, no staff training, nothing. The other teachers have been fumbling in the dark trying to address questions from students and figure out how to relate to him. I am lucky that he trusted me enough to come out to me first, so that I could provide some guidance to my colleagues—a job you should have done. Instead you let harassment and discrimination carry on under your nose. This is a failure of leadership!" He sits back, nostrils flaring, a muscle in his jaw twitching.

So the teachers have all been talking about me this whole time. Maybe Mr. Harrison didn't see what Blake was doing.

Maybe Ms. Rodriguez didn't notice the paper balls. Blake was always careful, until today. Never did anything that anyone could prove. But they could have done something before this happened.

They could have, and they didn't. All they did was talk.

Every tick of the clock over the door ripples through the room as Mr. Carter and Mr. Harrison stare each other down.

"For now, I have to deal with the problem at hand," Mr. Carter says, each word clear and slow. His face is red, the flush spreading up to the top of his bald head. "I can't have fighting on school grounds. You will both have a one-day suspension on Monday." He's looking at me now.

"What?" I burst out of my seat. "That's not fair!"

"This is bullshit." Blake shakes his head.

"District policy is clear. Students who engage in fighting are sent home." Mr. Carter stands up, and the room shrinks around his broad shoulders. "The office will call your parents." He walks to the door, opening it. "Miles, if you could stay." Mr. Harrison looks from Blake to me, his eyebrows raised. Mr. Carter gestures from me to the hall.

I grab my backpack and leave, walking fast, trying to get ahead of Blake. The hallway is empty, everyone in class, and I make for the back doors.

"You better watch your back," Blake calls behind me. I turn and he's standing in the middle of the hall. The office door closes with a thump.

"I've never even done anything to you," I say.

"You think I don't see how you are with Olivia?"

"What?"

He shakes his head, sneering. "Sure, play like you don't know. First Zoe, now Olivia."

Zoe's name jolts through me. When she transferred in last year, Blake flirted with her for a while, even stopping to talk to her at lunch when she started hanging out with us. He teased her in class, complimented her clothes, asked her to Homecoming and Winter Ball. She turned him down both times. His attempts at conversation got only polite smiles and dead-end answers. Finally, he gave up, around the time he and Olivia were cast as romantic interests in the musical.

"Are you serious?" I stare at him. "Zoe doesn't like you! She never liked you. I'm not even interested in Olivia."

"Whatever." He pivots and strides away. I watch him until he vanishes around the corner, and then I head straight out the door at the end of the hall, down past the parking lot, toward the bus stop. I need to get away from him, from all of them.

Outside, the damp and cold morning haze is still hanging around, fuzzing the world into abstract shapes. My thoughts twist and turn, filling my head until the street blurs. I walk past my bus stop and onward, lungs burning up the steep hill toward my neighborhood. The burning feels good, like if I walk far enough and hard enough, I can clear out my mind, clear out my body, forget who I am and start over. The fight flashes in my mind: Blake's face, the thud of his hands on my chest, Jared appearing. Fuck. My head aches all the way home.

CHAPTER TWENTY

I can't focus on anything that evening. Zoe texts me nonstop.
Jared filled everyone in after Blake and I went to the office, and
unread texts from Ronnie and Allison sit in my messages. Their
anger doesn't help, though. Mine has already left my body, and
I'm tired, aching all over, the places Blake hit me throbbing. I
lie on my bed, Robert Smith wailing in my earbuds, waiting for
dinner. My phone pings with texts. I turn it to Do Not Disturb.

When Dad calls my name down the stairs, I trudge up to
join them. In the doorway, I stop. Both of them are facing me,
on the opposite side of the table from my empty chair. Dad's
hands are folded on the table, Mom's arms crossed.

"You probably know why we want to talk," Dad says.

"I didn't do anything," I say, still standing. "Blake attacked
me. I tried to get away from him and a teacher made us go to
the principal's office. Then the principal suspended us."

"That's not what the voicemail said." Mom's eyes are bright with tears, a flush on her cheeks. "He said you'd been suspended for fighting. Both of you."

"Did you hear what I just said?" My voice fills the dining room.

Her eyes widen. "This isn't like you. Fighting in school, yelling at us. You never had these problems until recently."

"Maggie." Dad lays a hand on her arm. He looks at me. "Dean. Are you okay?"

I shrug, tears stinging my eyes.

"Why did this happen?" His eyes are steady on me.

I shrug again.

Mom makes an exasperated noise but subsides when Dad looks at her.

"Can I go?" I stare at them.

Dad sighs. "Okay."

I spend most of Monday online, reading articles about dysphoria. Halfway through the day, Zoe texts me.

It's weird without you here. I still can't believe Carter suspended you. How are you?

I'm ok.

Perfect time to catch up on homework, I guess. And an emoji with its tongue sticking out.

I know she's trying to joke, but it's not funny. I can't think of anything witty to text back. Yeah, I say.

We text about other things, but it feels like a chore. The sadness in my chest is small and tangled up with other feelings, but I leave it there. I don't know how to unwind it, and I don't want to think about what it might mean.

I go back to the YouTubers I used to watch every day. There are so many new videos. I haven't logged on in a while. I search for videos about testosterone, jump to Instagram, looking for people documenting their transition in photos. I scroll through the accounts I follow, looking for the smiling, round-faced, long-haired past selves beside the scruffy, sharp-jawed men five months, or eleven months, or two years on testosterone—it's clear from the pictures that everyone changes in different ways, at different rates. They talk about hair growth, fat redistribution, libido, hunger. I want to know about their emotions, their actions. Are they as different inside as they look on the outside? Do they like who they are? Has testosterone changed them? I don't want to turn into a Blake. I want to stay me.

Jade texts me later that night. Missed you at group today, she says.

Awww

What you doing Friday?

No plans

Wanna come hang at my place?

When I go back to school, nothing has changed. People stare at me in the halls, talk sideways to each other, fall silent when

I walk past, except now they aren't just talking about my gender but also the fight. I don't see Blake anywhere. Spanish class looms large in my mind. At the morning break, I go to the bathroom. I use the girls', because the thought of entering the boys' restroom makes me feel all shaky and weird.

The bathroom is empty, praise whatever god might or might not exist. I lock myself in a stall and try to breathe normally. I want to stay there, avoid Blake, avoid my friends, avoid everything. The bell rings. Someone comes in just as I come out of the stall: a tiny freshman girl who stops short, staring at me as I wash my hands.

"What's your problem?" I glare at her, ripping a paper towel from the dispenser. She backs away, rushing out of the bathroom. *It's not my fault I'm in here*, I shout at her silently. *It's not my choice.*

I stare at myself in the mirror, at the hair falling into my eyes and curling shaggily around my face. I clench my teeth and watch the muscle flex inside my jaw. Will I look more like Dad if I start testosterone? I try to picture my cheeks slimming down, a full beard coming in. Second bell rings. I shift the backpack on my shoulders and leave.

Ms. Rodriguez frowns as I walk into Spanish class. I scan the room. Blake is at the back of the class, in a different seat than usual. A seat on the opposite side of the room from mine. My heart jumps, but he doesn't look up. I start for my desk but Ms. Rodriguez shakes her head, pointing at the door.

"Ooooooh . . ." A murmur swells quietly from the back of the class. Ms. Rodriguez ushers me out of the classroom.

"I'm sorry I'm late," I say. "I was just in the bathroom. I'm not . . ." I swallow. "I'm not feeling well."

Her frown deepens. "I wanted to let you know I've been tipped off to what Blake's been doing to you in the class with the paper balls."

I shove my hands into my pockets, staring at the tips of my Converse.

"I will be watching him like a hawk from now on. You have any trouble, you tell me, okay?"

"Okay," I say.

We go back into the room and a few people look up, but most people are focused on the warm-up. As I sit down, Jared gives me the nod from his new seat next to mine. I jerk my chin in return and sit down. I'm aware of my whole body, my skin prickling like everyone is staring at me, but no one is. Not even Blake. Ms. Rodriguez starts the lesson, and her voice flows over me like a river. I breathe in, and out, and roll my shoulders back and forth. I'm here, and nothing bad has happened.

Yet.

At lunch, Zoe's glued to my side, head on my shoulder as she eats her sandwich. It's kind of nice, actually. Like we fit again, a little bit, the way we used to.

Ronnie's on my other side, Jared lying on his stomach on the floor in front of us, next to Allison, who's doodling in her sketchbook.

"We gotta do something about that fucker," Ronnie says.

"Like what?" I ask.

"I don't know." He stares at his cheese sandwich before biting into it.

Jared sighs. "Man, I know calling the cops isn't the move, but Blake really tempts me."

"Yeah, I get that," Allison says. She flips her pencil over her fingers one at a time. "Me and Nina were talking about this the other day. How going to the police doesn't always help people like us. Queers and brown people. Blake is a rich, straight, white boy. What are the chances of the police actually doing anything? The world is set up for people like him." She looks back down at her sketch and starts shading in the skin. "Even if he does get in trouble, he'll probably just resent Dean even more."

"It feels like he's just getting away with it," Ronnie says.

"Vigilante justice?" Jared half-laughs.

Allison shrugs. "Or social consequences. He's already getting backlash. People are ignoring him. Olivia broke up with him."

"And he's joking around in class like he doesn't give a shit," Ronnie says.

"We don't know what's going on in his head," Allison says.

"So what the fuck do I do?" I say, a little too loudly. Zoe squeezes my arm. "I can't just sit around waiting for the next time he flips out on me."

Jared studies the floor. Allison's pencil doesn't move. Everyone is silent.

"I'm sorry," I say. "I'm just—"

"Don't apologize," Zoe says. "You didn't do anything wrong."

Tears well up in my eyes and I clasp her hand where it's resting on the inside of my elbow. Ronnie leans his head on my other shoulder. Allison scoots closer, until her knee touches my foot, and Jared watches me steadily. We stay like this until the bell rings.

By the time sixth period rolls around, the anxiety is back. The hallway to the theatre goes on forever, like a nightmare where you just keep walking and walking and never reach the end. But I do. I take a deep breath and push open the auditorium doors.

Ronnie and Jared appear the moment I walk in, flanking me as I join the cast on stage. Mr. Harrison nods at us, his eyes finding mine, and then we start the warm-up game. Blake is on the other side of the circle. I avoid looking at him.

When we're done, Mr. Harrison clears his throat. "We'll be running Juliet's scenes with Lord Capulet, the Nurse, and Friar Lawrence today, but only during the class period. You've all gone above and beyond with this play, so I'm canceling after-school rehearsal in favor of set construction. Anyone who wants to stay and help the crew with that is welcome to do so. We'll resume normal rehearsals tomorrow."

We always have a set-construction day at least once during the run-up to a play, but the timing seems pretty convenient. I glance at Ronnie and he arches an eyebrow at me.

No one says anything or moves. Mr. Harrison claps his hands, and after a moment, people get to their feet, heading for their backpacks to do homework, or pairing up to run lines.

I head over to the costume closet. Ronnie's got a sewing machine set up outside the door, working on some alterations for Courtney's Nurse costume.

"I took your suit home," he says when he sees me. "Didn't want to tip off Mr. H. I wasn't sure if you wanted him to know."

"Thanks." The backstage couch has been moved next to the closet door, and I flop down onto it. The teal vinyl is ripped in several places, graffiti tags and unidentifiable stains dotting its surface. Zoe and I made out on it once. If legends can be believed, this couch has seen a lot of action.

"I have something else of yours at home," Ronnie adds. He doesn't look up from the sewing machine, but a smile tugs at his mouth.

"What?" I sit up.

"Your binders came."

"Oh my god." I clap my hands to my face.

"Want to come over tonight?"

"Hell yeah!"

He grins. "Excellent."

ACT FOUR

"What must be shall be."

—JULIET

Romeo and Juliet, act 4, scene 1

CHAPTER TWENTY-ONE

Ronnie leaves me alone in his room to try on the binders.
They're each in a different package: a flat box, a large cardboard envelope, and white plastic wrapping.

I strip out of my shirt and sports bra, and tear open the box. Arms through the armholes, neck through the neckhole, then pull down.

Pull down.

Pull. Down.

I can't pull it down.

I stare at myself in Ronnie's mirror, the binder caught at my biceps, arms sticking out like I'm a zombie on the hunt. News at seven: local teen trapped in undergarment.

I grab the hem of the binder and yank down. It's me versus the binder in a wrestling match to the death. Inch by inch, the binder slides into place, mashing my breasts against my chest. I stick my hands inside the binder like I've seen in the instructional posts online and pull my breasts up inside the fabric, so they look more like pecs.

My chest is completely flat, but I can hardly breathe. The binder cuts into the skin under my arms. No good. I try to pull it off, but it stops at my shoulders. Of course. Why did I think this was a good idea? I hop up and down, yanking the binder back over my biceps.

My shoulder sockets scream, but Binder Deathmatch Round Two goes to me. I fling the binder on the floor, sweating. If this is what binders are like, I don't know if I can do it.

I breathe deep and reach for another one.

This one is too big. My chest looks like it does in a sports bra, except the bottom of the binder doesn't lie flat against my skin, it just hangs loose. I guess this one would be good if I wanted some breeze.

I pick up the third package. Last one. A lump starts in my throat. What if this one doesn't fit either? I rip off the plastic wrap. The binder is a pale pinkish-beige, a little darker than my skin tone. I pull it over my head, ready to use force again, but it slips on easier than the others. It's a half binder, so my stomach is free, the cut of it like a cropped tank top, except way tighter. The arm holes are snug, but not painful. The squeeze of it on my ribs is more friendly hug than hungry boa constrictor.

I pull on my shirt over the binder and check myself out. I look good. The binder isn't as comfortable as a sports bra, but it looks right. Instead of the uniboob curve, my chest is flat. I smooth my hands down my front from collarbone to stomach and my chest fills up like I could cry or cheer.

Ronnie knocks. "You okay in there?" I open the door and he steps back, scanning me head to toe. "Nice!"

"I know, right?" I can't contain the grin spreading across my face.

He crosses the room to his closet and pulls it open, revealing the sewing desk inside, his clothes folded neatly on shelves above it. "So I've been working on your jacket." He riffles through the box of clothes next to the desk and pulls out a folded-up square of silver fabric. I gasp as he unfurls it.

The jacket is whole again.

"It was already a little big for you anyway," he says. "I was going to take it in." He hands it to me.

I take it, holding it up in front of me, and then I slip it on. I turn and look at myself in the mirror.

The jacket is a perfect fit. I turn, looking over my shoulder, and I can hardly see the seam up the back where Ronnie sewed it back together.

"The collar's a little weird now," he says, stepping up to me and fiddling with where it folds over at the back of my neck. "I'm not sure how things are gonna work with the pants. I've only made pants a few times. He cut it at the crotch, just to make it harder for me."

"Ronnie." I grab him in a hug so tight he squeaks. "Thank you."

The binder goes home with me and straight into the back of my underwear drawer. I want to wear it to school, but what if people notice? What if they say something? I don't know if I'm ready for that yet. But just knowing it's there makes me feel better.

On Friday, Jade texts to remind me about our plans that night. The text sends a ripple through my stomach. Will it be just me and her? What are we going to do? I don't really know why I'm nervous, but I am.

"Hey." Zoe pokes me at lunch. "What are you doing tonight?"

"Um." I don't want to make it weird, but I don't want to lie either. "I'm hanging out with Jade."

"Oh." She's silent for a minute, eating her pasta. "You talk to her a lot."

"I mean, we text sometimes." I shift on the hard floor of the hallway. "We don't talk that much, though."

Zoe doesn't say anything. Is she jealous? There's nothing going on between me and Jade.

"Sorry I can't hang out." I know I didn't do anything wrong, but I still feel like I should apologize.

"No, it's okay! I was just thinking maybe we could have a movie night." She smiles up at me, wiggles her shoulders. I know what she means. We haven't made out in a while, let alone done anything else.

"I'm sorry," I say again. "I can't."

"Okay. But soon though?"

"Yeah, totally." I put my arm around her and she snuggles close. We're quiet the rest of lunch, but it's an awkward quiet, both of us eating and watching the other three talk.

The day passes slowly. I told Mom and Dad I was going to Ronnie's house after school, like I usually do, so they wouldn't ask any questions. Jade's place is on Capitol Hill, near Lambert House, and I lurk at Caffe Vita until it's time to walk over. Her house is huge, rickety, and painted dark purple. The lights inside glow through the rainbow flag hanging in the front window, casting faint golden squares onto the dark front lawn. The living room is empty. Is Jade home? I take a deep breath, trying to calm my nerves.

"Behind you!"

I turn and jump out of the way of a large green bike, piloted by a person cloaked in a patch-covered denim jacket. The bike bumps over the curb, skidding to a stop at the bottom of the steps.

"You coming to dinner?" A quick smile to me, hands chaining the bike to the railing. "I'm Kestrel. *They* and *them* pronouns."

"Um, I'm Dean," I stutter out. "*He* and *him*."

"You're that high school kid!" Kestrel has piercings all the way up both of their earlobes and a nose ring. "Welcome to the Purple Straight-People Eater," they say, gesturing to the house. I laugh and follow them up the steps. Inside, under the light, I see that their hair is blue and spiked up in the middle.

Music is playing somewhere. Voices chatter from the kitchen, and I stop in the doorway, looking at the room full of people. They're all laughing, talking, some people chopping, one stirring a large pot, others standing around. Kestrel hugs everyone. A kitchen timer goes off and someone takes a pan of brownies out of the oven.

Jade emerges from the group, stopping short in front of me with her trademark small wave. Her hair is twisted into thick black locs now, the braids gone, and gold hoops hang from her ears. Her lipstick is bright pink, and she's wearing flowing patterned pants, a T-shirt the color of dusty gold cropped short to show her belly. "Everyone, this is Dean," she calls out.

"Hi, Dean!" Faces turn to me, people waving and smiling.

"Dinner's almost ready," she says. "Can you set the table? Dishes are in the cabinet over the sink." I nod, grateful for something to do.

In the dining room, I find the source of the music. A record spins on a player in the corner, a woman singing smoky and slow, as if she's tired and joyful at the same time. The record cover is balanced on the back of the player.

"You like Etta?" Jade wanders in, standing at the head of the table.

I shrug, setting out the plates. "Never heard of her."

Her eyebrows rise. "Are you serious? Etta James?"

I nod. To the left of the record player, wooden crates form stacks of shelves holding more records. I crouch down, running my finger along the thin spines. Jade comes up behind me. "All those are mine," she says, watching me flip through the records. There's music from every genre, but a lot of it is jazz—men with horns or saxophones, pianos, big bands, women singers in front of old silver microphones.

"My dad loves jazz," she says. I look up at her. She's staring at the John Coltrane record in my hands. "About the only good thing I got from him was my taste in music." Her laugh is short and dry.

"You mentioned you were in jazz band in high school."

She nods. "I was a singer. Tenor. Always got the leads." That smile, a bright flash and then gone.

"You don't sing anymore?"

"Hard to sing when your voice makes you feel like the punch line of a joke." She shrugs, but her eyes shimmer. "Nah. I'm going to be a social worker. Keep doing theatre stuff on the side."

"I'm sorry," I say. "About your family."

"Me too," she says. She watches the record spin, tapping her fingers on the back of a chair. "I miss them, but I don't. You know?"

I nod. "I think so."

"They can be great. My dad is funny as fuck. My mom is an amazing dancer. My brothers are both in honors classes. But then they turn around and refuse to accept what I say about myself. They love me, but only the version of me they want to see." The tears spill over and she looks up at the ceiling, blinking them back.

"Can I . . .?" I reach out a hand, and she nods. I put my hand on top of hers, on the chair's back, and squeeze.

She sniffs, running a finger under her eyes.

"I'm sorry if that was too personal," I say.

She shakes her head, half smiles. "It takes a lot more than a sensitive white boy to make this mascara run," she says. I blush and shove my hands into my pockets, but keep my eyes on hers. We stare each other down, and she giggles, the sound watery but happy.

"Let's eat!" Nina calls as people file in with dishes of food for the center of the table. Jade steps away from me to a seat on the opposite side, and people grab the seats around her before I can follow.

We do a quick round of names and pronouns, all ten of us squeezed in around the table, elbows bumping as dishes pass from hand to hand.

A nonbinary person whose name I've already forgotten shares that they've been approved to start estrogen, and everybody claps. Samir, a short man with brown skin and a Mohawk, ladles soup into my bowl. "So, Dean, you taking hormones yet?"

"Straight-to-the-point Samir, everyone." Kestrel snickers.

"What?" Samir says, spreading his hands wide, grinning. "I couldn't wait to start hormones when I was that age."

"That age!" Jade swats his shoulder. "Like you're so old? Okay, Grandpa."

Samir laughs. I keep my face still, hiding my surprise. Samir is trans. I look around the table, trying to figure out if everyone else is too. I know Jade, Nina, and Kestrel are, and so is their nonbinary friend.

"So?" Samir looks at me. "Do you want to?"

I shrug, wishing he would stop asking me. I'm pretty sure I do, but I have no idea when or how I'll get ahold of hormones.

"Come on, give him a break," Jade says.

"Okay, Mom," he says, with a smirk for her and a wink for me, and slurps a mouthful of soup.

The conversation moves on to other things: a protest some people are organizing; who's dating who in their circle of friends; a new book someone read and loved. I stay quiet, watching them trade jokes. What they're doing, who they are—I want to be part of it. This house full of friends, parties on the weekend, protests and craft nights and chosen-family kind of life. *Chosen family*: a phrase Jade used at group. As the words left her lips, the sparkle of another world enveloped us, a world that included me. My friends are part of my chosen family. I'm starting to feel like Jade and Nina are too. Maybe the people at this table can be. I want to make a difference in the world like they are, want to be out and proud, help organize Pride events.

After dinner, some people wash dishes; others drift to the living room, perching on the ratty couches, still chatting. I hover in the doorway. Kestrel nudges my elbow.

"I'm going outside for a smoke. Wanna join me?"

I follow them out into the backyard. They light up a joint and offer it to me, the sweet yet skunky smell of it wafting around us. I shake my head, shoving my hands deep into my pockets, trying to stay warm. I can't be high when I go home later. Mom will freak.

Our shadows stretch across the lawn, the porch light bright behind us. "Sorry about Samir." Kestrel exhales smoke into the darkness. "He likes to put people on the spot."

I shrug. "It's okay."

"I'm not ready to go on T, personally." They stare into the dark treetops above the house. "I've thought about it, but I don't know if I want all the effects. I'm nonbinary. I don't love being seen as a woman, but I don't really want to be seen as a dude either." They take another hit from the joint. "It would be cool to have a different body shape. But I don't know if I want a deeper voice, and I definitely don't want facial hair. Knowing my family, I'd get a full-on lumberjack beard."

We stand side by side in the cold night, the smell of wood-smoke curling through the yard from a neighbor's chimney. I'm slim. I know that. But in the mirror my hips are inescapable, unmistakable curves. If I unfocus my eyes, if I look at my figure like it's someone else's, my body is pretty nice. But that's the problem: It's someone else's body. Not mine, or at least, not yet, not unless it changes. Unless my curves fill in, like Kestrel is saying. Unless my voice lowers, like it does when I have a cold. The beard, though—I try picturing myself with a full, dark beard like Dad, and the image makes my brain itch.

"You'll know if it's for you," Kestrel says. "You've got time to figure it out."

"Thanks," I say, not really knowing why I'm thanking them.

They smile again. "Let me give you my number. If you ever want to talk about stuff, you can hit me up."

I nod. They pull out their phone, ask for my number, and text theirs to me. They grind the glowing nub of the joint into the dirt and we head inside.

CHAPTER TWENTY-TWO

"Have a good afternoon, everyone. Dean, if you could stay for a moment."

I gather up my stuff and stand in the front row, waiting as Olivia, Courtney, and the other kids clear out. None of the scenes we rehearsed today involved me and Blake. I'm glad. I'm not ready to face him on stage.

Mr. Harrison sits on the edge of the stage, legs dangling over the side. "Dean, I've been talking to Mr. Carter," he says once we're alone. "Under school district policy, Blake has committed both assault and malicious harassment toward you, since he has been physically violent toward you and has done so because of your identity. Normally, when we discipline students for these behaviors, they are also referred to the police. The principal is . . ." Mr. Harrison pauses for a moment, his jaw clenching. "Reluctant to do so, shall we say. However, if you pressure him in some way, or involve your parents, that could change." He looks at me. "Has Blake's behavior been a significant disruption to your education? Do you feel things are resolved now?"

I look down at the gray carpet, scuffing it with the toe of my shoe. Blake in trouble with the cops. Would they handcuff him at school, in front of everyone? I like that image. I'm tired of being afraid every day, tired of waiting and watching my back. But Allison's voice runs through my mind: *Blake is a rich, straight, white boy.*

Would the cops even do anything?

"I don't know," I say.

"It's your decision," Mr. Harrison says.

I nod.

He examines my face. "How are you doing since the fight?"

My mouth tightens. I jerk my shoulders up and let them fall.

"Dress rehearsals start tomorrow," he says. "Do you feel ready to act with him?"

I snort. "I don't really have a choice."

He looks down at his clasped hands. "I'm sorry. I wish I had an understudy for his part."

"It's okay," I say.

"I was also thinking about dressing rooms," he says. "I imagine you don't want to use the girls' anymore. Do you want to use the boys'?"

"Um." He's right. With everything else going on, I hadn't thought about it, but now that I'm out, using the girls' dressing room would be awkward. But using the boys' room? Being in there with Blake and his bros? "I don't know if that would be a good idea."

Mr. Harrison nods. "That's what I was thinking. At first, I thought perhaps you could use my office, but that wouldn't work for costume changes between scenes. What if we set up some privacy screens for you backstage? I've got some nice ones at home I can bring in. It's not ideal, I know."

I shrug. I don't really like the idea of being separate from everyone, in my own special space; it's like a neon sign letting everyone know that I'm different. But I guess it's what we have. "Yeah. That works."

"All right." He studies me, then sighs. "I'm sorry about all this."

"It's okay. Can I go?"

"Of course."

The walk out of the auditorium takes forever, and I can sense him watching me. Adults always try to hide their emotions, but they're never as good at it as they think. I know he's worried.

My backpack is light, most of my books still in my locker. Outside, it's cold but sunny, the afternoon light stretching long and golden across the parking lots, the grocery store, the dry, gray streets on the way home from school. As I crest the hill, breath in a cloud before me, I stop and stare down the road. Up here, I can see the blue of the Puget Sound and the mountains beyond. They're so clear today, jagged and white, as if cut from glass.

I pass my block and keep walking, down into the neighborhood. I know every pathway in and out of Carkeek Park. Among the trees, the sound of the street fades. I can hear the stream trickling below and my feet squelching on the muddy path still soaked by weeks of rain.

Cars are parked in the lot overlooking the water, people alone or in pairs inside their vehicles watching the sun sink. The mountains crouch shoulder to shoulder in shades of indigo, the sky red and pink behind them. *Red sky at night, sailor's delight.* The first half of Dad's favorite saying. I want it to be true, but I know it won't be. The sun might shine tomorrow, but we'll be one day closer to next week and opening night, one day closer to the end of the play, the end of Romeo. How fitting that my last moment on stage at Jefferson High is a death scene. I could write an English essay about that metaphor.

I sit on a log at the far end of the beach and draw my knees up close to my chest. I haven't let myself think about the end of the play, but in this moment, the thought adds itself to the weight dragging me down. Acting with Blake. Wearing the binder in public. My bio in the program. I still haven't told Mom and Dad, and I don't know if I can. I mean, I have to. But I don't know how. I grip my knees tightly, trying to hold on to myself. My jeans are rough under my fingers, the wind cold on my face.

I stay on the beach until the sun is just a glow over the top of the mountains. Most of the cars are gone when I walk through the parking lot. I take the path toward the south end of the park, walking in deepening shadows, heartbeat spiking with every rustle in the underbrush. My mind goes blank, my ears opening as the park sinks into darkness around me. Then, a faint amber glow begins to illuminate the path. I climb up the last steep incline and then I'm out, under the streetlights, the bus stop like a lighthouse in the night. I sit on the bench and wait to go home.

The bus driver nods when I get on, and the ride passes in silence, the seats all empty here at the start of the route. A few people get on, but mostly it's just me, avoiding eye contact with my own reflection, watching the neighborhood outside the window.

When I walk in the back door at home, Dad is in the kitchen chopping vegetables for a salad. A pot of mac and cheese is steaming on the stove, chili powder on the counter next to it. His whole face glows when he sees me.

"I can't eat dinner with you guys tonight," I say. "I have to catch up on homework." It's true. Rehearsals have me way behind. But also, I can't face Mom and Dad right now. I need to be alone.

I expect him to shake his head, coax me into joining them, but he just nods. "Keep that nose to the grindstone, kiddo. I'll bring you a plate."

"Okay." I walk toward the back hallway.

"Dean?"

I turn, and he's looking at me, really looking at me. "You know you can talk to me. Right?"

I nod. Another step. The door to the basement is so close.

There's a knot in my chest. If I stand here too long, his words will cut through it, and I'll tell him everything. *Dad, I'm trans. Dad, I'm a guy. Dad, I'm not your daughter. I'm your—*

I can't say it.

I open the basement door and go downstairs to my room.

On my way to sixth period the next day, a tap on my shoulder jolts me and I spin around.

"Just me! Sorry!" Olivia holds up her hands.

I let out a breath. "No worries."

"You ready for this?" she asks.

"Oh man." We walk into the theatre together. "I don't know." I laugh, but it sounds more like a strangled bark. Dean Foster, Dog Boy. "Maybe?"

"You'll do great," she says. "You're ten times the actor he is."

"Thanks."

My space is set up backstage, two tall folding privacy screens made out of smooth coppery wood. They form a large rectangle, inside of which is a small rack holding my costumes. A full-length mirror hangs from the side of one of the screens. I wonder if Mr. Harrison brought it from home too.

I take my binder out of my backpack and pull it on. Wearing it is like being hugged by Ronnie or Zoe. Then I put on my costume for my first scene: white linen shirt with rolled-up sleeves, trim slacks, and boat shoes. Romeo's kind of bougie, but I guess that makes sense. He is a nobleman, after all.

I stand there for a second, looking at myself in the mirror. It's strange to be alone in this moment. I'm so used to being in a crowded dressing room, everyone chattering, the excitement of dress rehearsals and approaching opening night buzzing in the air. How am I going to do stage makeup? Maybe I can bring a hand mirror from home and do it on the stage before we open, so I have good lighting.

My chest is tight. I don't want to be in the girls' dressing room, and I don't feel safe in the boys', but I still wish I could be with everyone, somehow. Even though I know it's not possible. At least, not right now. Maybe Jefferson will have a gender-neutral dressing room one day.

I find my position backstage as the opening scene begins. Across the stage, Blake is waiting for his cue, eyes closed, hands hanging loose at his sides. I watch him. His chest rises and falls, slowly. He looks like he's meditating.

Blake has a pre-show ritual. The thought is funny and confusing at the same time.

He opens his eyes and runs on stage. I watch, waiting for my moment, and I take a few deep breaths. Nothing can happen to me here. Blake won't do anything in front of everyone. I can do this.

I can do this.

I can do this.

I hear my cue, and I stride out of the shadows and into the spotlight.

After rehearsal, I keep my binder on. When I come out into the seats, Zoe's there waiting for me.

I smile. "How long have you been here?"

"Pretty much since school got out," she says.

"Sneaky," I say. "You're gonna have to pay like everyone else to see the show next week."

She gasps. "What do you mean? I'm the girlfriend of the star!" She emphasizes the last word, pressing a hand to her heart.

I laugh. "You're ridiculous."

"You love it." She smirks.

"I really do."

She stands up. "I was hoping we could hang for a while. I just got this new hair dye."

"Let me guess, you need my help."

She pouts. "I don't *always* make you dye my hair for me."

"Just most of the time." I reach out, trying to tickle her, and she jumps away. "Of course I'll help you."

When we walk in the door of her apartment, Sheena's in the living room, watching a soap opera. She waves, raising her glass of wine. "Happy Friday, girls."

Lava in my veins, instant and boiling. *Girls.* Zoe says hello, and I know I'm smiling, making conversational noises, but I can't hear myself talk. The word is wailing in my ears like a siren.

In the bathroom, Zoe lays out the supplies: hair clips, bleach, latex gloves, purple dye. I shut the door, lower my voice. "Does your mom not know I'm trans?"

Zoe's reflection meets my eyes, frowning. "You said not to tell anyone."

"Oh." I look away. "Yeah. I did."

She sighs. "Do you want me to tell her? Or do you want to?"

"I don't know." I'm tired of coming out, tired of telling people over and over. It would be nice not to do it again. "Yeah, maybe you could? If that's okay?"

"Sure." She clips her hair up section by section, leaving a layer free underneath.

"Maybe do it soon?" I sit on the edge of the tub. "If I start testosterone, she'll notice eventually."

"So you're going on hormones?" Zoe looks at me.

I shrug, palms flat on my knees, looking back. "Once I turn eighteen in April, I won't need my parents' permission."

"That's like four months away."

"I know."

"Okay." She turns back to the mirror. "I'll tell her."

She unbuttons her shirt, hanging it on the door. I can see a few veins tracing faintly through the skin of her chest, between her breasts, her white skin contrasting with her black bra. She's gorgeous. I want to touch her, hold her, but the few steps across the yellow linoleum from the tub to the sink stretch into miles of emptiness. I don't know what she's thinking, and I'm afraid to ask.

She grabs a towel from under the sink, stained with the

bleach and dye of past hair experiments, and ties it around her neck.

"All right." She looks into the mirror, hands on hips. "I'm ready."

I put on the gloves and take the bleach. Standing behind her, I cover the free hair, releasing it chunk by chunk, until Zoe's head is a sticky mass of white. Then I go back, saturating the roots. Our eyes meet in the mirror, and she smiles.

When I'm done, I step back, removing the gloves. She takes my place on the tub's edge, keeping her head still. The bleach drips onto the towel. I lean against the door and slide down until I'm sitting on the floor. She extends her foot out, touching mine, and we push back and forth.

"I could report Blake to the police," I say, just to fill the silence. "Mr. Harrison told me."

"Do you want to?"

I shrug.

She shakes her head. "He needs to know he can't get away with it."

I look at our feet, mine bigger than hers. "I just don't see how it will make a difference."

"We have to keep fighting, though." She leans forward. "Things change when people act."

"This isn't a movement, Zoe. I don't think anyone cares what one trans kid in Seattle does."

"It's not just about you, Dean." Her face is wide open, lit from within the way it always is when she talks about this stuff. "What you do could change things for someone else."

I bite my bottom lip. "I don't know."

"Did you know gay sex was still illegal in fourteen states until 2003?"

"What?"

"Lawrence versus Texas." She says the name as if she thinks I've heard it before. I turn my palms up, lifting my shoulders. "This guy in Texas got arrested and charged with a crime for having sex with another guy in his own home. They took it all the way to the Supreme Court and overturned all those laws."

I'm quiet, thinking. I can see it: Me, reporting Blake. Me, pushing the school district to change.

"That's cool," I say.

She stands up, and I move so she can wash the globs of bleach out. Bit by bit, we paint her hair purple, and then we sit back down, talk about school, the play, Allison and Nina, who apparently stay up late every night FaceTiming.

"You look nice, by the way," she says finally. "Your chest. Are you wearing a binder?"

"Oh." I look down and smile. "Yeah. I forgot to tell you. I bought it last week."

She nods. "Can I . . . can I touch?"

"Sure." I stand and she moves toward me. Her fingertips brush my chest, lightly at first, and then she lays her hands flat.

"Whoa." She runs her hands up and down my front. "It's so flat."

"I know." I grin.

She looks up at me and I put my hands on either side of her face. Dye streaks my knuckles, but I don't care. I bend and kiss her, slow and soft. Her mouth opens, her hands pressed against my chest. In my head, I imagine we look like a scene from a romantic movie, and the thought makes me smile against her mouth.

She steps back, smiling at me. "I have to wash this out."

I move to the tub's edge as she dunks her head under the faucet again. She turns her head side to side, purple rivers running off her hair into the sink.

"I love you," I say.

She smiles at me from under the cascade of water. "I love you too."

CHAPTER TWENTY-THREE

The last week of rehearsals zooms by. The costume crises, the missed cues, the forgotten lighting elements—four years in theatre means every mishap is familiar and expected. Perfection would be the only reason for worry, and we aren't perfect—people still missing lines here and there, the crew stretching a last piece of the backdrop into place during our final dress rehearsal on Thursday.

I'm so focused on the play that I don't even think about NYU. I'm sitting backstage Thursday, waiting for my cue, thumbing through my phone, when I get a notification. It's an email.

The sender's name makes my heart stop.

NYU Admissions.

I stare at the unopened email for a long minute, the world around me going quiet. This is it. This is the moment.

I click on the email and scan the first lines.

They address me by my given name, which makes me cringe, but I read on. "The Committee on Undergraduate Admissions has completed its review of applicants to the class of 2019 at New York University."

I shut my eyes. If I get in, I can start over. I can leave Seattle, go somewhere everyone just knows me as Dean. Knows me as a guy, instead of a girl. Except Zoe and Ronnie and maybe Allison, but that's okay. I can deal with that.

I read the next sentence. "The Committee carefully considered the credentials provided in support of your application, and it is with regret that I must inform you that we are unable to offer you admission."

Unable to offer you admission.

I stare at the screen.

Another notification. It's Zoe this time:

I GOT IN!!!!!!!!!!!!!!!

My heart drops like a stone into my gut. I put down the phone, listen to the lines on stage. It's almost time for me to go on. I can't deal with this right now. I run back to my dressing area, stuff my phone in my backpack, and head back just in time to go on stage.

After rehearsal, Zoe is there, waiting in the seats at the top of the center aisle. She jumps up when she sees me, grin stretching ear to ear.

"Did you get my text?"

I paste on a smile. "I did! I'm so happy for you!"

She squeals, jumping up and down, and I jump up and

down with her, the reality of my rejection growing heavier by the second.

"So? Did you get an email too?" she asks.

"I did."

"And . . . ?"

I can't hold it anymore. My smile slides away and her mouth falls open.

"Oh no." She sounds so disappointed. "You didn't get in."

I shake my head, tears stinging my eyes.

"Oh, babe. I'm so sorry."

"What are we going to do?" I ask, before I can stop myself.

"You can still come to New York," she says. "You could apply to another school, maybe? There's still Regular Decision."

"I don't want to go to another school in New York."

"Maybe community college? We can live together and you can do your pre-reqs and apply again?"

I shake my head.

"I don't want to leave you behind," she says, and now her eyes are starting to fill with tears too. Fuck.

"No, you're right," I say. "I still want to be in New York City with you. I'll figure it out."

She doesn't say anything, just looks up at me, blinking fast. The other kids stream around us, a few people glancing at us curiously. I keep my eyes on Zoe.

"We'll make it work." Now I'm trying to smile again, and she doesn't really look like she's buying it.

"Are you sure?" she asks, sniffing. "You just said . . ."

I nod vigorously, looking straight into her eyes, so she

knows how much I mean this. "We can do this. We're going to be together in New York City."

"Okay." She wipes her eyes and comes up on her tiptoes to kiss me. "New York City, baby."

It's a familiar refrain, one we've said so many times, but now it's hollow. I want this to work, I want to be with Zoe, so I have to find a way to make this happen.

Somehow.

On Friday night, we stand backstage listening to the auditorium fill up with chattering parents and friends. We take turns running out on stage to the tiny holes worn in the curtain, trying to spot people we know in the crowd. Mom and Dad are front and center like always, while Zoe, Allison, Ronnie, and Jared take seats a few rows back.

I can see the programs in my parents' hands, and it hits me like a lightning bolt. With all the rehearsals and then the NYU news and everything else going on, I never told them. I can't tell if they've read the programs yet. They're talking with Sheena, laughing about something. I step back from the curtain. There's nothing I can do about this now. I chickened out. All that's left to do is be the best Romeo I can be. Maybe that will be enough.

Five minutes before showtime, Mr. Harrison runs backstage and gathers us all into a circle for our traditional opening game. He starts out soft, chanting a line from the play.

"A rose by any other name—"

"—would smell as sweet," we whisper back.

"A rose by any other name—"

"—would smell as sweet," we say aloud.

"A ROSE BY ANY OTHER NAME!" he yells.

"WOULD SMELL AS SWEET!" we roar back, exploding into cheers, high fives all around, people jumping up and down. Then it's time for places and a held-breath moment before the curtain goes up.

"I do bite my thumb, sir!" The Montague and Capulet henchmen face off, trading insults and then carefully choreographed blows. I breathe as deeply as I can, my chest flat under my binder. I look down. It's real. I am real. I am Romeo.

And then it's time. Blake, in Benvolio's costume, greets me on stage, and I wax poetic about my sadness, my longing for Rosaline, the girl I'm pursuing, unaware that I'll soon meet Juliet. As we trade lines, I watch Blake. There's no flicker of rage on his face. He is his character, Romeo's cousin and friend, the reactions and inflections we've practiced so many times in rehearsal springing from his lips as if spontaneous. I hate thinking it, but he is a good actor. I know his parents never come to the plays, but I don't know why. He always brushes it off with a joke. I've never met his mom, and only once seen his dad—a tall, muscular figure in a spotless suit. He picked up Blake early for an appointment and never said anything to his son, just walked ahead of him down the hall as they passed me.

With a sigh, I cross to the bench at the edge of the stage, finishing my speech. Rosaline has rejected me. I am distraught, disheartened, alone. "Feather of lead, bright smoke, cold fire, sick health! Still-waking sleep, that is not what it is!" Drop head in hands, heave body as if crying. "This love feel I, that feel no love in this." I look up at Blake. "Dost thou not laugh?"

He shakes his head. "No, coz, I rather weep."

"Good heart, at what?" I ask.

A long silence. He stares at me, frowning.

"At what?" I prompt him.

We lock eyes for a long moment, and he takes a deep breath. Sits beside me. Puts a hand on my shoulder. "At thy good heart's oppression." The line, spoken hundreds of times, drops between us.

"Why, such is love's transgression," I say, sighing, letting the sadness fill my chest. He grips my shoulder tighter. "Griefs of mine own lie heavy in my breast." I carry on through the speech, Blake watching me.

"Farewell, my coz," I say at the end, and rise. Blake rises with me.

"Soft!" he says. "I will go along. And if you leave me so, you do me wrong."

I turn away with a shake of my head. "I have lost myself; I am not here. This is not Romeo, he's some other where."

He presses me, asking me to tell him who I love, who has hurt me so, trying to cheer me up, but I resist. Finally, I start to walk away, toward my exit. "Farewell. Thou canst not teach me to forget."

He catches up to me, slings an arm over my shoulder. "I'll pay that doctrine, or else die in debt."

As soon as we're off stage, he pulls away and we stand, staring at each other.

"Good scene," he says, quietly, as the next one begins.

"Same," I say.

He looks like he wants to say more, but then he turns away, hurrying to join the other guys on the couch for a round of fist bumps. I stand backstage, watching the play without seeing it.

The rest of the night rolls by. We cover for a few forgotten lines, ad-libbing or skipping ahead. Blake performs without hesitation, still in character just like I am, but we never reach the same realness as our first scene. There's a distance between us again, a wall behind his eyes, and mine too, if I'm being honest. For a moment in our scene, Benvolio and Romeo's friendship felt true, like it reached beyond the stage lights and into our lives. It was too weird.

Slowly, the moment fades away under the heat of the stage lights, and then we're on stage for the final bows, the spotlights in our eyes, the audience cheering and clapping. I dash to my makeshift dressing room, changing out of my costume. I smile at my flat-chested reflection in the mirror and leave the binder on.

Zoe tackles me in a hug as soon as I come through the double doors into the lobby. "You were so amazing!" She plants a lipsticked kiss on my mouth and I grab her waist, admiring her in a black velvet dress and fishnets. How could I think even for a second that I wouldn't be going to New York City with her?

"You *look* amazing," I say, and she blushes. The others hug me in turn.

"Dude, you *were* Romeo," Jared tells me. He's wearing the gold-collared red shirt from our thrift store run in September.

"Thanks." We all smile at each other and turn as Ronnie comes squealing up to us from the bathroom, arms outstretched, all of us collapsing into a group hug. When we separate, laughing, Mom and Dad are watching us.

"Great job, kiddo." Dad hugs me.

Mom smiles. "Really wonderful." Her eyes skip to my chest, flick back up to my face. "How did you make your chest so flat?"

"A binder."

"Well, go get changed," she says.

"I am changed," I say.

Ronnie clears his throat. Allison shuffles her feet. Zoe grabs my hand.

Mom's cheeks flush, her mouth a thin line. She taps the rolled-up program in her hand against her other palm.

"It's getting late," Dad says, voice stiff, his eyes on her. "Everyone have a way home?"

The crew mumbles an assent. I follow my parents out, glancing over my shoulder. My friends are lined up in a row, watching me go.

Good luck, Ronnie mouths.

And then we're gone.

The car ride home is silent. Mom stares out the window while Dad drives, his eyes on the road, hands at ten and two on the steering wheel. We hit every red light. When we get home, it's almost ten.

Dad puts the kettle on. Mom goes into the living room, and I hear the click of the furnace turning on as I take off my shoes.

"What does this mean?" she says.

She's back in the kitchen doorway opposite me, holding up the program. Dad is standing at the counter, staring out the window.

I guess this is happening. I reach down inside me and pull the words up one by one. "Do you know what transgender is?"

Dad nods once.

"I've heard the term," he says.

I swallow. "I'm transgender. I'm not a girl."

Mom's laugh makes my head jerk back. "What? You have . . ." She gestures at me. "What do you mean, you're not a girl?"

"I have certain parts." I blush. "But I don't feel like a girl inside. I never have. I just didn't have the words until now. I'm a trans guy."

Nothing. Silence. Dad turns and looks at me. I keep talking to push back the static roaring in my brain. "That's why I cut my hair. That's why I dress the way I do. That's why I wanted to be Tony."

"Tony?" Mom croaks.

"*West Side Story.*" I look at her. "Remember, you took me in fifth grade? I said I wanted to be Tony."

"I don't remember that." She shakes her head. Dad doesn't take his eyes off me.

"Well, I do." The tears rise, spilling out. "I've been so afraid to tell you, because you hate that I'm gay. The other night when you told me to move out when I was eighteen and yelled at me about my name, I thought you would kick me out for sure if you knew. I'm not a girl. My name is Dean." My traitorous voice breaks.

Dad clears his throat. "Nobody hates that you're gay, sweetie."

"You're the only one saying that, Dad." I look at Mom.

She stares back. "You're not a man."

"Yes, I am," I say.

"That's not possible."

"Well, I exist, so it is." The words snap out like a flag, proud and strong.

She's frowning now, nostrils flared, head drawn back like she doesn't recognize me.

"Maggie—" Dad puts a hand on her arm, but she's already walking toward me, and I step back, and then she's passing me, walking out of the room, down the hall. The door to their room slams shut. The kitchen tunnels around me until all I can see is her face, her eyes like a wall built between us. Tears blur my vision and I stumble for the back hallway, down the stairs, into my room. Dad doesn't call after me.

My room is dark and cold, the light dim through the curtain. I have to leave. Have to get out of here. I fumble with my backpack, throw in my books, my wallet, a pair of jeans and my favorite Bowie shirt, the one with his Aladdin Sane persona, the lightning bolt bright from forehead to chin. A present from Dad, for my fourteenth birthday. His voice rumbles in my head, the way he'd soothed me so many times when I was little: *Take a cool-down lap, kiddo.* I'd walk around and around our backyard, kicking up the fallen apples, or leaves, the detritus of whatever season.

I pull on my coat and creep up the stairs. I risk a peek into the dining room. It's empty. I look down the hall, but no sound comes from their bedroom. The door is closed. I cross the kitchen and then I'm outside, striding down the sidewalk, heading for the bus stop.

On the bus to Zoe's apartment, I call her. I have to do it twice before she answers.

"Dean? What's going on?" Her voice is sleepy.

"Hey." My voice cracks. "Babe. Can I come over?"

"Now?"

"I ran away."

"Wait, what?" She sounds more alert now.

"Can we talk about it when I get there? I just need somewhere to crash tonight." Outside the window, the world is a dark blur.

"Yeah, of course. Uh. Should I tell my mom? I think she's asleep already? But I could wake her up—"

"No, no. Let's just tell her in the morning." I don't want to deal with Sheena, with her hovering.

"Okay. I'll see you soon."

"Okay." I hang up.

When I get to Zoe's apartment building, the street is quiet. A single car passes, its headlights flashing over me standing at the callbox. I don't buzz the apartment; instead, I text Zoe, and a few minutes later she steps out of the elevator in an oversized Jefferson High T-shirt and pink joggers.

She opens the door and pulls me into a hug, then a fierce kiss that I'm almost not ready for. When she steps back, I try to smile, but I can't do it. My eyes fill up with tears instead.

"Let's go upstairs," she says, taking my hand, and I follow her into the elevator.

Her apartment is dark, and Sheena's bedroom door is closed. I trail behind Zoe into her room and we shut the door. I drop my backpack and flop face-first onto the bed.

"What happened?" she whispers, lying down beside me.

In halting words, I tell her, first about the bio, how I'd planned to tell them but never did, and then about our fight. Tears are rolling down my face and my voice keeps breaking, but I don't lose control. She sucks in a breath when I tell her the things Mom said to me.

"I'm so sorry, baby," she says when I'm done. My hand finds hers in the pile of blankets and we hold tight to each other. "Maybe they'll come around?"

"I don't think so," I say. "You didn't hear her. She just said it straight up: I'm not a man. How am I supposed to change her mind? I shouldn't even have to do that."

"Maybe she just needs time," Zoe says. "It's hard to see someone differently when you've only known them one way."

"Oh, is it?" I sit up, pulling away. "Ronnie didn't have a problem."

"That's not what I meant." She sits up too, and suddenly there's a huge canyon open between us, an abyss we're both sliding toward.

"What did you mean?"

"Just that—I don't know—it's just like, an adjustment, that's all."

I can't help it: I bark out a laugh. "My dad always fucking says that about her." I jump off the bed, backing away from Zoe. "I can't believe you're defending her."

"Well, it's hard for me too!" she says, and the words freeze us both into silence.

I stare at her. Has she been struggling with it this whole time? I thought she was okay with it, but was she thinking of me as a girl all along?

"I just never expected it, that's all," she says finally, but my ears are buzzing and I have to dig my nails into my palms to focus. "Everything is changing. You came out and you didn't get into NYU and now you're binding and using *he* pronouns and talking about testosterone." I start to speak and she cuts me off. "It's just a lot. I hadn't planned for it at all."

"Well, Jesus, I'm sorry my transition ruined your fucking plans," I spit out.

"I think you should go," she whispers.

"Yeah, clearly." I don't even bother to lower my voice. I grab my backpack and then I'm out of the room.

"Dean?" Sheena's right there, in her bedroom doorway, looking half-awake and confused. I ignore her, yanking open the front door, marching down the hall. The breath comes fast in my lungs. I have to get out of the apartment building, away from Zoe. She said she loved me. I thought I loved her. But it was all a lie. She never really saw me for the person I am. Where love was, now grief burns a hole in my chest, my heart dissolving into ash.

When I'm out of the apartment, I head for the place I should have gone all along. Ronnie's still awake when I call him, and he tells me to come over without asking me what's up.

It's almost midnight when I get to his house. I text him from the front porch, and he opens the door as slowly and quietly as possible, finger over his lips. I follow him down the hall to his room and we shut the door.

"I'm guessing shit went down with your parents," he whispers once I put down my backpack and kick off my shoes.

I nod.

"I'm so sorry," he whispers, hugging me tight.

He disappears into the hall and comes back with a sleeping bag and an air mattress. We set both up in silence, and then I sprawl out onto my back.

Ronnie sits on the edge of the bed. "Do you want to talk about anything?"

I stare at the ceiling. I feel dead inside, like everything that happened tonight is buried somewhere deep in my mind. More than that, I'm tired. So tired. "I think I just want to sleep."

"For sure." He nods. "Stay here as long as you want. You can sleep over after the play tomorrow too."

"Your parents won't mind?"

He waves a hand. "They'll be fine. I'll just pretend it's a regular sleepover."

When the lights are out, I lie there for a while, the evening replaying in my head. Finally, I grab my phone.

No texts. No missed calls. Maybe Mom and Dad haven't even realized I'm gone.

I text Dad. I left. I'm staying at Ronnie's this weekend. I see the ellipsis pop up, showing me he's typing back, but I exit the thread. I don't want to see what he's going to say.

CHAPTER TWENTY-FOUR

I'm lost when I wake up the next morning, not sure where I am for a few seconds, until the world rights itself and I remember that I'm in a sleeping bag on Ronnie's floor. And then it hits me like a train: the fight with my parents, the fight with Zoe. I squeeze my eyes shut and curl onto my side around the empty ache in my chest.

When I finally drag myself out of bed and walk into the living room, Arlene is sitting on the couch organizing her knitting basket, Janet Jackson playing on the CD player in the corner.

"Good morning, sunshine," she says.

"Hey." I yawn, avoiding her eyes.

"I hear you two had a surprise sleepover last night," she says.

"Uh." I'm not sure what Ronnie told her. "Yeah. Sorry I came over so late."

She waves a hand, the gesture exactly like Ronnie's. "Don't worry about it."

I join Ronnie in the kitchen. He slides me a Pop-Tart and I stick it in the toaster.

"What'd you tell her?" I whisper.

"You and Zoe had a fight and you were upset."

My eyes fill with tears and he frowns. "What's wrong?"

I stare at the toaster as it turns the sides of the tart golden brown. When it pops up, I handle it by the edges, dropping it onto a plate. I jerk my head toward his room, and he follows me, plate in hand.

He closes the door once we're inside and we sit down on his bed. The Pop-Tart looks so warm and delicious, but I can't eat when I'm about to cry. I tell him everything, the same way I told Zoe last night, except this time I tell him about what she said too.

"Shit," Ronnie says when I'm done. "That's awful."

I nod.

"Man." He shakes his head. "I don't even know what to say. They all suck."

"It's okay," I say. "You don't have to hate Zoe because of me."

"I don't hate her, but damn. I'm disappointed in her." Ronnie takes a bite of his Pop-Tart.

I do too. It's so good that it almost makes me feel a little better. Almost.

"Are you two . . ." Ronnie trails off.

I think I know what he's asking, and I don't know how to

answer it anymore. A week ago, even two days ago, I would have known. But now?

"I don't know," I say. "I mean, I didn't get into NYU, and now this . . ."

Ronnie is silent. My words hang between us like a knife waiting to sever something. All these months, and we never talked about it, what would happen if our plan didn't work out. Now it seems impossible that we didn't. How could I think everything would go perfectly, that I would get everything I wanted?

I should have known it wouldn't work out that way.

Saturday night's show goes by in a blur. I put on my best stage face and let the performance distract me from the pain that threatens to double me over the minute I let my guard down. Arlene and Jamal come, and they praise me and Ronnie afterward, and I smile and thank them robotically. They don't seem surprised that I'm sleeping over another night, and they bring us home without asking any questions.

Ronnie is up before me again on Sunday. When I open my eyes, his bed is empty, the door cracked open. The smell of bacon cooking drifts into the room. I sit up, stretching out the stiffness, and pull on the jeans and T-shirt from my backpack.

When I check my phone, missed calls and texts fill the screen. Five calls from Dad, and a string of texts I clear from the lock screen without reading. And then I see it: a text from Zoe.

Are you just going to ignore me?

The letters waver in front of my face.

I'm not ignoring you, I text back. There's so much more I want to say, want to ask, but my fingers are frozen over the keyboard. I don't know how to say any of what I'm feeling.

The ellipsis pops up, then goes away. I watch the screen, but it doesn't come back. I shove my phone into the bottom of my backpack and press my fingers against my eyes until the tears dry up.

In the bathroom, I scrub off the last bits of stage makeup still clinging to my face from the play the night before. There are only a few hours until the Sunday matinee, when I'll put on a full face of foundation all over again. Stage makeup has never felt feminine to me. It's always been a way out of myself, into whatever character I'm playing. Now it makes me more of who I am, and every time I darken my sideburns and eyebrows to create Romeo's face, my own features come into sharper focus.

Jamal is at the stove, flipping strips of bacon. Ronnie is sprawled on the couch in the living room, watching cartoons. A misty rain speckles the windows.

Jamal smiles at me. "You want any coffee?" Mom never lets me have coffee. I nod and he sweeps his arm toward the coffeemaker.

On the counter, his phone buzzes, and he grabs it, tucking it under one ear and gliding back to the stove where the bacon is sizzling. "Jamal speaking."

He glances at me, eyebrows furrowing. "Yes, what's going on?" He scoops the bacon onto a plate and sets the pan on a back burner, then turns to me, holding the phone out. "Dean, it's your father."

"I don't want to talk to him." I grip the mug with both hands. Ronnie appears in the doorway, silent, looking from me to Jamal, who stands still for a second. He puts the phone back to his ear, slowly.

"Did you hear that, Leon?" He listens. Arlene comes in from the hallway, wrapped in a navy-blue bathrobe. She arches an eyebrow, taking us all in. Jamal nods. "All right. Take care now." He sets the phone down, and then all three of them are looking at me. I look at my coffee, the steam swirling toward my face. The knot in my chest is back, tying itself tighter and tighter.

Arlene lowers herself into a seat at the table in the corner of the kitchen. "Dean, a while back, Ronnie told us you came out."

I can't move.

"Sorry," Ronnie whispers.

"Can you look at me?" Arlene's voice is soft.

I do. She doesn't look angry. "Did your parents kick you out?" she asks. "Is that why you slept over?"

I shake my head. "My mom was really mad. So I left."

"Did you tell them where you were?" she asks.

I nod.

"So why is your dad calling me?" Jamal asks, arms crossed.

"I've been ignoring his calls," I say. "I mean. He knows where I am. I just haven't talked to him since."

The two of them look at each other, Jamal nodding, Arlene making thoughtful eyebrows right back. Ronnie's got his fist to his mouth, like he can't decide whether to run or cheer.

"Why don't we eat breakfast?" Jamal says.

Ronnie just stares at him. I watch all of them. Is it really this easy?

"You can stay here another night if you need," Arlene says, getting up and shooing me away from the coffeemaker. "But you are going to call your father back today. And you are not drinking this coffee. Jamal." She shakes her head at him, smiling as she pours out my mug into the sink.

Jamal serves up the bacon with a side of eggs and toast, and Ronnie and I escape to the living room while his parents eat together at the kitchen table.

On the couch, Ronnie widens his eyes at me.

"I thought we were dead for sure," he whispers.

"Are they really cool with it?" I stuff an entire strip of bacon into my mouth. I could eat five breakfasts.

"I guess?" Ronnie stares unseeing at the TV. "They were cool with me being gay."

I watch the screen. I have no idea what's happening in this show, and I don't care.

"I'm sorry I outed you," Ronnie says.

I shrug. "I don't know. It's nice not to have to tell everyone."

"I should have told you, though."

"Yeah."

"Sorry."

"It's okay."

We sit in silence as animated characters chatter across the screen. I want to know what the difference is between Ronnie's parents and my mom, what makes it so simple for them. How could they accept what Ronnie told them without even questioning me about it? I'm on edge, like I'm post-car-crash and waiting for the whiplash. But it's not coming.

When we get home from the matinee show late that afternoon, the rain has stopped. Jamal and Arlene go out for a walk and Ronnie hermits away in his room, working on Math homework. I sit at the kitchen table, staring at my phone, and then out the window, trying to psych myself up to call Dad.

The neighbor's house is strung with multicolored Christmas lights. Every year, Mom and Dad and I take a drive, looking at the lights and displays in our part of the city. We always stop for peppermint hot chocolate at our favorite coffee shop, the one where Mom's water broke the night she went into labor with me.

I pick up my phone and call. Two rings. A third. I should hang up.

"Hello?" At the sound of Dad's voice I burst into tears, as sudden as a water faucet turned on. I can't stop, the sobs choking out of me. "Hey, hey. It's okay." His deep voice is soothing. I can picture him in his weekend sweatpants, kicking back on the couch.

I wipe my eyes. "You called earlier."

"That's right. I want you to come home, Dean."

"What about Mom?"

"We talked. She wants you to come home too." A pause. "She cried a lot after you left."

"She's the one who walked out." I press the nail of my index finger into the tip of my thumb, leaving lines in the skin. Mom could have reacted differently, but she didn't.

"I know. I think she regretted it right away. She just didn't know how to handle it."

"What about you?"

Another pause. "You remember my friend Phil?"

Phil. I know that name. "Your high school friend?"

"Yeah." He heaves a sigh. "She transitioned ten years ago. Changed her name to Tara. A few years ago, I found out she—" His voice breaks. "She passed away. Suicide."

On the other end of the line, he sniffs, and tears well in my eyes. I'd seen a picture in one of our photo albums, the two of them at a homecoming dance with their blond and smiling dates. In the picture, Dad is grinning, barrel-chested, dark hair slicked to the side. Phil—Tara—is expressionless, as if caught off guard by the camera's flash.

I remember Tara. A visit to the house once when I was in elementary school. Strong hands, one at my wrist and one at my ankle, swinging me around like an airplane while I shrieked and giggled.

"Why are you telling me this?" I whisper.

"When she came out to me—" His voice breaks. My whole body tenses. I want to run. I've never seen or heard Dad cry.

"I stopped talking to her. I didn't get it. I never even told your mom." His words hit me and I can't breathe, a fist around my heart squeezing it to dust. "I'm not going to make the same mistake again," he chokes out, and then he's sobbing.

I don't know what to say. Sadness surges in my chest like molten metal from the center of the earth, anger twisting it into a knot.

"Come home, kiddo." His voice is ragged. "I'll pick you up tonight."

I'm silent. Dad knew a trans person once. Which means I knew a trans person. Even if she wasn't out then. She was still trans.

And he cut her out.

How could he?

How could Mom treat me this way, look me in the eyes and tell me I'm not who I say I am, then cry and expect me to come home? Like everything's okay.

Everything is not okay.

"I can't," I say.

"Dean."

"I can't. Just leave me alone. I'm fine at Ronnie's." I hang up and turn off my phone before he can call me back.

CHAPTER TWENTY-FIVE

On Monday morning, I stand in front of Ronnie's mirror. I'm running out of time. But I can't make myself leave. Maybe my alarm hasn't gone off yet and this is all a dream.

"Dean!" Ronnie bellows from the living room. Time to go. I touch my chest self-consciously, grab my backpack, and book it out the door after him.

We make it to the bus stop a few steps ahead of the bus. As we rattle down the street, the light changes, blue dawn shadows melting into dark gold with the rising sun. Heavy clouds hang straight across the sky, sunrays peeking out from the thin clear line between the clouds and the horizon. I breathe as deeply as I can, trying to imagine how people will react. If anyone will notice. They've seen me binding in the play. And it's been a while since I came out to the cast. Probably everyone in the school knows by now.

And Zoe. Will she notice? Will we talk to each other at all? We still haven't spoken in person since the fight, and not since the last text I sent.

I touch my chest again, flattened under my binder. But I don't feel the way I did when I tried on my costume, when I was on stage. Maybe I was wrong. Maybe all of this was a phase. The sense of wholeness is gone and now there's a tornado spinning inside me. I zip my parka up and exit the bus, following Ronnie into school.

He breaks away for his locker and I head for mine farther down the hall. Ten minutes until first bell. I can make it that far. I open the locker, stuffing my jacket inside.

"Hey girl." The words ice me. I pivot. Courtney, Olivia's best friend, is there, smiling, high ponytail pulled tight.

"It's not *girl* anymore, Courtney." I try to smile. Play it off, play it off. She forgot.

"Oh my god!" She claps her hands over her mouth, giggling. "I am so sorry. I've just always thought of you that way." She steps closer, lowering her voice. "So what are you going to do? Are you gonna . . ." She motions to her chest.

"What?"

"You know." She raises her eyebrows. "Cut them off."

My mouth opens, words caught in my throat. Is this a joke? Did Blake tell her to do this?

She looks at me, hands curled around the straps of her pink backpack. "I'm sorry if this is too personal. I've just never met a transgender person before."

"Well, now you have," I say flatly, turning back to my locker.

"I'm just asking questions," she says. "You don't have to be rude."

I grit my teeth, pulling out the books I need. "Just leave me alone, Courtney."

She snorts, brushing past me. I slam the locker, then open it and slam it again. A group of sophomores giggle as they walk past me. I ignore them and walk to class, avoiding eye contact with anyone until I'm in my seat.

At lunch, I walk toward our usual hangout spot, legs heavier with every step. When I see Zoe's purple hair, see her smiling as she talks with Jared, sitting there on the floor of the senior hall, I want to run the other way. But I don't.

She looks up when I sit down next to Ronnie.

"Hey," she says, voice higher than usual.

"Hey." I manage a half smile.

Ronnie immediately launches into a recap of his new favorite Netflix show, and I focus on my food. I haven't told Jared or Allison about what happened with my parents, and I don't want to talk about it, especially not with Zoe around. Whenever I think or talk about Mom or Dad or any of it for too long, I start to get this hitch in my chest, like something bad is growing in there, blocking my breath. If I let it out, I'll lose control, and that can't happen. Shoving it down is the only option I have.

"Last shows are this weekend, right?" Allison asks me near the end of lunch. I nod. "Sweet. Me and Nina are going to come to the last one."

"Oh. Cool."

"Jade said she might come too," Allison said.

"We should all go," Ronnie says. "Bring the posse."

"I'm down," Jared says.

If I could, I'd smile, but I can't. Zoe doesn't say anything.

When the bell rings, she follows me like usual. We don't say anything until we're lost in the crowd, away from everyone.

She breaks the silence first. "What are you doing after school?"

"Probably going to Lambert House," I say.

"Oh." She plays with a long strand of hair, twirling it around her finger. "I was thinking we could hang out."

I know what she's really saying. We can hang out, and we can talk about the other night. Talk about us. But I don't know if I'm ready for that.

"Sorry," I say. "I promised Jade." I promised no such thing, but I need help saying no.

She stops. "Do you care about us at all?"

I turn. "What?"

"Us. This." She gestures between us, her face bright red, eyes sparkling with tears.

"Of course." The words grate in my throat.

"Then fucking talk to me!"

A few kids glance at us and away as they pass, hiding smiles. Everyone loves couple drama.

"Okay. I'm sorry."

She stares at me.

"Seriously. I'm sorry, Zoe. We can hang out. What do you want to do? Do you want to go to your place?"

She shakes her head. "Let's go to Beth's."

"Okay."

"Thank you," she says stiffly. "I'll meet you at your locker." Before I can say anything else, she walks away, taking the side stairs down toward her class. The bell rings. Slowly, I turn and head down the hallway.

Zoe and I are silent the whole way to Beth's that afternoon. The restaurant is quiet, a few people at the counter, a couple in one of the booths up front. The waitress takes us to a booth in the back.

"Thanks for hanging out with me," Zoe says when she leaves.

"You don't need to thank me."

"Well. I just know you'd rather be at Lambert House."

I frown. "That's not true."

She scoffs. "Come on."

"Why are you being like this?"

Her eyes fill up with tears. She stares down at her menu. "I'm sorry. Sometimes it just seems like Lambert House is more important to you than I am."

"How can you say that?" The clink of dishes, the chatter of the cooks in the kitchen, the music from the jukebox all sound far away.

"You spend all your time there. With Jade," she says, biting off the name like it tastes bad.

"What?"

"You see her all the time and you never invite me."

"That's not true. I only see her at group. And that one time we hung out. And you came to that open mic."

"Whatever." She rolls her eyes, looking down at her bright blue nails. A tear drops onto her hand. "You talked to her the whole time and completely ignored me."

Shit. I don't know how we got here, but I'm scared. It's like we're at the top of a hill, and one word will push us off the edge into a never-ending fall.

"Jade is my friend," I say. And okay. Sometimes I get this flutter in my chest like we could be, well. Something other than friends.

But I'm in love with Zoe.

I think.

"I'm sorry," I say. "Nothing is happening between me and Jade. I promise."

The waitress comes back. We stutter over our orders, asking for *pancakes? Yeah, and um. Hash browns. I think? Do you want that? Sure, that's fine.* The waitress leaves, and we sit in silence. I know I should say something, but I don't know what I can say. There's a rip in the fabric of us and I can't find where it started.

"I just." She swallows. "At opening night. I was watching you, in that suit, with that binder. You looked like a boy."

My heart lifts for a moment. "That's awesome. That's what I want."

"No." She shakes her head. "I mean. I know you want that. But I don't."

Her words blast a hole in my chest. I'm frozen in place, joints rusting closed. Robot Dean, shutting down.

I unhinge my jaw. Look for words. "I thought you were okay with it," I say.

"I tried," she chokes out. "I want you to be happy. But I don't want this."

"What do you mean?" It's warm in the diner, but I'm shaking. I grab my elbows, squeezing myself tight.

"I'm gay," she says. I stare at her. What does that have to do with anything? I want to speak, but I can't, all the words wound up inside my throat, petrified to stone. She throws her hands out. "I want to be with girls. I don't want to be some guy's girlfriend, Dean."

Sound rushes in, cars whirring past on the street outside, laughter from a nearby table, the jukebox playing a song I don't recognize. Zoe doesn't look like the girl I love anymore. She looks like a stranger.

"But I can't be a girl." Now I'm crying too, but I forge ahead. "The more I think about it, the more I come out, the more I realize how uncomfortable I am. I've never liked this body. I hate having hips. I want a flat chest. I'm not a girl. I'm a boy. I can't be something I'm not. I love you so much, but I can't do that. I have to be myself."

"Well, so do I!" she says.

"And I'm supposed to ignore who I am so you can be happy?" The words come out way louder than I meant. The cooks fall silent for a second and Zoe's eyes go wide. I lower my voice. "This whole time you acted like you were okay with it, and now you're treating me like I'm the one who did something wrong. You outed me to Jared and Allison! That was fucked up, Zoe." Tears are filling her eyes again, but for once I don't care. It isn't my job to make her feel better about how she's hurt me, and it isn't my job to keep quiet so she can be comfortable.

"I'm sorry," she sobs. "I don't want you to ignore who you are. I want you to be happy. I love you so much, but I—I don't know. It's so confusing. I want to be with you, but I don't want you to change."

"I have to," I whisper. And then I call them up, the words I didn't want to say, but it's the only thing I can do now. "I don't think we should be together anymore."

She sits still for so long, I'm afraid to move. I can't look away from her, hair tangled and stuck to her face, eyes swollen from crying. I want her to protest, say she was wrong, she can change her mind, love me for all of me, but at the same time I don't.

"Okay," she says. "I'm gonna go."

Before I can stop her, she slides out of the seat and disappears from the cafe. I stare at her side of the table, at the blank space where she used to be. She's gone.

She's gone.

And I'm alone.

I wake up numb. Ronnie watches me worriedly, but he doesn't press me. I told him what happened when I came back to his house after Beth's, and we drowned ourselves in ice cream and Marvel movies for the rest of the night. Arlene and Jamal were okay with me staying over a few more days.

"You and I are going off campus for lunch," he tells me when we sit down in first period. Allison's hello to me was awkward, and now she's sitting with her back to me, working on a drawing before class starts.

"Okay," I say.

I see Zoe from a distance a few times, and every time I turn and walk the other way as fast as I can.

In sixth period, while I'm studying for a History test, Mr. Harrison taps me on the shoulder. On stage, the Montague and Capulet henchmen are reviewing their opening fight scene, Olivia spotting for them.

"Dean, can you come with me?"

I start to stand.

"Bring your stuff," he adds.

What's happening now? I zip my backpack, my heart sinking, and follow him up the aisle.

In the lobby, standing with his hands in his pockets, is Dad.

I stop. "Why are you here?" Mr. Harrison is behind me, blocking the door back to the theatre.

"I'm taking you home, Dean," Dad says.

"No," I say.

"It's not a choice," he says. "I want you to come home."

Behind Mr. Harrison, I hear voices, some of the other actors asking what's going on. I can't do this in front of them.

"Fine."

Our silver sedan is waiting in the parking lot. Opening the

door, I slide into the passenger seat. In my periphery, I can see Dad looking at me. I look at my lap. I don't know what to say to him. After a moment, he faces forward and steers the car out of the lot toward home.

I stare out the window, waiting for him to say something. My whole body is buzzing, emotions ricocheting inside me. One second I want to cry, the next second I want to punch something.

He clears his throat. "Your mom and I talked." He turns the radio down. Christmas carols. He's a sucker for the holidays. "She wants you at home. But she doesn't want to discuss the gender stuff."

"Avoiding it won't make it go away," I say, staring straight ahead.

He sighs. "I know. But she's just not ready to talk about it. Can you give her that? Just some time to adjust."

The last word makes my teeth clench. She's adjusting. Always adjusting. As if she's the sun and I'm just a planet, revolving around her. But I have my own path.

"No," I say. "I don't care if she's not ready for it. I'm not hiding who I am to make her more comfortable."

"She may not respond well to that," he says.

"And you'll just let her, I guess?" I cross my arms tight against my smooth chest. He's silent, the car climbing the hill to our neighborhood. No mountains today. They're hidden behind the clouds.

"That's not fair, Dean." His voice is soft, calm, like he's talking to a little kid.

"You know what's not fair? Mom telling me I should dress differently my whole life. Me and my friends worrying about some jerk attacking us when we're just out living our lives. Me having to be a girl because no one ever told me there were other options." The words roll out of me, an avalanche flattening everything in their path. "You're not perfect either, Dad. You never told her to stop using my given name when you both know I hate it. You didn't stop her when she walked out. You didn't stop me when I left." Tears slide down my cheeks. "Tara shouldn't have died. You shouldn't need the suicide of your friend to realize you were wrong." I break into sobs and flop forward, hands clutched to my face.

Dad doesn't say anything. The car turns, then pulls to the side and stops. He turns the engine off. I cry harder, gasping and choking, head on my knees. I wrap my arms around myself. Everything spills out and I can't hold it in anymore. I want the life I never got. It's not fair that I have to play catch-up now, that I'll never know what it's like to be seen as a boy my whole life. I would have been a cool guy. I know it. I wouldn't be Blake, wrestling with my bros and saying awful things to people. I wouldn't be like the jocks at school. I wouldn't be the terrible dudes Zoe dated before she came out. It's not too late; part of me knows that. But another part of me thinks—what if it is? What if I never see myself in the mirror again? I can't go the rest of my life on glances and moments. I don't want to live that way. I want the world to see me as the boy I am inside. I want to grow up to be a man. I want to be good and kind and strong. I just don't know how.

After this weekend, Romeo is over. But who am I, without the play? Who am I, without the girl shroud around me?

Dad's hand touches my back. The sudden warmth startles me.

"You're right," he says, voice thick and gravelly. "You're right. Tara deserved better from me. And so do you."

I turn and curl into his waiting arms, crying into the soft flannel of his shirt. We bridge the center console, leaning toward each other, and it's uncomfortable, but I don't care.

"Everything's falling apart," I sob. "I came out to Zoe and I thought she was okay with it and we were going to go to New York City and be in love, but then I didn't get into NYU and this whole time Zoe wanted to be with girls, not with me." The last word comes out in a wail and Dad hugs me tighter.

"I'm so sorry, buddy," he whispers. "I'm so sorry."

I cry so hard I start coughing and he tells me to slow down, to breathe, so I try to, and gradually it gets easier. When we finally pull away from each other, he reaches into the backseat, grabbing an almost-empty box of tissues from the floor of the car. I blow my nose and wipe my face, and then I look at him. First his shirt, then his beard, then his eyes. When we make eye contact, he smiles, tears in his eyes. He grabs my face in both hands and squeezes it.

"This isn't the end of the road, Dean," he says.

My eyes fill with tears again. "You don't know that."

He looks at me. "I do know. I'm not going to lie to you, it's going to hurt. Maybe for a long time. But it's supposed to hurt."

"I hate it," I say, voice tiny.

He smiles, his eyes teary. "I know. I've been there." I lean my head against his chest and he pets my hair with a hand. "You've got such a bright future, kiddo. It's NYU's loss."

"I guess," I say, even though I don't really believe him.

"Come on. Let's get you inside."

I look over his shoulder. We're parked in front of the house. "Okay."

The walk up to the house feels longer than it is. He unlocks the back door and I follow him in. The house is quiet.

Mom steps through the doorway from the living room. "You're home."

Dad squeezes my arm.

"Yep," I say.

The silence settles on us like a smothering blanket. She's looking at me, and I'm immobilized by her gaze, my mind empty. I know I'm supposed to do something, but I can't say what I know she wants to hear. I'm not sorry for any of it. I'm not going to take anything back.

She waits.

I'm so tired. I can't do this right now.

"I'm going downstairs," I say, tearing my eyes away from her, and brush past Dad toward the basement. She doesn't say anything, just lets me go.

CHAPTER TWENTY-SIX

Somehow I make it through the rest of the week and through our Friday show. I avoid Mom as much as I can; whenever we're in the same room together, the silence is heavy with all the words we could say but haven't. I feel her looking at me sometimes, but I don't look back. I'm not ready to talk, and she doesn't try.

On the other side of the weekend is winter break. I won't see Zoe again for two weeks. The thought makes me feel like I'm ripping in half, but at the same time it's a relief. I can't understand it, how I can feel so terrible yet be glad at the same time.

On Saturday, I wake up in the late morning, and the hurt when everything comes back to me makes me roll right over and go back to sleep.

When I wake up again, my chest is heavy, as if there's a

weight pressing me into the bed. I'm still half in a dream. I'd been standing in front of the mirror, looking at myself, or trying to. Only a blurry outline was visible, like I was looking through fog. My body felt good—different in some way, as if a weight had shifted somewhere. On my face, I felt fuzz, the stubble of a small goatee. I smiled. I'd been waiting for this beard to come in for so long.

I touch my face without thinking. The fuzz is gone, of course. I've never wanted a beard before, but now it's a possibility. The good feeling from the dream dissolves, replaced by a ballooning of my hips, curves where there shouldn't be curves. My body feels heavy in a bad way.

I roll over, look at my phone, look again. *Shit.* I have to be at the theatre in an hour. Scrambling out of bed, I yank open the closet doors. Clothing. Clothing that doesn't suck. Jeans? No, too tight. Baggy black cargo shorts? Too cold outside for that. Back to jeans. I pull on my binder. Now a shirt. Gorillaz T-shirt from the floor passes the sniff test. A flannel over that and my parka, with a rain jacket on top. Blue beanie. I turn to the mirror, my least favorite part of getting dressed. All I can see is breasts and hips, a girl trying to be a boy. Just a tomboy, like people called me when I was a kid.

I jog to the bus stop. There's no one around, but I know I'm being watched. Everyone can see. Everyone knows. Girl, girl, girl, girl, girl.

I know this feeling now. It's what everyone in group talks about, what's followed me my whole life: dysphoria. Like everyone is staring at me, even when they aren't. Like I'm outside of my body, watching my life, or so far in myself I'm aware of every place my skin touches fabric, every place there's too much where there shouldn't be. My body parts aren't mine. They're curiosities, growths, attachments I can't get rid of.

Except I can. Not get rid of them, exactly. Just change them, with testosterone and top surgery. I want to talk to someone about this, but my friends can't understand. They're happy in their bodies, with the gender they were given.

I could talk to Jade.

I think about texting her, even pull out my phone and start typing a message a few times, but I always delete it. I feel nervous for some reason, and right behind that is guilt, Zoe's voice echoing in my head. Even though she had no reason to be jealous. Even though I don't want to start anything with Jade; I just want to talk to her, because I know she'll understand.

But still.

I put my phone away and board the bus.

Saturday is closing night. By the time I'm backstage in full costume and makeup, I can hear by the noise of the audience that we're playing to a packed house. I don't look through the curtain. I don't know who's here and who isn't, and I don't want to know.

Standing in the darkness, waiting for my first cue, I realize my nerves are gone. I'm not scared, I'm not excited. I'm just me. My chest is flat, my clothes fit. Romeo's pants and shirt aren't a costume anymore. Have I become him? Or has he become me? Or maybe I was always this person, and this role let me be myself for the first time. Either way, I'm ready.

The play flies by, the fighting, the swooning, the proclaiming all passing like a perfect movie under the lights. Olivia and I are on point, the onstage chemistry between us sparkling like fireworks. When I learn of her death, it shocks me like it's real, and tears sting my eyes, Zoe's face flashing through my mind.

When I stumble into Juliet's tomb, Paris is there, waiting for me. We fight, the movements rehearsed so many times with the stage combat instructor that the audience gasps when my final sword thrust seems to run him through. But he catches it beneath his arm, drops to his knees, and I pull it back.

I speak aloud, dimly recalling who Paris is, that he was supposed to marry my Juliet. I lay him out beside the tomb, a wooden platform the set crew built and painted to look like a flat-topped stone coffin. Olivia lies on top of it in a long white dress, one hand on her chest, the other stretched out. She could be sleeping, but Romeo knows the truth.

"How oft when men are at the point of death have they been merry! which their keepers call a lightning before death—" The tears choke me, but it's not acting, it's real. I stumble to Juliet's side, clasp her limp hand. "O, how may I call this a lightning? O my love! my wife!" I sob through my speech, every line a memory: Zoe's eyes, lit by her smile. Her arms, soft and warm around me. Her lips on mine. Her drive, her passion, how much she cared about me.

Her face, red with tears. Me, alone in the diner, staring at the empty space where she once was.

Finally, I stand, step back, gaze down at Juliet. "O, here will I set up my everlasting rest, and shake the yoke of inauspicious stars from this world-wearied flesh."

From my pocket I draw a small flask, a glass bottle no bigger than my thumb. The theatre is silent as I speak my last words, take in Juliet's face for the last time. Then I pull the bottle's cork and drink down the liquid inside.

I stagger forward, claw my way onto the top of the tomb beside Olivia. "O true apothecary! Thy drugs are quick." I press my lips to Olivia's, and stretch out beside her. "Thus, with a kiss, I die."

And I collapse onto her chest, closing my eyes against the bright lights and the darkness beyond them.

The last scenes blur together as I watch from off stage, and then we're on stage again for curtain call, the clapping and cheering ringing in my ears as if from far away. I smile out at the audience and take my place beside Olivia in the line. We swing our hands up, then down as we bow, and the curtains close.

In my dressing room, I change back into my street clothes and scrub off the stage makeup in the mirror. The familiar rush of a post-performance high fills my body, and I shake all my limbs, jump up and down, grin at myself in the mirror. I want to whoop out loud but everyone will hear me.

It's strange, feeling this good after a death scene, one that felt so real while I was acting in it. I always thought, before this play, that *Romeo and Juliet* was a love story. Two people who meet by chance, forbidden to be together, who die rather than be parted. But now I know it's not a love story at all. Romeo and Juliet, in the play, are so young, younger than me. They hardly get to know each other at all before deciding to marry. And their deaths are a mistake based on miscommunication; if Romeo had known that Juliet was faking her death, he never would have swallowed the apothecary's poison. He never would have had it to begin with. And why is it considered romantic to die because you can't be with someone you love? It's not romantic. It's just sad.

I've spent the last three months being Romeo, and now that the play is over, I realize just how little we have in common. I don't want to die. I want to live. I miss Zoe so much; the hurt is still right there, right under the surface, so sharp it stings me at the faintest reminder. But I know who I am now, and I'm excited to be that person. To be myself. I don't need to be with Zoe to be whole.

One by one, I hear people go out to get their flowers and their hugs until it's just me backstage. I put each costume back onto its hanger, picking pieces up from where I scattered them on the floor during my costume changes. When I get to the suit, I hold it up, smoothing it out before setting it back on the rack. I stand a moment, holding the sleeve of the jacket, touching the soft velvet lapels. The tears are back, blurring my vision. I let out a shuddering sigh, blinking them away, staring at the costume. *Goodbye, Romeo. Thank you.*

I step out of my dressing room and look around: at the set pieces, looming in the dark; at the open door of the empty dressing room; and out at the stage, still bright with lights even though no one is left under them. It's over. The realization fills me up, makes me want to smile as much as cry. This is the last time I'll be backstage at Jefferson as an actor.

And now I know. Who I am, what I want—now that I've played Romeo, I can never go back to girl roles. Maybe I won't look how people think a boy is supposed to look, but that doesn't mean I'm not one. And if I start testosterone, that will change. One day, someone might cast me for a male role without knowing that I'm trans. I'll be in a dressing room with guys and none of them will be laughing at me. I'll be one of them.

I am one of them.

Ronnie appears on the empty stage and points when he spots me. "Last but not least." He comes closer, smiling. "All your adoring fans are waiting."

"Zoe came?" I ask without thinking.

His mouth turns down and he shakes his head. "Sorry, boo."

Even though I knew she wouldn't come, it still hurts that she isn't here.

Out in the lobby, almost everyone is gone. Standing there waiting for me are Jared, Ronnie, Jade, and Allison and Nina, holding hands. Behind them, Dad smiles at me.

"You're here," I say, looking at him.

"Of course. I wouldn't miss your last show." He folds me into a hug and I let him. He stands back, hands on my shoulders. "You looked great in that suit."

"Thanks, Dad."

"We were thinking of going to Beth's," Allison says. "Jade and Nina have never been."

"Sure," I say.

"No cast party?" Dad asks.

"I don't really feel like going," I say. The party is at Blake's house. And it's not like the people in the cast are really my friends. Maybe Olivia. But everyone else? Nah.

Dad hugs me goodbye again before waving us off to the bus stop. There's too many of us to ride in the car, and I'd rather be alone with my friends right now, anyway.

Beth's is full, but not too full, the late-night rush barely beginning. We snag a booth in the back, the waitress dropping crayons, paper, and menus on our table. I glance at my phone.

Nothing.

The others talk high school horror stories, which pop stars are actually talented, show each other their favorite Instagram meme accounts.

"You're quiet," Jade says, drawing the outline of a mermaid on her paper.

"Zoe and I broke up," I say.

Jade sets down her crayon. "Damn."

"Holy shit," Jared says. "I'm so sorry."

Allison is quiet. Nina watches me, her arm over Allison's shoulders. "What happened? If you want to talk about it."

I tell them what Zoe said.

"That's some bullshit," Jade says when I'm done. "I'm sorry."

I shrug, swallowing down the tears. "Can we talk about something else?"

Everyone nods, murmurs *yeah of course, sure, sorry.* Ronnie passes me another blank sheet of paper. I grab a crayon and start coloring it in, all purple. I'm not sure what I'm going for, but whatever.

The jukebox fills the silence with a terrible old rock song from the early 2000s. Jared spreads his arms wide and caterwauls along with the lead singer, and everybody bursts out laughing, even me. Jade digs a handful of change out of her pocket and marches over to the jukebox. We shout song requests and she scrolls through the catalog, the coins clinking into the machine.

The conversation rolls on and I try to stay in the moment, focus on my friends' smiles, their words, but I can't. The pancakes are thick in my mouth. Too sweet. I set them aside and wait for the others to finish.

Afterward, we pay and walk Jade and Nina to their bus stop, waiting with them. Nina and Allison are making out like they're never going to see each other again, and Ronnie shields his face, making us all laugh. My eyes are scratchy, my body drained of all the adrenaline from the play.

Jade smiles at me. "You were great, Dean." She reaches out, curling her hand around my upper arm, squeezing slightly. The night folds around us like we're alone on the dark curb, cars zooming by, the lake black through the trees on the other side of the street.

"You've got this," she says, looking me in the eyes for a long moment.

"Thanks," I whisper.

"How have you been doing other than . . ." She waves her hand.

I know what she means. Besides the Zoe stuff. "Um. I've been okay. I've been dealing with some dysphoria."

She laughs. "I know how that goes."

"I was actually wondering . . . could we hang out sometime? Just you and me, and talk about it?"

"Yeah." She smiles. "That sounds chill."

"Cool." I still feel a little guilty, but I know I don't need to. I'm not doing anything wrong.

The bus pulls up and we wave as Jade and Nina board it, and then we wait on the curb for Arlene to pull up in the minivan.

When I finally get home that night, it's way past midnight. I'm half-afraid Mom will be up waiting for me again, but the house is dark, their bedroom door closed.

Downstairs, I collapse onto my bed without taking off my clothes. I put in my earbuds and find my song: "Rebel Rebel."

Bowie's voice fills my ears. I wrap myself in a blanket in the center of my bed, the binder a comforting pressure around my ribs. I'm looking at the collage on my wall again, but this time all I can see is Zoe. A picture of the two of us from the beach this summer, both soaking wet. Us in the photo booth at the mall: kissing, smiling, tongues out and eyes crossed. The first picture the five of us ever took together: Zoe in the center, her arms stretched out, the camera turned to our faces all smushed together, side by side so we can all fit in the shot. We're in Jared's basement, stoned, though you can't tell from the picture, and the flash is bright, our eyes squinting.

The guitar churns, Bowie's voice over it as if he's asking me: How can I know? How can I know, even now, even after what Zoe said, that I'm going to keep transitioning, keep binding, start testosterone as soon as I can?

I don't know how I know. It just feels right.

The song fades and the next one comes on. I wanted us to be heroes, but maybe we're just humans.

My chest rips open and I sob until there's nothing left.

ACT FIVE

"Ah me! how sweet is love itself possess'd,
When but love's shadows are so rich in joy!"

—ROMEO

Romeo and Juliet, act 5, scene 1

CHAPTER TWENTY-SEVEN

I can't get out of bed the next day. I stay curled under my cov-ers, heat cranked, marathoning shows on Netflix. The play is over. Zoe and I broke up. I didn't get into NYU. I know Dad said it would hurt less eventually, but I don't know if I'll ever feel better. Everything I loved, everything I was hoping for, is over.

After a while, I switch over to YouTube, catching up on the guys I follow. One of them has a new video, all about testosterone and its effects.

I know I need parental approval to start testosterone right now. But in four months, in April, I won't. Can I wait that long? It feels like forever. The binder helps, but it's also made me that much more aware of everything else I want to change. At least, I'm pretty sure I want those changes. But I'm scared too. What if I don't like them? What if too much changes too fast?

I turn off the computer. I can't deal with all of this at once.

My phone lights up, but not with a text. It's Ronnie, on FaceTime.

"How are you doing?"

"Great," I say flatly. "Just fantastic."

"I'm coming over, okay?"

I don't have the energy to put him off. "Okay."

An hour later, the front door opens upstairs. I can hear Mom's voice, dulled to a murmur through the walls, followed by Ronnie's, and then footsteps on the stairs.

A knock.

"Come in," I mumble. I'm still in bed, back to the door.

I hear it open, and then a weight presses down the mattress behind me. "I brought a chocolate cupcake," Ronnie says.

I try to laugh, but it comes out as a sob. "I thought she loved me."

"I know she did."

"I thought she was okay with it. But she was hiding the way she really felt the whole time."

He doesn't say anything.

"I just don't understand." I close my eyes, tears leaking out, sliding across my nose and cheeks into the pillow.

He puts a hand on my shoulder. Upstairs, I can hear footsteps moving around in the kitchen.

"Maybe she never loved me at all. Maybe she just wanted her perfect girlfriend fantasy." I make my words into a knife, dig them into my heart. If I can be mad at her, maybe I won't miss her.

"I saw the way she looked at you," Ronnie says, voice low and fierce. "Nobody looks at anyone like that unless they are in deep."

I draw a shaky breath.

"You went through some shit this year," he says. "It wasn't right in the end, but that doesn't mean it wasn't right at all."

Another knock.

"Thank you so much," Ronnie says to whoever's at my door.

"Let me know if you need anything else." It's Mom. I start to roll over, but the door is already pulling shut, and she's gone.

"You need to eat," Ronnie says.

I struggle upright. "I don't get hangry like you do."

"Please." He rolls his eyes. "Maybe that's true, but if there was a word for sad and hungry, that would be you."

I snort. He hands me a peanut butter and jelly sandwich, and we eat together.

I spend Christmas Eve day in Jared's basement, playing video games. His parents are atheists, so they don't celebrate the holiday. Between the rat-a-tat of guns on the screen and the spread of candy and chips in front of us, I almost forget that I'm missing out on Christmas hot chocolate with Mom and Dad. Jared doesn't ask me about Zoe and I don't bring her up.

On Christmas morning, I wake up to Frank Sinatra crooning through the ceiling, and follow the smell of coffee up to the living room. Mom is curled against Dad on the couch, both of them with steaming mugs.

Mom smiles when she sees me, the first smile she's cracked since my return. I look around the room. The tree is decorated in years of handmade ornaments, glittery paper wrapped around the presents underneath.

"We missed you last night," she says.

I stare at the presents, at the bright sparks of Christmas lights reflected and caught in the wrapping paper shine. "I didn't think we would be doing that this year," I say. Dad shifts, propping one ankle up on his knee, studying the tree.

"Why not?" Mom actually sounds surprised.

I frown at her. "Uh, because you don't want to be around me."

Dad takes a slow sip of his coffee.

"That's not true," Mom says.

"Well, you don't want to talk about gender stuff. I don't know if you've noticed, but that's a big part of who I am." I cross my arms. As long as I stay mad, it's not hard to look at her.

Tears glitter in her eyes. "That's not all you are."

"But it's important to me!" My voice is loud in the small living room.

"Dean." Dad looks at me over his coffee cup.

I throw myself into the armchair across from the sofa. "Can we just open presents and get this over with, please?"

"No," Mom says. "We have to talk to each other. I'm not living like this anymore."

"How am I supposed to talk to you when you can't accept me?"

She closes her eyes, takes a deep breath, then looks at me. "I know. I'm sorry. I need you to know that I'm trying."

"Really." I don't even try to soften the sarcasm. Everything I've ever done against Mom's wishes became about her embarrassment, not my happiness. I cut my hair and she wailed about what my grandmother would think. I started dating Zoe and she got all upset, saying she'd never have grandchildren. As if I was a trophy, not her kid. As if I was some award she got for living her life the way everyone expected. And then I ruined everything.

And now she expects me to be okay with her, just because she's trying?

"Yes. Your father brought home some books, and I've been reading them." She glances at Dad and he reaches out, taking her hand.

I'm quiet. She's never done that before.

"I know you might not believe me, Dean, but I love you. It's hard for me to understand, but I am trying."

My name, from her mouth, rings in my ears. I think it's the first time she's ever said it. I don't say anything—she doesn't get cookies for doing what she should have done all along—but I shift forward in my chair.

"I want to understand," she says. "I really do."

"Mom." My voice cracks. "You don't have to understand. You just have to accept it. I'm not going to change. I'm trans. I'm a boy."

She takes another deep breath and nods. "Okay. I hear you."

"Okay." I can tell she wants to hug me now, but I'm not ready for that. It's too soon.

"Well." Dad clears his throat. "Should we open some presents?"

"That sounds wonderful," Mom says, smiling at him. He moves forward and grabs the first gift, passing it to me.

CHAPTER TWENTY-EIGHT

On the first Monday morning after break, I pull on my binder like it's armor, trying not to think about how I'm going to get through the day. The pain is still sharp, and I know I can't avoid Zoe forever. I'm nauseous the whole bus ride to school.

In English, Allison turns around the second I sit down behind her. "Hey."

"Are you mad at me?" I ask.

She shakes her head. "I know I've been kinda weird. I was just trying to figure out how to still be friends with both of you."

"I get it." I look down at the desk. "It's cool if you pick her." It isn't, but I don't want to fight Zoe over our friends.

"Oh, I'm not picking sides," Allison says. "She knows that."

"Is she okay?"

Allison shrugs.

I push the hair out of my eyes, rubbing my forehead. "I'm sorry. That's a silly question."

"I can't say anything," Allison says. "I'm not mad at you, though. I understand why you did it."

"You do?"

"Yeah. Hey, this is for you." She flips through her sketchbook and tears out a page, handing it to me.

I look at it. It's me. My face. Now I remember the drawing she was working on, the day she'd let me know that Zoe told her I was trans.

This is the drawing. It's my face, but different: the jaw more of a square than a point, the sideburns defined, the hairline farther back, with a little bit of a widow's peak, curls flopping over on one side.

It's me. Or what I would look like, if I had grown up with testosterone fueling my body instead of estrogen.

"Allison." Tears sting my eyes. "This is amazing."

She smiles. "Thanks."

I tuck it carefully into a folder where it can't get wrinkled. "So you probably know I'm not going to New York."

"Yeah." She fiddles with a colored pencil, flipping it over her fingers.

"What are you going to do?"

"I'm still planning on it."

"What about your parents?"

"I mean. They're not happy about it."

"They know?"

She sighs. "It got a lot harder to lie when all the application due dates passed. There was a full-on interrogation. I caved."

"Shit."

She shrugs. "I don't know. At least it's out in the open now. It kind of sucked, hiding so much from them. They're not happy about it, but they're not fighting me anymore. Not right now, anyway. I think they maybe realized my art isn't just a phase."

Ronnie bursts into class as the bell rings and sits down behind me, squeezing my shoulder. I grab his hand and squeeze back. Ms. Porter calls the class to order and we face front. I take a couple deep breaths. I'm not sure how the rest of the day will go, but the tension in my chest has eased a little bit.

After group that day, Jade and I head to Caffe Vita. I told Mom and Dad about the group, finally, and I could tell Mom wasn't thrilled at the idea of me staying out afterward to hang out with someone she hadn't met, but she just nodded. Growth, I guess.

"How's the house? The Purple . . ." I try to remember the name Kestrel called it. Jade and I sit across from each other, her with tea, me with a mug of hot chocolate, because Mom isn't here to tell me it's too late for sugar.

"The Purple Straight-People Eater?" She smirks.

"What does that even mean, anyway?"

"It's a reference to an old song."

"Oh, like the eighties?"

She dies laughing and I hide my face as people around us stare. "Come on! You're literally only a year older than me, you can't make fun of me for not knowing!"

"Sorry!" She waves a hand, catching her breath. "My grandma just used to play that song for us all the time when we were kids. I forget not everyone knows it. It's this novelty rock song from the fifties, basically like their version of a viral song. It's called 'The Purple People Eater.' When I found the house and we all moved in, we were joking about naming it. I referenced the song, Samir added the *straight* to it, and it stuck."

"Ohhh . . . kay." I laugh. "That's weird, but I like it."

"Anyway. We're good. How are you?"

"Ugh." I bang my forehead lightly on the table.

"That good, huh?"

I heave a sigh. "It fucking hurts. I just want it to stop."

"I know." She watches me. "Remember that girlfriend I mentioned? The bi one, the one I was dating when I figured out I was trans?" I nod. "When we broke up, I didn't get out of bed for like six months."

"Great. So I have more pain to look forward to."

She laughs, shaking her head.

"I didn't get into NYU either." I take a sip of the hot chocolate.

"Damn. You're going through it."

"Yup." We drink in silence. "And the play is over."

She eyes me over the top of her cup. "You know, it's not New York City, but we have a pretty amazing queer performance scene here," she says.

"Yeah?"

"My friends and I are planning our first show as a collective right now. It's going to be a burlesque and drag rendition of *Mean Girls*. We're putting it on at this small theatre here on the Hill."

"What?" My eyes widen. "I've never seen drag or burlesque. Isn't that like, stripping?"

"You say stripping like it's a bad thing." Jade arches an eyebrow. "Burlesque involves stripping, yeah. It's also historically been a way of satirizing or commenting on politics, making people laugh, showing off your sexuality or your body—it's hella queer. We've got a great scene here in Seattle."

"Wow. That sounds really cool."

"You should hang with us sometime. See what we're about."

"Okay." I grin. "Yeah, I will."

"Good." She smiles at me, and I feel that flutter again, like I did when we were standing in her dining room, Etta James's voice weaving around us. "So how are your parents doing with everything? Did they come around yet?"

"Sort of. My dad's chill. Mom is . . . she's calling me Dean now, but the pronouns . . ." I sigh. "Not even close."

"Relatable," Jade says. "My mom used my pronouns for the first time last week."

"That's great! I mean, not great that it took so long. But still."

She smiles. "Sometimes it's baby steps. It shouldn't be that way, but I don't want to cut them out of my life, so."

"Yeah. I feel bad complaining about Mom sometimes. I know other people have it worse."

"I don't know about that." Jade shrugs. "There's always something worse, but is it really productive to compare hurt? She's not kicking you out, sure, but that doesn't mean you have to be okay with what you get."

"I guess."

"Do you know what you want to do? About transition?"

"I've been thinking about testosterone," I say. Jade hums thoughtfully, watching me. "My dysphoria keeps getting worse."

"That happens," she says. "Coming out unlocks a lot of emotions."

"It's like . . ." I tap the sides of my mug. "Like my body literally doesn't fit me. Like it's a piece of clothing that shrank in the dryer. It's not terrible most of the time, but it's weird, and I don't even want to get out of bed because everyone's going to see me and stare at me and all my parts are too big." I wave my hands at my hips. "How do you deal with it?"

Jade laughs. "I wear what I want and I avoid mirrors like I'm a vampire."

"I feel like a vampire afraid of not seeing his reflection," I say.

"Do you think testosterone would help you see yourself?" The question hangs in the air, not a judgment, just an open door.

I look at her. "There's only one way to find out, right?"

The week is hard. Zoe doesn't sit with us at lunch anymore, hanging out with some kids from the Queer Alliance instead. I've never been interested in joining, but she's mentioned it a few times. Allison goes with her sometimes, so it's just me, Jared, and Ronnie. But it's okay. We're getting closer, the three of us, in a way we weren't before. Like we're a unit, instead of me and Ronnie, and Jared the set-crew friend.

Blake ignores me. He looks happy, even though it hasn't been that long since Olivia broke up with him. All her friends give him the silent treatment in solidarity. Except for Courtney. She's the Marian to his Harold in *The Music Man*, our spring show. He finally has the lead. Off stage, she laughs at all his jokes, sits next to him when Mr. Harrison talks to the class, talks loudly with him about their plans to study lines after school.

"Dean!" Mr. Harrison catches me in the hall on Friday. "How is everything?"

I shrug. "It's okay."

"Have you given any thought to what we discussed?"

Right. Reporting Blake. I haven't thought about it at all, but I don't want to. I've given him enough of my time this year.

"I think . . ." I bite my lip. "I think I just want him to leave me alone."

"He seems to be doing so," Mr. Harrison says.

"Yeah." I shift my backpack on my shoulders. "I mean, if he messes with me again, I'll report it. But as long as he stays away from me, we're good."

"Okay." Mr. Harrison nods. His bow tie is black, with a small rainbow pin on it. "Well, then. A glooming peace this morning with it brings. Or afternoon, rather."

I recognize the Prince's last lines from *Romeo and Juliet*. "I guess."

He looks at me, really looks at me, his eyes steady. "Dean, no matter what happens, I'm proud of you."

I look down. I don't feel like I've done anything special, but it's nice to hear. "Thanks, Mr. H."

On Sunday, I'm doing homework on the couch when I get a FaceTime from Ronnie.

His face appears on screen when I answer, his eyes wide. "Dean." The living room is darkening as the sun sets. I reach over and turn on the lamp. He draws a shuddering breath. "I need to tell you something. Don't be upset."

"Uh." I'm on alert. "Okay."

"I got in."

"You got in?"

"To Parsons."

"Oh my god." I stand up. "Oh my god."

"I got into Parsons." Ronnie's voice is slow, warm, hesitant, a smile spreading across his face.

"New York City, baby!" I scream, and then he's screaming, and we're screaming together. Dad comes to the doorway, one eyebrow arched.

"Ronnie got into Parsons!" I shout, and Dad lifts his arms, pumping his fists. I'm so excited I leap onto the couch, bouncing on the cushions until I fall onto my knees.

"Why did you think I'd be upset?" I ask.

"I don't know. I just didn't want to bum you out. You know. Because you didn't get into NYU."

"Ronnie." I shake my head. "I can handle it. I'm so happy for you."

He grins. "I gotta talk to Dad."

"You can do this." I clutch the phone with both hands.

He laughs like a runaway train. "I don't know. I don't know. I have to go to Parsons, Dean. There's no other option."

"Just talk to him," I say.

"Okay," Ronnie says, and the word sounds like a promise, an anchor, a sunrise. "Okay."

CHAPTER TWENTY-NINE

The Music Man is my least favorite musical. My two least favor-
ite people as the leads doesn't help.

Ronnie hates it too. "If I have to listen to one more round
of 'Shipoopi,' I'm going to shipoop all over the costume closet,"
he says backstage on Wednesday. I collapse in laughter over
the backdrop I'm hammering together, the other set-crew
kids snickering behind me. They've all switched my pronouns without saying anything, only a few mistakes here and
there. With them I'm not the school trans boy; I'm just Dean,
good with a hammer, one of the only actors who ever works
on the tech side.

We work through the class period while the cast plunks
through note by painful note. When the bell rings, most people leave, but I stay. Hammering nails is very satisfying. Especially when I pretend the nail is Blake's face.

"Hey."

The voice startles me, makes the hammer slip and pound my thumb instead. I curse, holding my hand, and look up.

"Oh my god." Zoe stands there, hand to her mouth. "I'm so sorry."

"It's okay." I stand up, facing her. She's so close, only a few steps away.

She shoves her hands into the pockets of her denim skirt. "Can we talk?"

The backstage couch has been moved close to the set, where the crew kids like to kick back during construction. We sit at opposite ends, her with one leg tucked under her body, the other on the floor, as if she's about to push off and run at any moment.

I look at her, at the violet blaze of her hair. I remember the afternoon we dyed it, how she touched my chest over the binder and told me she loved me. She's so close to me, but so far away, like she's on the other side of a bridge hanging charred and broken.

"I miss you." Her voice breaks.

I know what I could say, what I would have said if this was months ago, and the words ache like too much sugar in my teeth. All I can tell her is the truth. "I miss you too."

And I do. But I know our missings aren't the same.

"I think about you every day," she says, the honesty as raw as sandpaper on my skin. "I messed up. I still want to be with you. You're still the same Dean, and I love that person."

Something in her voice makes me shift, move an inch

away, the arm of the couch poking into my back. I'm not the same Dean: not the Dean of a month ago, when we were still together; not the Dean who sat beside her at the open mic; not the Dean in Romeo's suit who stared himself down in the mirror backstage. Even when we started dating, I was already changing, spending night after night online watching transgender YouTubers, getting up the next day and bottling it all up.

"Please say something." She stares at me, hands clasped tight in her lap. On stage, the chorus stomps through their choreography.

"I don't know." I look into her eyes, as dark as the distance between her words and my truth. "I miss you every day. But I'm not the same, and I'm going to keep changing. I'm going to start taking testosterone as soon as I can. You're moving to New York City. Every time you come back, I'll be different."

She opens her mouth, but I have to keep talking. "I loved you, Zoe. I loved you and I still do, but you said it yourself. You don't want to date a boy. You're a lesbian. And I'm not a girl. I never have been, and I never will be."

"We can try," Zoe says softly.

My heart is screaming, looking for a way out, a way back to her. I move closer, reach out, take her hand. She clutches it like I'm a lifeboat taking her to shore. I swallow the tears, focusing on the warmth of her hand, our fingers woven tight.

"We already did," I say.

She sucks in a breath and lets it out shakily, staring at our joined hands. "I thought we'd be together forever," she whispers. "You're my anchor. Nothing in my life has ever felt as perfect as being with you."

I shake my head. "Perfect isn't real."

She pulls her hand away, covering her face, sobbing, and my heart crumples. I slide through the space left between us and she falls into my arms.

I can smell her hair, that orange-juice sweetness, her body warm against mine. I know we're not meant to be, I know it isn't right, but for a moment I wish it was. Our love is as familiar as a puzzle I've done a thousand times and can still finish, even though it's missing the pieces I need the most.

Finally, she pulls away, wiping her eyes. "I don't know if I can be around you for a while. It hurts too much."

"If you want, I can go hang out somewhere else at lunch." She looks up at me, and I scoot back. We're too close, and it's too comfortable. "Ronnie and Jared are your friends too."

"It's okay." She doesn't look away. "I still hang out with Ronnie outside of school. Jared wants me to help him pass History." She rolls her eyes. "That kid has terrible study habits."

I laugh, the sound half relief, half amusement. We're back on safe ground, the bridge still burned, but not unmendable.

She smiles, the corners of her mouth trembling. "Parting is such sweet sorrow," she says.

Juliet's goodbye to Romeo. It's a key unlocking my own tears. She grabs my hands, squeezing tight. I try to memorize the round sun of her face, the arch of her brows, the wings of her black eyeliner smudged and swooping away from her long eyelashes. Her beautiful brown eyes. The ghost of a kiss floats between us, and for a moment, I think about leaning forward. But she lets go of my hands and rises, heading through the half-built frames of the set, down the stairs off stage left. I watch her walk away, but she doesn't look back.

I'm alone again, sitting on the couch. It's quiet backstage, the cast circled up now. I can barely hear the low murmur of Mr. Harrison's voice giving them feedback. The first time I walked into this theatre, I was fourteen, and it was the summer before freshman year. It was Picture Day, and the photographers waited on stage with their backdrops and their lights and their big cameras, but all I could see was the hundreds of seats, the wide sweep of the stage, the rose-red curtain framing it all. I wanted to be on that stage.

I wipe my eyes. Slowly, I walk toward the bench I'd been working on. I scoop up the nails from the floor, the hammer from where I set it down. I put them away in the tool closet and grab my stuff. The chorus is singing now.

I push out the door at the back of the theatre into the cold January sunlight, and let it close behind me.

CHAPTER THIRTY

I zoom down the side of the bowl, gliding across the bottom and sailing back up into the sky, the wind freezing my face. The streak of sunny winter days has lasted into the weekend. I woke up this morning and actually felt kind of okay for the first time in days—the first time since the breakup.

The clack of Jared's board snaps across the empty skate park as he ollies again and again. As I spiral around the bowl, the speed and the wind clear my mind. I'm a boat with a wake of worries, and I'm going to outrun them all.

I take a break, sitting on a bench in the sun. Jared rolls up, zigzagging back and forth in place in front of me. He's in cutoff knee-length shorts, impervious to the wind chill.

"When did that happen?" I point at the scabbed-over scrape covering his right knee.

"A few weeks ago."

"Ouch."

"Yeah." He jumps up, balances on his board, then flips it, his too-big white T-shirt billowing around him. "So. How is everything?" He doesn't look at me, focused on the trick.

"I don't know. I feel okay today. But in general . . . still shitty." I stretch my legs out in front of me, staring at my toes.

"I'm sorry, dude." He sits down on his board, elbows propped on his knees, and looks at me, one hand shading his eyes. "What are you going to do about NYU?"

I stare across the bowl, the sun on concrete making me squint. "I don't know. I mean, I'm not going to New York. I got in a couple other places. I might just go to school here."

"That'd be cool," he says. "I'm staying in Seattle too."

"Oh yeah?"

"Yeah, I didn't get in anywhere, so I think I'm going to go the community college route. You know, get my pre-reqs done, figure out what I want. I'm thinking being a teacher would be tight."

"A teacher?"

He grins. "Don't sound so surprised."

"Sorry."

"It's all good. I know people think I'm a slacker." He rolls back and forth a little. "But I was a lifeguard last summer and working with kids was pretty fun. Plus you get all the breaks and summer off."

"Good point."

We're quiet for a while, and then he clears his throat. "Can I ask you about, like, trans stuff?"

"Sure." I'm hesitant. Jared's seemed so chill with me so far. I hate that I'm not certain what he's about to ask.

"How is all that going?"

I smile in relief. "I might start testosterone." From the playground across the field, children's voices echo, high and excited.

"Wow." He nods slowly. "So . . . you're going to become a dude?" He grimaces. "Sorry. That came out wrong."

"Yeah. It's not really about becoming a guy. I know I am one, I just don't look like it to the world," I say. "But I don't want to end up like Blake. I don't want to be some asshole dude. I just want my body to change."

He squints at me. "Do you know any guys besides Blake?"

I blink. "Uh, yeah. You and Ronnie, obviously. My dad. Mr. Harrison."

"So why are you afraid you'll end up like Blake?" I open my mouth, then close it. He barrels on. "He's just one kind of guy, a typical piece of shit. But I'm not like that. Neither is Ronnie. You're not automatically going to become like the worst of us just because you take testosterone."

I sit, silent. He's right. Dad, Ronnie, Jared; none of them look anything like the muscle-bound trans men online, or behave like the stereotypical entitled cis man.

"That's one of the things I like about skating," Jared says. "Yeah, a lot of the other dudes are just as macho and gross as guys who don't skate. But nobody cares if I have long hair, or dress grungy, or if I'm quiet."

"Have people really made fun of you for your hair?"

He laughs. "Actually, Blake used to rag on me all the time. Called me a women's hairstyle model."

"I'm really sorry," I say.

He shrugs. "I just ignored him. He stopped after a while. Found other people to fuck with."

"Didn't it bother you?"

"At first. But then I thought about it and I realized being compared to women isn't offensive. Blake just does that stuff because he's insecure, and that's his shit to deal with." He jumps up. "Come on, I'm hungry."

We wander down toward the coffee shops and restaurants along the main street. He skates ahead, jumping on and off the curb, then zooming back up to me, only to skate ahead again. I watch him, long blond hair whipping in the cold breeze, hoodie zipped to his chin. I imagine myself as a guy: narrow hips, flat chest, squared jaw. Flannels and faded jeans. Maybe even long hair. The idea of growing my hair out doesn't seem so awful if I'm a guy. For the first time, I can kind of see it, see him, who I am, who I will become.

On Sunday, Ronnie and I lounge like slugs on his couch, bingeing his new favorite Netflix show, another Marvel adaptation.

"I talked to Dad," he says.

"What?" I sit upright. "And?!"

He stares at the television. "And nothing. He said he'd think about it."

"Dang." I slump down again. "I mean, that's something."

"I guess."

We watch superheroes fight on screen, destroying the bad guy. I get up and go to the kitchen, toasting myself another Pop-Tart. The front door opens.

"A little help here," Jamal calls out, and the television pauses. I join Ronnie in taking a few bags of groceries from Jamal's hands, carrying them into the kitchen. When that's done, we go back to the couch. I can hear Jamal rummaging around, cabinets opening and closing.

"Ronnie?" We sit up and turn around. Jamal's standing there, leaning on the doorway, looking at us. "I wanted to talk to you about something."

"I can go," I say, but he shakes his head.

"No, no. That's not necessary."

I look at Ronnie. He's staring at Jamal, head pulled back into his neck just a little bit as if his dad is a Marvel villain and he's waiting for the final death blow.

"I just wanted to tell you." Jamal cracks his knuckles. "I thought about what you told me. And I'll sign the loan."

Ronnie jumps up, mouth making shapes without sound.

"One condition, though. You have to get a part-time job." Jamal half smiles as Ronnie starts to splutter. "That sound fair?"

"Oh my god. Oh my god," Ronnie says.

Jamal grins. "I'll take that as a yes."

Ronnie dashes around the couch and tackles him in a hug, knocking him back against the refrigerator. Jamal laughs, squeezing Ronnie tight, kissing the top of his hair. Ronnie lets go, spinning toward me.

"I'm going to Parsons!" he screams. I jump up, and we land a high five so hard my hand burns like fire, but I don't care.

"I can't believe this," he says, turning back to Jamal. "I can't believe this."

Jamal just smiles, shaking his head, crossing back to the half-empty grocery bags on the counter.

Ronnie looks at me again and I grin back at him. "We need to celebrate," I say.

We end up heading for Capitol Hill. When we get off the bus, we walk toward Caffe Vita, Ronnie jumping up and down every few feet, shrieking for joy. It's still cold, but the sun is out, peeking through patchy clouds.

In the cafe, we sit across from each other. He's got a grin on his face, staring out the window dreamily. "I can't believe I get to have this."

I grab both his hands, squeezing them. "You're going to New York City."

He smiles at me. "I'll get enough financial aid for an apartment, which I'll share with Allison and Zoe, of course," he says.

"Of course." I smile at the thought. "And I'll visit and crash on the couch, and you'll take me for a slice of New York pizza."

"You'd be okay with that? With Zoe being there?"

I stare out the window at the people passing by, then look back at him. "Yeah."

He narrates his first year: the boys, the clothes, the discovery of his talents by a famous Broadway director. A few tables away, a boy our age looks over for a moment, then back to his laptop. He's wearing a soccer jersey from another school, the blue bright against his light brown skin, his dark curls shaggy around his face.

"And my boyfriend, who visits every month from Seattle," Ronnie whispers. We laugh. He looks at me. "I wish you were coming. Are you sure you can't make it work?"

"Yeah." I turn the cup around in my hands. "I don't know. I'm still sad that I didn't get in. But now, with Zoe and me broken up, with everything changing . . . it just doesn't feel the same."

"I get it." He watches me. "How are you feeling about the breakup?"

I snort. "It sucks. I miss her. But I know I'm missing something that can't exist anymore. It did for a while, but even if we tried to make it work now, it wouldn't be the same."

Ronnie nods. I let out a heavy sigh. We sit, him in his thoughts, probably about Parsons, maybe about us, our friends, how so much is different from what we thought it would be. I'm thinking about that part too, how at the beginning of this year, I imagined this moment as something distant and gold, a nebulous happiness shaped like loving Zoe and knowing I was going to NYU at the end of the year. And now happiness looks so different. I'm sad, but I'm closer to being myself than I ever have been. I wouldn't trade that for NYU acceptance. I wouldn't trade it to be back together with Zoe. I wouldn't trade who I am for anything.

"Wanna walk?" Ronnie asks.

We set our empty cups in the dish bin and leave. The wind blows around us, through our hair, Frisbee players shouting from the field as we walk alongside Cal Anderson Park. The telephone poles are covered in layers of posters, a patchwork of color as high as a person can reach. One jumps out at me: *Trans Pride Seattle.*

"Check it out." I point the poster out to Ronnie. We step closer. The poster is ripped and faded from rain and sun, but I can see the date is from last year, with a lineup of performers. It happened in the park.

"I didn't know we had a Trans Pride March," he says. "I thought Pride was just the big parade downtown. We should go."

"Yeah," I say, studying the poster. "We should." I smile. Pride isn't until June, but I'm already excited. Maybe I'll be picking classes at the University of Washington. Maybe I'll move out on my own, or maybe a room will open up at Jade's house. Maybe I'll start performing with her collective. Maybe I'll be on testosterone by then. I don't know.

The possibilities are endless.

ACKNOWLEDGMENTS

I'm a Leo, and we love a good speech, so I've been writing this in my head for a long time. If I forget anyone: thank you, love you, that's my bad. Here we go.

Thank you to my incomparable agent, Lauren Abramo, for your wisdom, humor, and passion for this book (and all my work). My editor, Maggie Lehrman, for understanding and loving Dean and his story right away. I feel so lucky to work with both of you! Emily Daluga, for all your work and especially for key feedback that changed the ending for the better. This book is stronger because of you!

Everyone at Abrams/Amulet who helped make this book happen: Marie Oishi, managing editor; Hana Anouk Nakamura, cover designer; Kim Lauber, Hallie Patterson, Jenny Choy, and Brooke Shearouse in publicity and marketing; Elisa Gonzalez, sales director; Jenn Jimenez, production manager; and Andrew Smith, publisher. I could not ask for a better team.

Susan Hae-Jin Lee, my cover illustrator: thank you for bringing Dean to life through your art.

Abeni Jones and Quincy Drinker, my sensitivity readers: thank you for your time, energy, and valuable feedback and insight.

Brian Kennedy for the early feedback, mentorship, and cheering me on; you are the best stage parent. Wendy Heard, thank you for befriending me on that wild #DVpit day; you are so great. ZR Ellor, your feedback is always impeccable, on writing and many other things; I told you I'd mention in my acknowledgments that you were right about that revision. YOU WERE RIGHT!

Beth Phelan, for #DVpit and for being an all-around awesome human. Thank you for creating the space for my work to find an agent and for me to find a community. Bethany C. Morrow, for uplifting me as a very new author by including me as a contributor in *Take The Mic: Fictional Stories of Everyday Resistance.*

The Richard Hugo House in Seattle and the panelists who chose the 2016–2017 Made at Hugo House Fellows: your early support was critical to the existence of this book.

The Made at Hugo House Fellows 2016–2017: Shankar Narayan, Willie Fitzgerald, Beryl Clark, Gabrielle Bates, and Katie Lee Ellison, and our guides Christine Texeira, Sonora Jha, and Anastacia Renee. I'm so grateful to have met and been mentored by you all.

Hugo House again, for creating the Scribes program, an early version of which I attended in high school, and Roberto Carlos Ascalon, for running that Scribes group. You held space for us to express ourselves more fully. Thank you.

The weekly writing circle folks at Old Growth Northwest, for reading the very early vignettes of this story and helping me realize Dean should be the center of it.

The 21ders! I'm so happy to be debuting with you all. Special shout-out to the Queerever 21s, and super-special shout-out to my fellow trans debuts (and all trans young adult and middle-grade authors). I'm not naming you, because by the time this book comes out there will (hopefully!) be even more of you and I don't want to leave anyone out, but you know who you are. I'm honored to write alongside you.

The students, teachers, and staff at Seattle Country Day School, who were so supportive and enthusiastic about my writing life and this book during the 2017–2018 school year. Special shout-out to the third graders—I can't believe you're in sixth grade now! To those whose names I promised to put in a book: don't worry, I haven't forgotten.

Ms. Middleton, my eighth-grade language arts teacher, who wrote in my yearbook that she expected to see my books on shelves one day. Here's the first one, and there are more on the way.

Dylan, for enthusiastically listening to early scenes as they were written, and for your validation of my right to write the story and my identity as a nonbinary person.

Vanessa, for hyping me up, supporting my writing, and pushing me to dream bigger in writing and all things. I admire you so much.

Tanya, for nearly a lifetime of friendship. Here's to twenty more years.

Katie Lee Ellison again, for the continued friendship, literary fellowship, laughter, discussion, and more.

Jules, Eli, Teagan, Avi, and Natalie, for being part of my friend-family and cheering on my writing accomplishments (and me as a person).

A special shout-out to Erika for reading my very first draft when only half of it existed, and for asking me whether Dean was going to visit Jade's house. The scene at the queer purple house exists because of you.

Lee and Jeanne: I feel so loved and supported by you.

Eggplant House members past and present: Caitlin, Nathaniel, Kait, Matt, Morgan, Grant, Jen, Molly, Simone, James, Egg, Erika, Kate, Postyn, and the current fam, Doug, Kevin, Bex, Jillian, and Hayden. My love and gratitude for you would need a whole book to itself. Thank you for being my family and for letting me mine your good, bad, and embarrassing teenage moments for my books.

Mom, Dad, Hannah: My first family, I love you so much. Thank you for always supporting my writing, for nurturing my inner wisdom, for seeing me, for sharing your pain and joy with me, and for being there no matter what. Through everything. I am who I am because of you, and I'm so grateful.

Hayden: Love of my life. Being with you is one of the best things to ever happen to me. Thank you.

Queer and trans people everywhere: You are an endless source of wisdom, motivation, inspiration, imagination, innovation, beauty, joy, and resilience for me. We're here, and we're not going anywhere.